Soul Bonded

For free previews of Meghan's next release visit us at

Soul Bonded

by

Meghan Malone

SOUL BONDED

ISBN 13: 978-0-9886009-2-8

This Trade Paperback Original Is Published By
North Bay Press
Santa Rosa, CA 95403

CREDITS
COVER DESIGN BY TY JUSTICE

Acknowledgments

Every book I've written has been a team effort, and this one is no exception. First and foremost, I want to thank Ty Justice, my designer, publisher, and marketing guru, who has worked tirelessly to help bring this book to fruition. I also need to thank Angie Williams for her support, creative input, and for helping me find time to write. And to Jodi Justice, who helped brainstorm ideas for titles, each one more inappropriate than the last.

I would also like to thank my team of editors and beta readers: D. Jackson Leigh, Anne Rose, Daishonique Davis, Lisa Gebhart Longhurst, and Kris Ridste. And so many other people for their encouragement and support, including Toni Whitaker, my parents, my sister Kathleen Riek, and the readers of my lesbian fiction who have expressed interest in crossing over to read my work in a new genre.

Dedication

To readers of romance novels

CHAPTER ONE

Four days after losing control of her car and sliding into a mercifully shallow embankment during a Sierra Nevada snowstorm, Katie Connelly's entire existence had been pared down to only one thought: I don't want to die. Amazing, the way four days of freezing cold and hunger could change one's priorities. Last weekend her biggest worry had been that she would grow old alone. Now it was that she would never grow old at all.

She'd started out optimistic in the hours after the accident. Despite the fact that her cell phone got no reception this far into the woods, she'd never dreamed that help would prove so elusive. Too far from town and without proper clothing to hike to safety, she'd told herself that a car would surely come along and spot her eventually. After all, she couldn't possibly be the only idiot to ignore a winter storm warning and venture out onto the back roads. It might take a day, even two, but rescue would come. While she waited, she sang to keep up her spirits, read the bestseller that had been languishing in her backseat for the better part of six months, and rehearsed what she'd say to whomever freed her from her frozen prison. When that first night had fallen, she'd drifted off to sleep shivering but full of hope that she'd awaken to the sight of a clear sky and some sign of humanity.

The second day in the car had been more difficult—

natural biological urges reared their ugly head and hunger set in. She started to worry about the snow that was drifting perilously high around her useless car. Day three consisted of a lot of crying, mentally cataloguing all her regrets, and cursing her lack of foresight in not packing more food. And now, day four: she was emotionally numb, starving, so cold she feared she might never thaw out, and quickly losing hope that anyone else was stupid enough to drive around in a raging blizzard.

Mostly, she really, really didn't want to die.

And all because she'd left girls' weekend in Tahoe a day early. If she'd waited until Sunday to head home, as planned, the storm would have already been in full swing. She wouldn't have even made it out of town. Being snowed in would have pissed her off, but at least she wouldn't be preparing for a slow, untimely demise. Spending one more day feeling lonely and pathetic among her happily partnered girlfriends sounded like a dream compared to a slow death inside a cheap economy sedan. One whose payment was now two days overdue.

This really was the perfect ending to a shitty weekend.

Sighing, Katie burrowed deeper into her sweatshirt and glanced at the window. It was completely covered in snow, so she couldn't determine if the weather had started to clear. She hadn't been able to see outside since yesterday morning. For all she knew, her car was buried to the point where it couldn't be seen from the road.

That was a terrifying thought. This wasn't a well-traveled route, to say the least. She couldn't count on many people passing by even on a good day, so she desperately needed to attract the attention of anyone who did. She wasn't going to get many chances.

She considered her options. She could try to dig out the car or else leave the possibility of rescue to ever-diminishing luck. Getting out of the car didn't feel like a good idea, but neither was ignoring that the odds of being found were close to zero if nobody could see her. Pretty soon she wouldn't have enough strength left to do anything about that problem. She had no idea how many more days she could survive with no food and only melted snow to drink. As it was, the idea of stepping outside into the frigid, wind exhausted her—and it wouldn't get any easier if she waited. This was truly a now or never kind of situation.

"Damn it. I don't want to." She'd been talking to herself a lot over the past few days. The sound of her own voice comforted her like nothing else could. Proof that she was still alive, she supposed. What could be more comforting than that?

Not going outside, her brain supplied. Staying in the car. Her fingers were already frozen, she'd been trembling for what felt like weeks, and all the clothes from her suitcase couldn't keep her warm even within the confines of her car. If she got wet or even lingered outside too long, she might never warm up. Hypothermia was a serious, persistent threat, and going out into the weather could mean speeding up the process of freezing to death.

Then again, doing nothing might easily lead to the same fate, if the starvation didn't kill her first.

"Damn it," she whispered again. Mustering the very last of her energy, she fumbled through the small mountain of clothing she'd piled on top of her body to stay warm. Her mind was cloudy and her movements felt sluggish, like she was a children's toy that was slowly winding down. Worst was that she couldn't stop shaking. "Focus. Focus." If she was going to clear off the car, she needed to get as much extra clothing on her body as possible. Anything to keep the heat she had left from escaping into the frigid Northern California air.

Layering shirt-upon-shirt, she stopped only when it became too difficult to move her arms. Pants were even harder to manage. She tugged on a pair of pajama bottoms over her jeans, but she couldn't fit another pair of jeans over those. The final touch to her ridiculous outfit was the adorable blue hat and gloves set that she'd purchased especially for this trip. At the time she'd thought the snowflake pattern was darling. Now she no longer cared how well the color complemented her auburn hair and fair complexion. If she never saw another snowflake, it would be too soon.

Girls' weekend had been a bust in every way—this was just the icing on the cake. She'd arrived full of pride about her booming web design career and excited to catch up with college friends, but by the end of the first night, it had become clear that she was the pathetic old maid of the group. At least that's how the rest of them treated her. Stripped of the vibrant, unique personalities she remembered from school, now each of them seemed singularly preoccupied with alternately bitching and waxing poetic about the men in their lives. And when they stopped talking about their love lives, they'd start in on Katie's. After just twenty-four hours, their repeated, well-intentioned reassurances that she'd find someone, too, threatened to drive her crazy. None of her many accomplishments mattered to those people. Just the fact that she was thirty-three and perpetually single.

Katie tugged the snowflake hat onto her head, then scowled at the gloves. They were totally impractical for this situation. Knit wool was adorable in the store, but it would never keep her hands dry. Leave it to her to buy stupid, girly, useless gloves.

"Worst weekend ever." She took a deep breath and opened the car door. Or tried to, at least. It moved less than an inch, then got stuck in the snow that had blown and drifted over the past few days. She grimaced as a stream of powder fell over her hands and onto the car seat. "Shit!"

She pulled the door closed with effort. The car was covered, all right. And she was trapped inside.

Katie lay back against the seat and closed her eyes. Every bit of her energy went toward not bursting into tears. She didn't want to cry. It wouldn't help, and even if the hot tears felt good on her skin for a moment, they would quickly freeze and make an uncomfortable situation even worse.

Exhausted by the effort she'd just exerted, Katie struggled against the seductive pull of sleep. The last time she'd roused from a nap, hours ago now, she'd promised herself she wouldn't fall asleep again. Not until she was rescued. She'd worried that next time, she wouldn't wake up. But now she was so tired and so very powerless, making it difficult to hang onto her resolve.

A sudden sense of calm washed over her. Things were well and truly out of her hands. There was nothing she could do except sit and wait. The thought freed her somehow, and she sank down into the peaceful oblivion of sleep once again.

CHAPTER TWO

Eventually time ceased to have meaning. Katie didn't know how long it had been since she tried to open the car door—probably hours, maybe days. Each time she drifted into consciousness, she was less tethered to reality. Her perceptions were muddy and it was painfully difficult to stay awake. So she slept whenever she could. Her lucid moments came less frequently, then seemed to stop altogether.

She dreamed—of rescue, of not being able to find her classroom on exam day, of being in love. The last one was her favorite. It made her feel safe, like everything would be okay no matter what happened. Waking from that dream was particularly disappointing, and she immediately yearned to float away again into the refuge of her own mind. Reality had nothing to offer her anymore.

At some point her dreams took a strange turn, and in a moment when she'd actually thought she was awake. But she couldn't be awake, because she saw bare hands begin to clear away the snow on the windshield, and that was impossible. The hands were attached to muscular arms—also bare—that worked furiously to dig her out.

She managed a weak chuckle. Naturally she would imagine a rescuer who wore even more impractical winter clothing than she did. She closed her eyes and listened to the muffled sound of digging, the moving of snow, then the startlingly loud crunch of a fist crashing through the frozen windshield. A frigid blast of air stole her breath, violently shattering her numbness. She curled away from the icy wind on instinct.

Then she was floating, cradled against solid warmth that barely penetrated the chill that had settled into her bones. She tried to get closer to that heat, to cuddle up to it, but she just couldn't get enough. The cold surrounded her, she was drowning in it, and no matter how badly she wanted to claw her way out, she lacked the strength and, sadly, the will.

Was this what it felt like to die?

Katie surrendered. Relieved, she sank into the strong arms that cradled her and waited for the cold to abate. Surely she wouldn't be forced to endure this icy chill for eternity.

Images came in disjointed flashes. Snow. The trees. Impossibly warm, bare skin against her frozen cheek. Then a cabin lit by a golden glow from within. Perhaps that was heaven. All she wanted to do was get inside that glow, to bathe in it. To forget that she had ever frozen to death alone.

The next time she came to, her body hovered between intense pain and razor-sharp ecstasy. Her skin tingled as though a thousand bees were stinging her at once. She wanted to scream, but a heavy pressure building low in her belly caused her to moan instead. Waves of incredible pleasure nearly overwhelmed the agony of whatever was happening to her body, leaving her breathless and disoriented. The sensation was like teetering on the edge of orgasm, and she wanted nothing more than to tip over into oblivion and leave the pain behind.

As though the universe had finally decided to cut her a break, the excruciating sting receded until all that remained was bliss. And now she could feel—soft sheets against her naked skin, the firm press of a male body against her own. Swept away by swift, aching need, she snuggled closer to her dream companion, desperate to sate her desire. Still foggy, she struggled to find the friction she craved, hands roaming over coarse hair and hard planes, but total satisfaction proved elusive.

She had a vague thought: Why do my sex dreams always end in frustration?

Then another: I'm safe.

With that, the last trace of her consciousness slipped away.

CHAPTER THREE

Katie clawed her way out of sleep with fierce determination, aware that something wasn't right even before she opened her eyes. Her mattress was too firm. The air carried the unfamiliar scent of cedar. A solid shape rested against her side, breathing evenly—one that was far too big to be her cat. Alarm quickened her breathing as she finally broke free from her heavy slumber and took stock of her surroundings.

She was in a strange bed in a strange room. Wood paneling covered the walls, log cabin style. The framed nature photographs hanging from them gave the space a rustic feel, as did the redwood furniture that looked handcrafted. A lamp served as a dim sentry on the nightstand beside her, casting soft light over the large, brown mixed-breed dog curled up at her side. He stared at her with soulful chocolate eyes and then yawned, clearly unmoved by her rising panic.

Heart pounding, she sat up slowly. Where the hell was she? What had happened?

She dropped her head into her hands and tried to make sense of her jumbled memories. She vividly recalled the accident. Her internal debate about whether to walk miles in the desolate cold or wait for help. The four long days huddled in the backseat of her car. Losing track of what was real and what was delusion, dreaming of rescue one minute and death the next.

Then nothing. And now this.

Clearly she had been saved, but by whom? And how was it possible that she'd just woken up feeling so...refreshed?

Improbable as it was, she was in tip-top condition: rested, healthy, and most importantly, toasty warm. Confusion about how she'd gotten here aside, her mind felt sharp and alert in a way it hadn't in days. Except for the intense hunger that twisted her stomach, she was in far better shape than someone who'd just spent the past few days stranded in the frigid cold with only two candy bars and a snack-size bag of pretzels had any business being.

She lifted the comforter that covered her body, unsettled to discover that she was dressed in a pair of men's sweatpants and a baggy T-shirt. The clothes didn't belong to her, which meant that someone had undressed her. Like, really undressed her—she wasn't even wearing a bra. She snuck a hand beneath the waistband of the sweats and confirmed that she didn't have panties on, either. Her rescuer had obviously gotten an eyeful.

Just as the thought crossed her mind, the bedroom door opened and a man stepped inside. He stopped short when he saw her. "Oh."

She snatched her hand from the sweatpants and opened her mouth to say something, but the words caught in her throat. Dark and rugged and handsome, with vivid green eyes she could see from across the room, the stranger pretty much ticked all her 'perfect man' checkboxes. He was powerfully built, exuding strength and physical confidence, yet seemed to have as much trouble meeting her gaze as she did forming a coherent sentence. The dog perked its ears and whined at his master, but Katie could only manage a weak nod.

"You're up." The man hooked his thumbs in the pockets of

his well-worn jeans and nodded at the dog. "I hope Shilah didn't startle you. I left him here to keep you warm."

She forced herself out of her stupor. "No, Shilah was fine. And very warm."

He shivered almost imperceptibly, still not meeting her eyes. "Do you remember what happened?"

"I had an accident." She pulled the comforter up around her body, slightly uncomfortable with the way he refused to look directly at her. Maybe he was only trying to protect her modesty—though it was a bit late for that, if he was the one who'd undressed her—but his uneasy avoidance seemed to hint at deep-seated guilt. Between his obvious discomfort and her instant, uncontrollable attraction to a complete stranger, Katie felt painfully vulnerable. Determined to act normal, she mustered a polite smile. "I lost control of my car. I was afraid I'd freeze to death if I tried to walk for help, so I decided to wait for someone to find me. But...nobody came."

"You'd nearly frozen to death by the time I got to you. You were unconscious, then delirious." The man leaned against the doorway, angled away from her. Almost as though he was ready to bolt at any moment. "Do you know how long you were stranded out there?"

"No." She gathered the comforter closer. "I lost track of time after the fourth or fifth day."

"I'm not surprised nobody found you. Your car was almost completely buried under the snow." He folded his arms over his chest, drawing her attention to his firm, muscled physique. She couldn't help but wonder what he looked like without his shirt. "It's lucky I spotted you when I did."

"Yes, very lucky." She dragged her gaze from his biceps to his face. The tender concern in his voice was at odds with his distant demeanor. "So where am I now?"

"In my cabin, about three miles from where your car ran off the road." Hesitating only momentarily, he walked across the room to the window and drew back the curtains to reveal angry, swirling flurries and frozen trees blanketed in white.

13

"Storm picked up again this morning—it's Friday, by the way. All the roads are closed, otherwise I would've taken you into town."

"Friday," Katie whispered. It had been almost a week since she'd left Tahoe. No doubt her clients wondered where she was. Not to mention her parents and her older sister. Oh, God. Alarmed, she threw the blankets off her body and scooted to the edge of the bed. "Do you have a phone I could use? I need to let my family know I'm not dead—my clients, too. Everyone probably thinks I am."

The man raised his hand and took a step closer. "I don't have a phone. Listen, be careful. You're probably very weak."

No phone. That meant she was trapped in a cabin in the woods with a strange man, and with no way to let anyone know where she was. A very real feeling of helplessness overwhelmed her, followed by a jolt of stark fear. She didn't know the first thing about this guy, who had apparently seen her naked already. Desperate to regain at least the illusion of control, she struggled to stand. "How about a computer? With Internet?"

"No, I'm sorry, but—"

He stopped talking and raced forward as she finally pushed up off the mattress, and caught her around the middle when her legs dissolved beneath her. Cradled in his powerful embrace, she felt instantly safe. Protected. The sensation triggered another burst of memory—being held in these arms, surrounded by this scent, his naked skin against hers. A hot surge of lust rocketed through her body and wrenched her back into the present. Gasping, she stared at him in shock.

He took a shuddering breath and carefully placed her back on the bed. Then he stepped away quickly. "Let me get you something to eat. You need to regain your strength."

Katie wasn't sure what frightened her more—her strange, uncharacteristic lapse, or the realization that she was completely dependent upon a stranger. Careful not to reveal her unease, she crawled back beneath the comforter and arranged the blankets over her chest. She had no idea whether her body's memory of this man was delusion or reality, but the way she'd just reacted to his touch rattled her to the core. She'd never felt anything like it before. The fact that the guy acted like he couldn't bear to be around her only made it worse.

"I know you want to contact your people, but there just isn't any way to do that from here. As soon as the storm lifts, I'll take you to town. I promise." He turned away, but not before she noticed the impressive bulge in his jeans. That he was in a similar state of arousal didn't comfort her in the least. The man was a stranger. Nobody knew she was alone with him in his home. She was having strange flashes of lying naked in his arms, yet she hadn't been conscious in days. And apparently she was too weak to walk, let alone fight him off if it came to that.

"Are we all alone out here?" She wrapped her arms around her stomach and tried not to let on how terrified she suddenly felt.

He hesitated. "Yes." For the first time since entering the room, he made brief eye contact. "But you're safe here with me, Katie. I swear it."

When he looked at her, she nearly forgot to breathe. It wasn't just the impact of those piercing eyes finally landing on her, but also the way they seemed to see her in a way that she wasn't sure she'd ever really been seen before. She knew it was ridiculous to feel this way—not even a minute ago, she'd been worried that he was getting ready to attack her—but that didn't change how his gaze made her feel inside. He looked at her as though he loved her. As though he would even die for her. She couldn't fathom what would inspire that level of devotion from a man who didn't know her at all. It frightened her. So did the sudden realization that he'd called her by name.

"I looked at your driver's license," he said, answering her unspoken question. "Your purse is next to the nightstand, on the floor. And your clothes are drying now. I can bring them to you when they're ready." He tore his gaze away from hers. "They were soaking wet by the time I got you home. I tried not to look at…you…any more than necessary."

Katie blushed. "Given that you know so much about me already, maybe you can tell me your name?"

"Rafe Whelan." He walked to the doorway and paused with his back to her. "I'll bring you lunch, then leave you alone. I've got books, if you like to read, or paper and pencils, if you wanted to write or draw. No television, I'm afraid. No computer, either."

She doubted she would be able to relax enough to do anything except sit and worry. Her life was literally in this man's hands. His very strong, masculine, sexy hands—which could be serial killer hands, for all she knew, or those of a sadistic sexual predator. After her reaction to having those hands on her, she couldn't shake the feeling that he'd not only undressed her, but also initiated some kind of intimate contact she only vaguely remembered. And now he reeked of guilt and shame. How could she read or draw or nap, especially, with that hanging over her? Afraid to alert him to her growing suspicion, she scooted back against the headboard and pulled her knees to her chest. "A book would be nice."

He nodded and started out the door, but something made her call out to him. "Wait!"

Rafe stopped and glanced back in her direction. "Yes?"

"When do you think the roads will be open?"

"I don't know." He turned and stared at her with an intensity that raised the fine hairs on her arms. "Soon, I hope. I want to get you back to your people just as badly as you want to go. Believe me."

Hearing the sincerity in his words, but unsure what to make of it, she gave him a reluctant nod. She didn't want him to know that she distrusted him. Not while she was a prisoner in his home. "You saved my life. Thank you."

"You're welcome." Something that looked like regret passed across his face, but he covered it nicely with a smile that made Katie's stomach flip-flop despite her best efforts to remain unaffected. "If you're still cold, I can prepare a hot bath for you. And give you privacy, of course."

She couldn't think of a worse idea. "That's generous of you, but I'm okay. Thanks."

He left with a curt nod, the smile vanishing from his face before he'd even turned away. Katie shuddered as he closed the door. Alone with his dog—Shilah—she sank her fingers into the coarse fur that covered the back of his neck. "Are you here to keep me warm, or to guard me?"

Shilah rolled onto his side and exposed his belly in a clear attempt to solicit a stomach rub. She complied, feeling a little silly about her fleeting paranoia. The dog was just an overgrown puppy. Perhaps his master had a similar soft nature.

There was no real reason to assume that Rafe meant her any harm. So far he had been polite and respectful, and he was clearly trying to keep his distance—even if to an unsettling extent. If not for the guilt in his eyes and the downright disturbing flashes of what might have happened while she was unconscious, she would have no reason to see him as anything other than a hero. But it was obvious that something was off. He seemed overly anxious for her to go, as though he couldn't stand being around her. Somehow she felt like both an intruder and a prisoner—unwelcome but stuck in his house, unable to leave.

Yet despite all that, her body stirred as she thought about him. Dark-haired with a couple days worth of scruff covering his chiseled face and a leanly muscled body, he was her fantasy man come to life. And those eyes…Katie whimpered as her inner muscles clenched, sending a ripple of pleasure down to the tips of her toes.

For a moment she sat stunned. Then she slowly eased her hand beneath the waistband of her sweats and sought out her labia with tentative fingers. Slick wetness coated her trimmed hairs, her inner thighs, her almost unbearably sensitive folds. She'd never felt anything like it. Gasping, she tore her hand out of her pants and wiped her fingers hastily on the sheets.

This wasn't normal. This wasn't her.

Had he slipped her some kind of drug? Taken advantage of her when she was unconscious? Even if she had vague memories of wanting it, she hadn't been in any condition to consent. Had he done something to put her in this state so that if she remembered what he'd done, she would think it was her idea?

Katie closed her eyes and fought to recall the details of her rescue. She'd been so out of it mentally that she'd thought Rafe's appearance was a dream or even a dying vision—being taken out of the car, carried through the cold, then eventually warmed in his embrace. But it hadn't been a dream. At least not all of it. That something had happened between them was obvious.

She wasn't sure how to stay in Rafe's house without knowing what it was.

CHAPTER FOUR

Rafe knocked on the door again some time later, startling Katie upright in bed. She'd only meant to rest for a minute, not wanting to be vulnerable when her host returned, but Shilah had put his head on her belly as soon as she'd lain down and she'd lost track of time petting him. Now Shilah grumbled as she shot ramrod straight against the headboard before calling out, "Come in."

The door opened and Rafe walked inside without glancing in her direction. He carried a bowl, a piece of crusty bread, and a glass of water. Clearly in a rush, he set the food on the nightstand and backed away. "I hope you like chicken soup."

The savory aroma hit her in the face and made her mouth water. Any concern she might have had about being drugged disappeared at the prospect of filling her stomach. She snatched up the bowl, then gave him a sheepish nod. "This is perfect. Thank you."

"You can have more if you'd like." For the first time, a trace of humor crept into Rafe's voice. "But you should probably take it easy. Your stomach needs to acclimate to having food inside it again."

"I'll keep that in mind," Katie said as she shoveled a spoonful into her mouth. She moaned, undone by the warmth and flavor of the broth, not to mention the promise of sustenance. Never again would she take food for granted.

19

Ever. "Oh…this is so good."

She looked up and Rafe quickly averted his gaze from her chest. Swallowing, he rasped, "I'm glad."

Though he'd traded the snug jeans he'd worn earlier for a pair of loose sweatpants, Rafe's arousal remained obvious. She tried not to stare. Had he been excited this whole time, or was he reacting to her unselfconscious enjoyment of her lunch? Either way, she vacillated between being frightened, embarrassed, and pleased by the evidence of his desire. The longer he went without trying to initiate physical contact, the more convinced she became that he wasn't planning on assaulting her. Not while she was conscious, at least.

She frowned. If she wanted to know what had occurred while she was unconscious, she would have to ask him. Even if he wasn't willing to tell her the truth, she might learn something from the way he responded. "Can you tell me what happened after you got me out of my car?"

Panic flashed in Rafe's eyes. "What?"

"After you dug me out of my car…I don't remember much, and what I do recall, I'm not even sure really happened." Katie hesitated, unsure how much she wanted to say. She hated to accuse him of behaving improperly when he hadn't done anything overtly threatening. So maybe he was a little aloof and a lot awkward. The guy lived in the middle of the woods. People skills probably weren't among his strengths. She decided to start with an easy question. "Did you carry me back here? I swear that's what I remember, but…it seems a little crazy, in my head."

Rafe crossed the room and opened the trunk that sat in the corner. He pulled out a folded comforter, but instead of offering it to her, he held it in front of his crotch, hiding his erection. "I did carry you. I went out for a hike that afternoon on foot, so…" He cleared his throat and glanced longingly at the bedroom door. Once again, he seemed desperate to leave. "Why don't I let you eat? I'll bring your clothes when I come back for the dishes."

"Wait." She set down the bowl of soup. No way was she going to let the food distract her from her most important goal. She needed to know what she'd gotten herself into. "What happened after you brought me inside? I must have been in pretty bad shape."

"You were hypothermic." Rafe's expression softened. "When I got you here, I took you straight to the guest room. Your clothes were soaked through from the storm, so I undressed you. Then I put you in dry clothes and covered you with blankets. I sat with you for a while to make sure your condition didn't deteriorate as you warmed." He glanced at Shilah, who thumped his tail against the mattress the instant he received his master's attention. "You're strong. You're a fighter. Once you were warm and I was confident you were stable, I put Shilah in bed with you to provide body heat. Then I left."

It was a good story. She wished she believed it. She didn't know how she knew it wasn't the whole truth, but she did, in her bones. Rafe was lying to her. His dishonesty was so obvious it made her cringe. While it shouldn't have hurt her on a personal level—she didn't even know this man—the deceit stung. Inexplicably, it felt like a betrayal, as though she'd actually expected more.

He finally met her gaze, swallowing visibly at whatever he saw in her eyes. "Let me get your clothes." He practically dashed out of the room.

Katie gave the soup a sidelong glance. Her stomach growled painfully, and against her better judgment, she picked up the bowl. Yes, Rafe was lying to her. That didn't mean he'd put something in her food. It didn't mean he wanted to hurt her in any way. Or at least that's what she tried to convince herself as she took another tentative bite. She needed to eat. If she didn't, she wouldn't have the strength to defend herself, if it came to that.

Realistically, he'd had ample opportunity to hurt her if he'd wanted. Chances were, he was just socially awkward or something equally innocuous. He had promised to take her into town as soon as the weather cleared, and right now she had no choice but to believe him. So she was going to eat.

She was surprised when he knocked on the door only minutes later. She placed the empty bowl of soup on the nightstand and called out, "Come in."

This time Rafe held a pile of folded clothing. "Looks like you were wearing everything you had with you." A smile tugged at the corner of his mouth, but he sobered quickly. "I'm sure you'll be more comfortable in your own clothes."

Actually, she was certain that his T-shirt and sweatpants were worlds more comfortable than anything she'd packed for girls' weekend, but she wasn't going to say that out loud. "I appreciate that. Thank you."

Rafe took a deep breath, then dragged his gaze to meet hers. Once again, a heady rush of passion and need flooded through her body and settled between her legs, where it swiftly became a gnawing, yearning ache. She swore she could see her desire reflected in the flaring of Rafe's nostrils, the darkening of his eyes, the quickening of his breath. Katie leaned forward in anticipation, sensing that he was about to open up to her, that he may even say something that would help explain the chemistry between them.

A muffled knock came from somewhere outside the bedroom, startling both Shilah and Rafe and drawing their attention to the door. Rafe's face fell at the interruption and a look of cold dread chased away the longing in his eyes. Katie's heart rate picked up as he strode to the door. "Wait here. I'm not expecting anyone."

She nodded and rested her hand on Shilah's head, grateful that the dog made no move to leave. There was no mistaking Rafe's reaction to this visitor. He was nervous. And why not? He lived in the middle of the woods and the roads were supposedly closed. It did seem unusual that someone would just drop by. Very unusual.

Was this guest really unexpected? Or was Rafe nervous

for another reason?

Perhaps his surprise had been feigned. Maybe he didn't want her to know that he'd invited someone over? Or that there was someone else living in the house? The possible implications of her increasingly paranoid thoughts turned her insides to ice.

Cautiously, she scooted to the edge of the bed. Mindful that her legs hadn't supported her the last time she'd tried to stand, she gripped the edge of the nightstand and slowly got to her feet. After a slight wobble, she found her balance and then, gradually, her strength. She wasn't sure what she hoped to accomplish, but she couldn't just sit in that bed and worry about who had come calling.

Katie tiptoed to the bedroom door, holding up her hand to Shilah in a silent plea for him to stay. He whined low in his throat as she eased the door open a couple of inches, but didn't move. Not wanting to leave the safety of the room, she closed her eyes and rested her forehead against the doorframe, listening hard.

Two male voices. As she strained to make out their words, a deep, unfamiliar baritone rose in anger.

"What the hell are you thinking?"

Rafe said something too quiet for her to hear, then added, "I had no choice."

"Of course you did."

"What? Let her die?" Rafe practically snarled. "That wasn't an option."

"Why not? She's a human, for fuck's sake. You should never have gotten involved."

Katie's eyes flew open. Rafe's visitor was a straight-up crazy person. He'd spat out the word human as though it tasted bad in his mouth. As though he truly believed he was something else. Something better. She waited to hear Rafe's response, praying he wouldn't say something equally as insane.

Unfortunately, another low whine from Shilah drowned out

23

Rafe's response. She tossed a glare over her shoulder at the dog, shutting him up with one hard look. Then she turned her attention back to the conversation, which had grown even more heated.

"She can't stay here." The stranger's voice radiated anger. "It's far too dangerous. She'll attract trouble. She'll be killed."

Katie's heart stuttered, then pumped into overdrive. Killed?

"You think I don't know that?" Rafe's easy acceptance of the man's warning raised gooseflesh on her arms, as did the anguish in his voice. Now she knew she wasn't simply being paranoid. Her life was in danger.

"Then why is she still here?"

"What do you want me to do with her?" Rafe lowered his voice, forcing Katie to open the bedroom door another few inches so she could creep into the hallway to listen. "The roads are closed. She's not strong enough to walk out on foot, or even travel by snowmobile, if that were possible. If we ran into anyone on the way into town, I don't know if I could protect her. You know what it's like out there tonight. Trouble would find us, and it wouldn't be a fair fight."

"Tonight is nothing compared to how it'll be tomorrow." The stranger matched Rafe's quiet tone, but she still made out what he said next: "You could kill her, Rafe."

She held her breath as she waited for Rafe to respond.

"I won't." He didn't sound wholly confident.

"How can you possibly—"

Rafe cut him off with a harshly whispered reply, too soft for Katie to hear.

"What the fuck is wrong with you?" The stranger's booming reaction shook the walls, startling her backward a step, right into the doorframe.

"I didn't know it would happen." Rafe growled the words, meeting anger with anger. "That it even could happen."

"You should have just let her die."

"I couldn't." Rafe paused. "I know you don't understand, but even before...I couldn't do that."

"At least it would've been an easy death. A clean death. Now she'll most likely be raped, tortured, and murdered tomorrow—and I still think there's a good chance that you'll be the one to inflict one or more of those fates. It would have been better to let her go peacefully, brother."

This time Rafe growled for real. "I will not let that happen."

"You said it yourself—you won't be able to protect her. You know how they are. They catch one whiff of human pussy in these woods, and you'll be up against a goddamn horde trying to get at it."

"Like I said, you think I don't know that?"

More than anything, Katie yearned to close the door and stop listening. But her feet stayed rooted to the floor as she hung on every horrifying word. Terror didn't even begin to describe what she was feeling inside. The urgency in their voices was real, even if nothing they said made sense. They might be crazy, but each of them clearly bought into their shared delusions. That meant they were beyond dangerous. Both of them.

"So what are you going to do?" Now the stranger sounded weary. Defeated.

"I'm going to keep her hidden. Keep her safe."

"And then?"

"Then I'm getting rid of her." Rafe fell silent for so long that Katie thought maybe both men had left the cabin, even though she hadn't heard a door open or close. She considered venturing farther out of the bedroom, just to take a peek, but froze in place when Rafe spoke again, brokenly. "I promise. Day after tomorrow, she's gone."

"If she's still alive."

"She will be." Rafe sounded hollow now. "She has to be."

His ominous, sorrowful words hit her directly in the gut. Nauseated, she willed her body into motion and retreated into the bedroom. Her knees wobbled as she eased the door closed, taking care to stay silent. She didn't want them to know she'd been listening, even if she wasn't sure how to interpret their conversation.

Whatever it all meant, one thing seemed clear: she was in deep, dark trouble.

CHAPTER FIVE

Katie paced back and forth in front of the bed while she waited for Rafe to return to the room. The chicken soup had given her the much-needed energy to exercise her legs and regain some sense of physical confidence. For that she was grateful. Based on what she'd just overheard, she was going to need her strength.

No matter how sexy Rafe was, no matter how protective he might have seemed at times, there was no non-threatening explanation for the things he and his friend had just discussed. Hearing the words raped, tortured, and murdered tossed around so casually—and with such acceptance—scared the hell out of her. That his friend had suggested that Rafe himself might commit one or more of those acts upon her was beyond comprehension. Rafe's insistence that he wouldn't might have reassured her more if he hadn't seemed to indicate that something had happened between them after her rescue—something bad enough to draw his friend's anger.

Overwhelmed, Katie stopped pacing and forced back the sob that threatened to escape. The worst part of this whole nightmare was not being sure whether she could trust Rafe. He'd sounded sincere when he told his friend he wanted to protect her, but at the same time, he was clearly a liar. He'd been lying to her from the moment she woke up. And he was crazy. Batshit crazy.

So how could she possibly trust him?

"Oh, God," she whispered. Her eyes brimmed with tears and she swiped them away, frustrated. She had no idea what she was going to do, but crying wasn't an option. The pissed-off part of her wanted to confront Rafe and demand the truth, while her more pragmatic side urged her to hide the fact that she knew something was amiss. If he reacted to her accusations with violence, she had no way to protect herself, nowhere to hide. Even if she managed to escape the cabin, she didn't know how to reach civilization—and the cold would likely kill her before she could.

She inhaled deeply, trying to steady her nerves, but immediately regretted it when Rafe's pleasantly male scent flooded her senses and turned her legs to jelly. Anger surged through her, fiery and all-consuming. How was it possible that the mere hint of his smell on her borrowed clothes could make her body forget that he was obviously a lunatic? She was at a total loss, and resented the hell out of him for that.

At what was almost certainly the worst moment he could have chosen, Rafe knocked on the bedroom door again. "Katie?"

Startled, she stumbled backward a few steps and brought her hand to her chest, shocked to feel her heart thumping in nervous excitement. Infuriated that her mind and body were on completely different wavelengths when it came to this man, she barked, "What?"

The door creaked open and Rafe peeked inside. "Are you all right?"

At the sight of his face—square-jawed, rugged, and handsome—and the concern in his beautiful eyes, Katie's thin hold on her control snapped. "No, I'm not. I am definitely not all right."

Rafe's expression changed instantly, as though he was dropping some pretense he realized she wasn't buying. His entire countenance hardened, even as his throat jumped in a clear indication of anxiety. "Do you need another bowl of soup?"

No, she wanted to shout, she needed to know what was going on. But she held her tongue, afraid of pushing him too far. "Who was at the door?"

He studied her as though trying to decide why she was asking. Or maybe he sensed that she already had an idea. After a long hesitation, he said, "A neighbor."

"I thought the roads were closed."

"They are. He has a snowmobile. And he doesn't live very far." Rafe took a step closer, prompting Katie to step back. The complex mix of emotions on his face confounded her. "Tell me what you're really asking."

Katie tamped down the urge to keep retreating. She could see a hint of danger in Rafe's eyes and feared that the artifice of civility was about to dissolve between them. Her gaze darted around the room as she tried to decide what she would do if he came after her. He stood between her and the door. The bed blocked her only other route of escape.

She really didn't want to get anywhere near that bed right now.

"Did you tell him about me?" Katie said. Though it wasn't what she really wanted to know, she suddenly, desperately, didn't want to push her luck. "I was just wondering…could he take me into town?"

Rafe relaxed slightly. "Yeah, he knows you're here. He agreed that the roads are impassable right now, even by snowmobile."

"And let me guess…he doesn't own a phone, either?"

Rafe's guard went back up. "No, he doesn't." He paused, then said, gruffly, "It's a different lifestyle out here. We don't rely on technology the way your kind does."

"My kind?" She took another inadvertent step backward. His labeling her as some sort of other reminded her of the way his neighbor had spat out the word human.

He looked away. "City folk."

"Of course." She no longer cared about getting answers. She only wanted him to leave the room. "Okay. Thank you."

But he didn't leave. He didn't even react. Instead he stood eerily still as some kind of internal battle seemed to play out, one that Katie could plainly see but didn't understand. When he suddenly lifted his hand to reach for her, she gasped and flinched away.

He jerked as though she'd struck him. "You think I'm going to hurt you."

She shook her head in weak denial.

"You do." Rafe moved out of her space. As he did, Katie's attention drifted downward, to the incredible bulge in his pants. He followed her gaze and scowled, covering himself with his hands. "I'm not going to hurt you."

"Then why are you lying to me?" Katie's hand flew to her mouth as soon as the accusation escaped. She hadn't meant to say that.

"I'm not going to hurt you." He stepped closer and she backed up until she bumped up against the edge of the mattress. "Look at my face, in my eyes. I could never hurt you."

She did look, not that she needed to, because what she saw in his face was the same thing she heard in his voice. Utter and complete sincerity. Devotion. The scary part was that she believed him. But he still hadn't answered her question. With courage she didn't understand, she said, "Tell me why you're lying to me."

"What do you think I'm lying about?"

"What happened after you brought me home?" He claimed that he couldn't hurt her, and at this point, she assumed she was about to find out. "You did something to me, didn't you?"

Rafe turned and walked to the door. "Do you need anything else before I turn in for the night?"

"Are you just going to ignore me?" Somehow, his avoidance was almost worse than the anger she'd expected. Without thinking, Katie followed him for a few steps. "Rafe, please tell me what happened. Whatever it is. What did you do to me?"

"Nothing." He swiveled around and glared at her. "Listen to me: you are going to stay in this bedroom. Use the bathroom if you'd like. I will bring you food and water and whatever else you need. Just ask. You can keep the door closed, and I'll only bother you to cater to your every need. If I had some way to allow you to lock me out, I'd let you do that, too. All I can do is promise that I will not enter this room without your explicit permission."

The genuine hurt in his tone reduced her to feeling like an ungrateful bitch. "Rafe—"

"I don't know what you think I might do to you, but I promise that I will not touch you, hit you, kiss you, fuck you, or otherwise injure you in any way. When I brought you back here last night, all I did was try to help you. I warmed you up. That's all I was trying to do."

He sounded so genuine, but she knew what she'd heard. Disappointment burned in her chest, making it hard to breathe. She desperately wanted to believe him, to take comfort in his presence and view him as her protector, but she couldn't trust anything he said. Not when he was keeping secrets. At the risk of insulting the man who'd saved her life, she allowed her anger to surface. "Fine. Then go. I don't need anything else from you."

"Fine." He threw open the door and stepped into the hallway. "Now be a good girl and stay in your room. Don't make this any harder than it needs to be."

"It doesn't need to be hard at all," Katie snapped. "All you have to do is be honest with me."

Rather than answer, Rafe shut the door in her face. Stunned, she stared at the wood grain in disbelief. She was infinitely more upset about her situation now than she'd been only an hour ago. Apparently tomorrow would bring grave danger, and the man who swore he wanted to protect her was not only crazy, but also a liar. She wasn't safe here. Not at all.

With that thought, Katie stalked over to the pile of clean

clothes and tugged off Rafe's T-shirt. She couldn't stand to smell him on her anymore.

CHAPTER SIX

She had to leave.

When it came down to it, that was her only option. Katie wasn't sure how she would sneak away or where she would go, but that wouldn't dissuade her from the only course of action that made sense. Remaining here meant willingly putting her life in Rafe's hands. Better to take her chances on her own. The bad weather and their isolated location meant escape could very well be a suicide mission, but according to Rafe's friend, she was as good as dead if she stayed. She didn't know what to believe anymore. In her heart she somehow couldn't imagine Rafe hurting her, but there was no real reason to trust him. Not after what she'd heard. Maybe he was just a really good actor—sociopaths usually were, right? Given the choice between that and being raped, murdered, and/or tortured, she'd take the cold any day.

Shilah sat on the bed at her side, ears pricked. He seemed to sense her unease, whining low in his throat and nudging her with his nose. She stroked his head to shush him, not wanting Rafe to have any reason to come back. Outside, the sky had gone dark. Rafe had indicated that he was going to sleep soon...she hoped he was at least being honest about that. Once he was asleep, she would investigate the cabin to see if he'd been lying about not having a telephone. If she could call for help, maybe she wouldn't need to venture into the night by herself. She could just blockade herself in the bedroom until help arrived.

Of course, she had no idea how she would direct the police to her location. Katie sighed deeply. "This just keeps getting better, doesn't it?"

Shilah lay his head on her thigh and matched her exhalation. Laughing despite her fear, Katie flopped back onto the mattress and closed her eyes. She had some time to kill before Rafe went to bed, no doubt, and conserving her energy was probably the best way to do it. Careful not to get too comfortable, she allowed herself to doze lightly.

Jerking awake some time later, Katie blinked in confusion, then craned her neck to glance out the window. Inky blackness stared back at her. She sat up in a rush, heart pounding as she tried to decide how long she'd been out. Shilah picked up his head and blinked, looking at her expectantly.

"What do you think?" she whispered. "Is your daddy asleep?"

Shilah thumped his tail against the mattress, clearly pleased by the sound of her voice. She stroked his head—he really was a very nice dog—then stood slowly, not wanting him to follow. She held out her hand. "Stay here."

Shilah immediately leapt off the bed and stretched with exaggerated languor. Katie rolled her eyes and stepped between him and the door, hands on her hips. "I said stay." She gestured. "Sit." She was relieved when he obeyed without hesitation. "Now stay."

She walked to the door and, when Shilah didn't move, pressed her ear to the cool wood. Silence. She couldn't hear anyone walking around, which could mean he'd gone to bed, or else he was just sitting quietly somewhere in the cabin. Unfortunately, the only way to know was to look.

"Okay." Katie took a deep breath, resting her forehead against the door. "If he's awake, I'm going to tell him that I think you have to go outside to potty. Deal?"

Shilah's tail smacked against the ground a couple times, then stilled. When she glanced over her shoulder at him, he stared back eagerly as though waiting to see what she would do. With a quick plea to the universe, she gripped the doorknob and twisted it open. A nightlight plugged into a socket near the floor illuminated a dim path to the end of the short hallway, leaving her to wonder what lay beyond. She closed the door behind her, not wanting Shilah to follow. Before venturing any farther, she waited to see if Shilah would bark and alert Rafe to her movement.

The bark never came. Katie stood completely still and strained to catch any noise that would signal that Rafe was awake. Nothing. All she could hear was the sound of her pulse racing, and the rush of adrenaline through her veins. The silence quickly turned oppressive, startling her into action. Frightened or not, somehow the thought of doing something seemed so much less terrifying than continuing to stand there dumbly.

Her legs quivered as she crept down the hall and turned left to find another hallway, this one with two doors, one open, one closed. The open door was a bathroom, which she was sorely tempted to use. She hadn't peed in a long time, as far as she knew, and the very thought made her bladder burn. Unfortunately, she would have to wait just a little longer. If she wanted the freedom to explore the cabin without attracting Rafe's attention, making a pit stop wasn't exactly the height of stealth.

Pushing aside her biological needs, Katie moved past the closed door on tiptoes. There was a good chance that was Rafe's bedroom. The thought stirred an unwelcome tug of arousal that she couldn't begin to explain. Surely the fact that Rafe was definitely a liar and probably a crazy person should mitigate her inexplicable attraction to him. Right? So the fact that one part of her wanted to push open his bedroom door and crawl into bed with him had to mean that she was crazy, too. Or that he really had drugged her.

Sickened by the thought, she made her way to the end of the hallway and found herself in a large room that had been sectioned off into a kitchen, a dining area, and, separated by a long bar complete with stools, a sitting room with a couch and fireplace. The light from the nearly full moon shone in through the room's windows, allowing her to make out the dim shape of the furniture, though not the details of the pictures she could see hanging on the walls. What struck her was that everything looked so normal. Nothing about this man's home suggested that he was insane or murderous—though, she wasn't exactly sure what she'd expected to find. A pile of bodies? Guns and knives? A sex dungeon?

Did it really matter that Rafe's cabin wasn't littered with evidence of evil intent? She knew what she'd heard. Determined not to linger in the common area any longer than absolutely necessary, she made a slow circuit around the room, starting in the kitchen. She searched the counters for a telephone, dismayed when she couldn't find one. She'd nearly convinced herself that Rafe had been lying about not having any way for her to contact her parents or her sister, but maybe he was telling the truth. She found a flashlight in a drawer next to the pantry, which she took. Then she raided the pantry, taking some beef jerky that looked homemade, a package of crackers, and a banana. It wasn't much, but she wouldn't last in the elements for very long, anyway. If she didn't find shelter before running out of food, she was as good as dead.

More and more, that seemed like the most likely outcome to this situation. Stay or go, she would be lucky to make it home alive.

She performed the rest of her search in efficient silence. From what she could see in the low light, Rafe was a man who enjoyed reading, photography, and music. His bookcase overflowed with fiction and non-fiction, still more framed nature photos lined the walls, and he had an expensive-looking sound system—by far the most modern piece of technology she'd seen in the place. The fact that he liked such human diversions made him only slightly less ominous.

There were probably plenty of serial killers and rapists with good taste in music. The fact that their music collections were nearly parallel—plenty of classic rock, with a smattering of 80's gothic rock favorites—meant nothing. It didn't mean he wouldn't kill her if that's what pleased him.

Her next big find was a closet where she found a heavy fleece jacket. She snatched it off the hanger and tucked it under her arm. It looked a lot warmer than her own winter coat, and big enough to layer over the rest of her clothing. If she was really going to make a break for it, she would need the extra protection.

She saw the two-way radio just as she was about to leave the sitting area. It sat on a desk in the corner farthest from the window, cloaked in shadow. At first she didn't recognize what it was, but the distinctive shape gave it away. Her skin prickled as she crossed the room to examine it. Rafe had said there was no way to contact the police or her family. If the radio worked, and she had no reason to assume it didn't, then this was evidence of another lie.

She hesitated. If she could use the radio to call for help, she wouldn't have to actually step out that door into the cold night. She could just sit and wait for rescue. Again. Katie frowned. Last time, that hadn't exactly worked out. Even if she could figure out how to use the radio to call for help, Rafe might catch her. It could be loud enough to wake him up, and what then? She'd be dead long before help arrived. But going outside...the closer she got to having to really make a decision about what to do, the scarier the thought of fleeing into the woods became. She would almost certainly get lost. She had no sense of direction in the best of times, and the flurries that continued to fall outside would only further disorient her. Not to mention the fact that she had no idea where she was. Rafe said they were three miles from her car, but in what direction? Besides, that could also be a lie. She could be miles and miles from civilization—too far to walk.

After a lengthy hesitation, she picked up the two-way

radio and ran her hands over unfamiliar buttons and dials. She had no idea how to use the stupid thing, but she found herself twisting a knob next to the antenna anyway.

Beep.

Katie startled and nearly dropped the radio, bobbling it between her hands frantically before finally regaining her grip. Her finger pushed another button, causing another loud beep. The front display glowed green, intensely bright in the darkened room. Shaking, she turned the knob to power it down, then stayed statue-still as she waited for Rafe to emerge from his bedroom. But there was only silence.

She looked at the radio in her hand, tempted to put it back where she'd found it. But she knew the better move would be to just take it with her. Away from the cabin, she could try to call for help without worrying about being overheard. Leaving her only way to communicate behind would be a dumb move, one she would surely regret if she wound up lost and alone in a blizzard.

Katie swallowed. She supposed this meant she'd made up her mind.

She had to leave.

CHAPTER SEVEN

After Katie made her decision, she moved fast. Rushing back to the guest room, she put on her heaviest winter clothes and the fleece jacket, then made a terrible discovery. Her shoes were nowhere to be found. She hadn't even looked for them before, not wanting to make noise while she skulked around the cabin. It had never occurred to her that they wouldn't be nearby. Rafe had obviously taken them off when he undressed her, but he hadn't left them in her room. Her cynical side urged her to see that as yet another sign of his ill intent. Luckily, she'd seen a pair of his boots near the front door. They would be far too big and make walking more difficult, but they would have to do.

She tucked the food from the kitchen into one of the large pockets in Rafe's coat, the flashlight and two-way radio in the other. Shilah sat next to the guest room door and watched her preparations, wagging his tail in excitement. She frowned at him, worried that his enthusiasm would give away her escape. At the door, she reached into her pocket and tore off a piece of jerky, then tossed it into the far corner of the room. Shilah looked at the spot where it landed, then at her, tongue lolling.

"Go get it!" Katie whispered. "And then stay."

Shilah took off running, but he didn't linger to watch him enjoy his treat. Instead she slipped out of the room and sprinted past Rafe's bedroom to the front door. She pulled on his boots, certain that at any moment, his door would click open down the hallway. She was surprised when it didn't, and even more shocked when she pulled open the front door and slipped outside without eliciting any barking or activity from any of the cabin's occupants. A frigid blast of wind stole her breath and large flurries landed wetly on her face, but Katie had never been so relieved to be out in the cold.

She was free.

In the guest room, her plan had been to carefully survey the landscape and identify where the snow-covered road began. But that wasn't how it went down. The noise of the cabin door closing behind her triggered a fearful, primitive reaction. She ran for her life.

Or at least she tried. Thigh-deep snow sent her toppling forward when her lower body didn't move as fast as she expected. Cursing under her breath, she picked herself up and brushed off the front of her coat. This was going to be a difficult walk.

Rafe's truck was parked to her right, trapped in snow that had piled up over the bottom of the tires. She could only assume that he'd parked in the driveway, and that he'd driven straight in. There was a clearing in the trees behind the truck, probably a road. She trudged in that direction, clumsy in Rafe's oversized boots, and concentrated on walking in a straight line. It didn't take long before she had trouble seeing where the road ended and dirt and trees began. Panic kept her walking forward even when she grew less confident that she was going in the right direction. By the time she lost sight of the cabin behind her, she had no idea where she was. She'd somehow wandered off the clear path through the trees, and when she pivoted in place after finally stopping short in confusion, she realized that she had absolutely no idea which direction to go.

Oh, God. This was a bad idea.

"No," Katie whispered under her breath. "No, this was my only choice."

But was it? Maybe she had misjudged Rafe. Maybe he'd

only humored a crazy neighbor, played along with his delusion. It was possible. She looked back over her shoulder, in the direction she thought the cabin might be. No longer in motion, the cold settled into her bones and she shivered. Maybe she should go back.

"Don't be stupid." She swiped at her face when her eyes teared up, partially from the cold, but also from frustration. Life had placed her in an impossible situation and she'd made a choice. Now she just had to make the best of it. She exhaled, watched her breath drift out into the night, and agonized over what to do next. Rafe could be awake by now. He could even be looking for her.

That's when she remembered the two-way radio in her pocket. She pulled it out with trembling, glove-covered hands and turned it on. The beep sounded startlingly loud in the middle of the peaceful woods and the display glowed like a giant, neon-green beacon. Paranoid, she glanced around, then squinted at the controls frantically. It took her only seconds to realize that she had no idea how to work the device. She pushed a couple of buttons and watched names flash across the display. Cooper. Dale. Alpha. She frowned, not exactly relishing the idea of calling up one of Rafe's buddies. She already knew what the friend who'd stopped by earlier thought Rafe should've done with her. He wasn't going to help her if she called him up.

Cooper. Dale. Alpha. Which one sounded the least threatening? She decided on Cooper, for no other reason than the face she conjured up for that name seemed kinder than the others. She pushed a couple more buttons, cringing at every beep. "Hello? Is anyone there?" She scanned the trees around her as she waited for an answer, half expecting Rafe to burst onto the scene. Engaging the talk button again, she whispered, "Please, I need help."

She was about to twist the dial to call 'Dale' when a familiar voice came over the radio. "Does Rafe know you're calling me, little girl?"

Katie gasped and dropped the handset. An eerie green light emanated from the snow where it landed, transforming the dark woods into a spooky, almost alien landscape. Her throat went dry as she cursed her instincts. She'd just called the man who'd told Rafe she was going to end up raped, tortured, and murdered—maybe even by Rafe himself.

"You there, girl?" The snow muffled his gruff voice. "Listen to me. Turn off the radio, go back to bed, and trust that Rafe will protect you. He's the only chance you've got."

A mournful howl in the distance snapped Katie out of her temporary paralysis. She snatched up the radio and twisted the knob to power it down, then walked in a small circle, scanning the woods. She could try to call Dale or Alpha and hope for a better result, attempt a blind walk out of the woods, or simply make her way back to Rafe's cabin. Her jaw chattered as she struggled with indecision. Another howl cut through the stillness of the night, much closer than the last.

All at once, she realized that her biggest danger might not be getting lost. Despite the weather, she wasn't alone in the woods. She hadn't realized that the Sierra Nevada mountains even had a wolf population, but now she worried about a whole new threat. She would have to walk for hours to find help. What were her chances that the wolves she was hearing wouldn't find her before then?

Shit. Katie turned back in the direction of her own footprints, determined to retrace her steps. She was disheartened to see the deep imprints from her boots already filling with drifting snow, becoming less and less visible every second it took her to slog her way through the powder. She'd only taken a few steps when an ear-piercing howl rose up all around her. The sound bounced off the trees, making it impossible to pinpoint the source. Her heart thundered in her chest and she stumbled before she regained her balance and continued her frantic high-stepping through the snow.

It was official. This was a very, very bad idea.

A large white wolf leapt out from behind a tree in front of

her, blocking the path made by her disappearing bootprints. She opened her mouth to scream, but no sound came out. Only a puffy white cloud of terror, which floated away uselessly into the atmosphere. Unable to move, she stood frozen in place and waited to see what would happen next. Maybe it would decide to go away if she didn't move. Part of her yearned to bolt in the opposite direction, but she could never outrun a wolf and even if she did, she would only end up more lost.

The wolf stared at her. She averted her eyes, not wanting to challenge it in any way. The hair on the back of her neck stood up at movement in her peripheral vision. She turned her head, horrified at the sight of another wolf—this one gray— standing even closer than the first. Before she could react, the gray wolf surged forward and caught her leg in its mouth. Her many layers of clothing offered some protection, but sharp teeth tore into her flesh deep enough to pull a hoarse cry from her too-dry throat. Burning agony shot through her calf as the wolf jerked her violently enough to throw her off balance and into the snow. It released her leg only to reclaim it seconds later in an even fiercer grip. He shook his head back and forth, ripping her flesh.

The bloodcurdling horror inside her finally burst free from her mouth in a scream that sounded like it came from a stranger. The surreal vocalization of her own fear and suffering echoing through the desolate cold frightened her even more than the malevolence in the wolf's soulless eyes. Just when she thought he was going to tear her apart, the wolf retreated. Her stomach turned over at the sight of blood oozing from a ragged tear in her pants.

Adrenaline coursed through her veins. She scrambled to her feet and took a slow, hobbling step backward. She didn't want to encourage the wolves to chase, but she was too frightened to play dead. Both wolves drew closer, making her tremble so violently that she nearly lost her balance again. The wolf that had bitten her advanced, baring blood-stained teeth in a terrible grin.

Then the impossible happened. In one fluid, surreal motion, the wolf's shape changed. Fur receded, smoothing into tanned skin. Paws turned into hands and feet. Rising up on its back legs, the wolf became a man.

A very naked man, whose large erection jutted out from between his legs like a weapon.

In a single breath, Katie's terror deepened beyond anything she could have imagined. Her entire sense of reality shattered at the sheer insanity of watching beast turn into man. The wolf-man licked her blood off his lips. "It tastes delicious."

The white wolf morphed into a well-built blond man whose arousal rivaled his friend's. "It smells delicious, too."

It. She was nothing to these two—only prey. Katie turned and tried to run, but a solid shape hit her from behind and knocked her forward into the snow. The gray wolf, a man no longer, grabbed onto her other leg, wrenching a pained gasp from her lungs.

"Hey!" The blond man yanked his partner away from her leg. "Don't chew it up until I have a chance to fuck it."

The gray wolf shifted back into human form, his mouth dripping with her blood. "Chewing's my favorite part."

"Well, fucking's mine." The blond bent and rolled her onto her back, pressing her deep into the snow. Claustrophobia overwhelmed her as cold surrounded her on all sides. The man ripped open Rafe's coat, then wrenched it off her shoulders. "Just give me a few minutes and then you can do whatever you want. But I'm not screwing your leftovers."

Katie twisted away from the blond man's hands, but without leverage, she couldn't pull herself out of the snow grave he'd created using the weight of her body. Tears spilled over and she sobbed as both men began to tear away her clothing.

"Fuck, you're overdressed." The man who'd bitten her released his handful of her ripped shirt and backhanded her across the face. "Stupid bitch."

She squeezed her eyes shut as tight as she could. She didn't want to watch. She couldn't stand to see what they were doing. They'd barely even started and already she wished they would just kill her.

A vicious snarl arose from somewhere near. Katie opened her eyes in time to see a dark shape slam into the blond man, taking him down into the snow beside her. The newcomer, a jet black wolf, bit the blond man, who changed back into his beast form and threw himself into the tussle. Their enraged snarls filled the air as the fight migrated away from where she was entombed.

"Fuck this." The biter continued to pull down her pants. "I'm not waiting around so some other wolf can use you up."

She pushed against his chest in a futile attempt to fend him off. He caught her across the face with his knuckles, lazily, as though swatting away an insect. Then he went back to work, grabbing her thin undershirt and rending the material with his hands.

A sharp, keening whimper caught the biter's attention. He released her and stood up, growling in the direction of the other wolves. "The fuck?"

A familiar voice responded. "She's mine."

Katie's muscles turned to water. Rafe had found her.

CHAPTER EIGHT

"Yours?" The biter laughed, then spat in Katie's direction. She struggled to sit, desperate to escape from her frozen prison. "I found it first."

"Actually, you didn't. I found her a couple days ago." Rafe met her eyes when she finally sat up. Naked and also fully aroused, he stood over the crumpled body of the blond man, blood staining the snow around his bare legs. The blond's throat had been torn out and Rafe's chin dripped with crimson. He pinned her with a hard look. "I simply misplaced her tonight."

"Oh, well." The biter twisted her hair in his fist until she cried out. "Finders, keepers. I thought your pack didn't go for humans, anyway."

"We don't hunt them, no." Disdain passed over Rafe's handsome face. "We don't kill them."

"So then what do you care?" He dragged Katie up and held her against his naked thigh. "You want a turn after me? I can't promise I won't chew her up a little. I'll leave her face, though. Keep her pretty for you."

Rafe's expression hardened. "You're not going to touch her. In fact, I suggest you take your hands off her right now."

The biter sniffed, staring Rafe down, then nodded at the body on the ground. "He dead?"

Rafe's icy stare never wavered. "Yeah."

"You killed one of your own kind for a human. Think your

alpha will agree with that?"

"I'll deal with my alpha." Rafe took a step closer, never breaking eye contact with the biter. "Let Katie go. Now."

"Katie?" The hand in her hair jerked sharply, bringing fresh tears to her eyes. "It has a name?"

Rafe lunged forward with a primal growl. "I said, let her go. She's mine. Do you understand?"

The biter loosened his grip on her hair, surprise written all over his face. Staring at Rafe, he leaned in close and pressed his nose into Katie's neck, inhaling deeply while she shuddered and tried to pull away. Laughter shook the biter's powerful frame as he shoved her back into the snow. "With a human? That's disgusting."

"You know I'll kill you if you touch her. Just like I killed your buddy." Rafe stalked closer, openly appraising her body as he approached. "Is it really worth it?"

"You tell me." The biter puffed up his chest and stepped away from where she'd fallen. The two naked men faced each other, squaring off. Incredibly, neither of them seemed affected by the cold. "Is she worth it?"

"She's mine. That means I'll die to protect her. Even if she is just a human." Rafe ran his worried gaze over her bare skin, which had gone numb in the freezing wind. The reason for his fierce devotion was a mystery, one that should have unsettled her. Instead it made her feel safe. Protected. Her eyes met his. "Go take your friend's body back to his mate, if he had one."

"He does. A mate, and a son."

Rafe cringed. "No one else has to die tonight. Just leave us. This was a misunderstanding, but now it's over."

The biter chuckled. "Oh, this isn't over. Not at all." With one last, dismissive glance at Katie, he walked over to his friend's corpse and nudged it with his foot. "This murder won't go unanswered. I promise you that."

"He was going to rape and kill my bond-mate. Nobody will fault me for protecting her."

Shivering at Rafe's words, Katie gathered her torn clothing around her exposed body. His bond-mate? What the hell had happened while she was unconscious?

"We'll see." The biter loped toward Rafe, shooting him a stern sidelong glance as he passed. "Take your human slut and get out of here." He paused in front of Katie and gripped his erection in his hand. "I'll see you soon, Katie. Next time I'll bring more friends. Hope you're ready."

Rafe moved between them, a flesh-and-blood shield. "Come back and I'll kill you. All of you."

"Good luck with that." The biter winked and melted back into wolf form. He threw his head back and howled, then took off running through the trees.

As soon as he was gone, Rafe rushed to her side. "How badly are you injured?"

"I..." Katie's head swam with everything that had just occurred. She didn't know what was most disconcerting: the fact that werewolves existed, Rafe's delicious nudity, or her desire to fall into his arms and let him protect her. "I'm not sure."

He knelt in the snow, took her leg in his hands, and gave her a careful examination. "He bit you. I won't know how badly until we get back to the cabin. Which we need to do immediately, by the way, before any more come." He shoved the oversize boots back over her socks, which were soaked through and heavy.

She let Rafe help her to her feet, then fiddled awkwardly with her torn clothing. Modesty seemed ridiculous in this situation, especially since he'd already seen her naked, but it was the only thing she had left. Being treated like a piece of meat had stripped away her humanity; denying Rafe the right to see her body helped restore a tiny piece of what made her who she was.

"Here, put this on." Rafe draped his coat over her shoulders and pulled it closed over her chest. "I'll lead you back in wolf form. Someone took my boots, and my feet are starting to get cold."

"I'm sorry." Katie felt well and truly chagrined. "Rafe, I—"

"We'll talk when we get back to my place. Until then, be quiet." She tried not to stare at his perfect ass as he turned away from her. He glanced over his shoulder, catching her gaze. "Full moon tomorrow. The woods are crawling with my kind tonight."

She shivered and limped after him. "Okay."

He transformed into a wolf and stared at her with glowing eyes. She lowered her gaze and followed as he led her back over the faint path she'd made during her walk in. He trotted through the snow at a fast clip, stopping every few feet to wait for her to catch up. Her toes were like ice in the soaking wet socks, her legs hurt, and her mind raced with all she'd just learned. Werewolves were real. One of them was claiming her as his bond-mate, whatever that meant. She'd almost just died. And apparently the woods were teeming with wolfmen who could leap out and attack at any moment.

The trek back to the cabin seemed to take forever. She hadn't realized she'd walked so far, and wondered whether she would have been able to find her way on her own. When a baleful howl echoed through the trees just as the cabin came into sight, she stumbled and caught herself on hands planted in the deep snow, then straightened and used one last burst of energy to run to the front door. Rafe made it there before she did, shifting back into human form and ushering her inside. He locked the door and stalked after her, anger evident in his every step.

Katie stopped just inside the door, not wanting to track water through the house. She was so cold. The pain in her legs worried her just as much as the imminent possibility of her murder by werewolves. She didn't know whether she would make it through the night alive, and the one person who had shown her any kindness was furious with her.

She met Rafe's steely gaze, breath quickening at the fire in his eyes. For better or worse, she was going to have to trust this man.

He really was the only chance she had.

SOUL BONDED

CHAPTER NINE

"What the hell were you thinking?"

Katie shrank away as Rafe's shout rattled the walls. Shivering, she wrapped her arms around her chest. All she wanted was to get out of her soaking wet clothes. She wasn't sure she had the strength for a dressing down when she was this cold. "I said I was sorry."

"Sorry?" His hands shook as he ran them through his wet hair. He engaged the heavy deadbolt on the door, then stomped past her to the kitchen sink, where he washed the rest of the blond man's blood off his face. "You could have been killed!"

"I didn't know—"

Rafe spun around and glared at her. "You didn't know that you could freeze to death out there? You didn't know that you had no idea where the hell you were even going?" Rage contorted his handsome features. "Forget the fact that it's the night before a full moon and we're right in the middle of major werewolf territory. I get that you didn't know that part, but surely you realized that running off into the night, in sub-zero temperatures, was colossally, dangerously stupid."

"I didn't know what else to do." It sounded weak, even to her.

"So suicide seemed like the best option?" He advanced on her, his erection bobbing menacingly with each step. She flashed back to the feeling of rough hands pawing her body and cowered, closing her eyes. Her whole body tensed in anticipation—of what, she didn't know.

His footfalls stopped abruptly. For a moment she heard only his labored breathing, then he exhaled and walked past her. She opened her eyes in time to watch him tug on a pair of sweatpants that had been left pooled on the floor in the foyer. Relieved that he'd given her a little space, she turned to meet his gaze. "Suicide wasn't my intention."

"But it was nearly the result." His expression was hard, almost cold, yet she sensed volatile emotion beneath the surface. "Just tell me what possessed you to do something like that. What did I do that was so horrible that you decided it was better to take your chances out there alone?"

Katie straightened. "I was worried you were going to hurt me."

"Were you?" He studied her face. "Really?"

She lowered her head. "It wasn't anything you did. I overheard you talking to your friend. He said I was going to end up getting raped and murdered—maybe even by you— and your side of the conversation didn't exactly make me feel any better. I heard him call me a human, so full of disdain. I thought he was crazy—that both of you were crazy, maybe." Katie exhaled. "He told you that you should've let me die. And meanwhile you were making me feel things that I had no reason to feel. Emotions." She paused, embarrassed. "Other stuff, too. I didn't know what you'd done to me to make me feel that way. I didn't know why you and your friend said the things you did. So I was frightened. That's all."

Rafe's expression softened. He folded his arms over his muscular chest, as though he was suddenly aware of how threatening he actually seemed. "Look, we need to get you warmed up. Again."

Katie nodded, too exhausted and frozen to argue. She followed Rafe into the guest room, greeting Shilah with a sheepish pat on the head. "Hi, boy."

Rafe pinned him with a hard look. "You're in the dog

house for real, boy. You were supposed to be watching her."

Shilah wagged his tail, clearly pleased to be addressed by his master, whatever the context. Katie couldn't help but laugh. "He doesn't seem terribly concerned."

"He knows I'm all bark and no bite." Rafe gestured at her body. "You need to take those clothes off. Especially if I'm going to clean your wounds."

Shy but chilled to the bone, Katie shrugged off Rafe's coat before hesitating. "Could I have some privacy?"

Rafe nodded. "Meet me in the bathroom down the hall once you're undressed. Go ahead and use one of my T-shirts from the dresser. I think you still have some..." His gaze darted to the pile of her laundry he'd left stacked on the floor. "Just leave your legs bare so I can treat the bites."

"All right."

He stood at the door, hands laced in front of his crotch. "I'm not going to hurt you. Honestly, Katie. Never."

She believed him. "I know."

Rafe left the room with Shilah at his heels. As soon as he shut the door she began to strip off her wet clothes. Her fingers were so numb they barely worked and her shivering increased exponentially as soon as the air hit her bare skin. As a result the whole process took her longer than she wanted, and drained her completely. She probably needed Rafe's help, but believing that he wasn't going to kill her didn't mean that she was ready to let him undress her again.

Once her upper body was bare, she braced herself for the hard part. She took a deep breath and stripped off her pants, sickened by the sight of a deep bite wound on her right calf. It was still bleeding lightly, but didn't hurt nearly as much as it looked like it should. No doubt it would be really painful once the feeling returned to her body. The bite on the back of her other calf was shallower and not nearly as bad, but seeing so much of her flesh torn open and raw turned her stomach.

Naked, she limped to the dresser by the closet and got a worn T-shirt out of the top drawer. Rafe's scent wafted up to greet her, instantly comforting. She inhaled deeply as she tugged the shirt over her head, then cursed under her breath. He'd called her his bond-mate, and the wolf who'd bitten her had clearly sensed some connection between them. Was that why simply smelling Rafe made her feel like this? Like... She shivered again. Like she was home.

"Katie, are you okay?" Rafe's voice came from just outside the bedroom door.

She walked stiffly to the pile of laundry and pulled a pair of her panties off the top. She had to struggle to make her limbs move so she could put them on. "I'm just so cold." She shuffled to the door and threw it open, beyond caring about her lack of clothing. All she wanted was for Rafe to dress her wounds so she could crawl under the blankets. She never should have left in the first place. "I feel like I'll never be warm again."

Rafe's gaze slid down the length of her body. His throat jumped when he saw her mangled legs. "He really got you."

"Yeah." She glanced down at her calves and shrugged, teeth chattering. "I can barely feel it. I can't really feel anything right now."

Rafe glanced over his shoulder at the bathroom door, then at her. "Why don't you let me warm you a little before we look at the bites?"

Something about his tone told her that there was a reason he was asking permission. "What does that involve, exactly?"

He smiled, almost shyly. "A hug. Basically."

"A hug." She wasn't sure she liked the idea. It almost felt like a trick. It was certainly too much for him to ask after what those beasts outside had put her through. But if there was any chance it might really help her fight off the ice that had settled into her bones, she was willing to take a leap of faith. "Okay."

He seemed surprised by her easy acquiescence. "Okay." He hesitated. "It would probably work better if we were skin-to-skin..."

Katie frowned. "No."

"All right." He held out his arms and looked into her eyes. "Come here."

She surprised herself by stepping into his embrace without hesitation. He curled his powerful arms around her back and pulled her close enough to feel his heartbeat thumping in rhythm with her own. Within seconds, exquisite heat spread throughout her body, starting at her chest and flowing into the tips of her extremities. Katie gasped and nearly pulled away, but Rafe kept her close.

"It's okay," he murmured. "It's normal. Let it happen." He rubbed a hand up and down her spine, as though comforting a child. "I've got you. Just hold on to me."

Katie clung to Rafe tightly, overwhelmed when the warmth that flowed from his body to hers bloomed into an intense rush of emotion. There was so much to process that she couldn't separate everything she was feeling—love, safety, devotion, protectiveness, peace. The rhythm of his breathing shifted to match hers, making her feel as though his body was merely an extension of her own. She buried her face in his neck, overwhelmed by the all-consuming joy of being in his arms. His scent surrounded her, drawing out a low, needy moan that made her blush. Despite her embarrassment—despite everything that had happened tonight—she had to fight the urge to raise up on her tiptoes and kiss Rafe on the mouth.

Instead, she cried out in shock when sensation returned to her calves in the form of burning, throbbing pain. Rafe released her, wiping away her tears with his thumbs. "Your wounds?"

Katie nodded dumbly. Now that their embrace was over, the surreality of the entire situation hit her hard. Not only the existence of werewolves, but Rafe calling her his bond-mate and her body's incredible reaction to his touch. Hell, her soul's reaction to his mere presence. Trembling, she placed her hand on Rafe's warm cheek and looked deep into his tender green eyes. "Rafe—"

He shook his head and took her hand. "Let's go to the bathroom so I can clean your wounds. We'll talk about it there." His shoulders slumped almost imperceptibly as he led her down the hallway. "I'll explain everything."

CHAPTER TEN

Katie winced as Rafe guided her more gravely injured leg beneath a stream of warm water from the bathtub's faucet. He poured some anti-bacterial soap into the wound and carefully but thoroughly washed it. The soap and water stung like a bitch, and despite his careful touch, she had to restrain herself from lashing out. "Fuck."

Rafe raised an eyebrow. "I'm sorry. I really am trying to be gentle."

"I know you are." She brought her other foot up onto the edge of the tub and rested her cheek on her knee, not caring that Rafe could see her panties. Maybe it was foolish, but she no longer feared him. On the contrary, an unexpected thrill crawled up her spine when his gaze slid to the space between her legs. Beyond a discreet flaring of his nostrils, he betrayed no reaction. She watched calmly as he turned his attention back to her leg, flushing out her wound with a tenderness she never would have expected from a man of Rafe's size and strength.

"It's good that you were wearing so many layers. This could've been much worse."

"Believe me, I know." She tried not to think about the way those two werewolves had talked about her—like she was a piece of meat to be violated and then eaten. A couple of bite wounds were nothing compared to what could have

59

happened. If this was her worst souvenir from tonight, she considered herself lucky. The thought triggered a sudden, horrifying memory of werewolf lore drawn mostly from films and television. Nausea rolled over her. "He bit me. Does that mean..." She swallowed, certain she would be sick. "Am I a werewolf now?"

Rafe surprised her by laughing. He shot her an easygoing grin, so handsome it took the sting out of his amusement. "No, it doesn't work like that. You have to be born this way."

"Oh." Katie considered that as her heart rate slowed. Then she realized how her disgust might have come across. "No offense intended. I'm sure it's not like being a werewolf is the worst thing in the world."

He snorted. "I appreciate you saying so."

"It's just that I—"

Rafe shook his head. "You don't have to apologize. I understand."

She joined in his examination of her deeper wound. Even if it didn't turn her into a werewolf, the bite was going to leave a scar. The entire attack would no doubt linger within her subconscious mind forever. "Do you think I'll need stitches?"

"No, we need to let the wound stay open to heal." He stared at her leg as the water rinsed over it, then furrowed his brow. "It'll lower the risk of infection."

She nodded. The concern in his eyes made her belly flutter in the most pleasant way. There he went again, looking at her like she was his entire world. She knew they had to talk about whatever this bond was between them, but she was almost afraid to ask. Not ready to be direct, she said, "I'm lucky to have such a competent savior."

"You're lucky in more ways than you can imagine." Stormy emotion tightened his features. "I could have lost you, Katie."

"You barely know me." Clearly this wasn't exactly true, and she was pretty sure he already knew that she'd caught on. A surge of courage emboldened her to challenge him to be honest. "Why do you care?"

Rafe averted his eyes and held out his hand. "Let me see the other bite."

She extended her bent leg, suppressing the urge to whimper when he cradled her ankle and guided it beneath the water. To hell with waiting for Rafe to come clean. If he wasn't going to come out and address his big revelation, she would. "You told that—" She paused, hesitant to offend him with her labeling of his brethren. "What do you call yourselves?"

"Just call him a wolf. That's all he was. A mean-ass wolf."

Beneath the cold judgment in Rafe's eyes lurked a hint of shame—for his own kind, she assumed. He was obviously made of different stuff than those animals in the woods, or even his friend, Cooper, who'd urged him to let her die. But why did Rafe care about her seemingly worthless human life when none of the other wolves did? What set him apart? She sensed that it had everything to do with the answer to her next question. "You told that wolf that I was your bond-mate. What did you mean?"

Pain and sorrow radiated from his tense frame. "It's…complicated."

"Yes, it does sound complicated." Katie waited a beat, then said, "Tell me. Please."

Rafe rattled her with a look of genuine fear. "You were so cold, Katie. So cold. And unresponsive." He continued to cradle her ankle as he spoke. "You were dying—and I had to do something. So I just…followed my instinct."

"What did you do?"

He exhaled slowly. "I warmed you just like I did a few minutes ago. I took off my shirt and got beneath the blankets with you, then held you while I focused all my energy on raising your body temperature with mine. And it worked." Guilt tightened his features. "But something happened. Something I didn't expect."

Enough with the build-up. She needed to know. "Rafe—"

His next words came out in a rush. "We bonded. I had no

61

idea it would happen—that it even could happen. It's rare enough for two werewolves to bond, so I never imagined that it would be possible for me to do it with a human."

"We bonded?" Katie wrestled with disbelief as he turned off the faucet and opened the drawer beneath the sink. She had no idea why it would be a struggle to accept the concept of bonding souls on a night when she'd seen men transform into wolves, but her logical mind rebelled at the idea. She wasn't even sure what it meant. "Explain what that involves. Please."

He avoided her eyes as he uncapped a tube of antibiotic ointment and began spreading it over her wounds. "It means our souls are connected."

She waited for more. When he didn't elaborate, she huffed in exasperation. "And?"

"When you hurt, I feel pain." His fingers glided over her skin, so very careful. "When we're together, I'm whole. And when we're apart, we'll both...feel that loss. Acutely."

Katie couldn't wrap her mind around what Rafe was telling her. When she hurt, he felt pain? Did that go both ways? "What do you mean, we'll feel the loss? How?"

"It's my understanding that separation will mean tremendous suffering for both of us. But I can't say for certain...I've never experienced it before." Rafe shook his head and closed his eyes, pausing in his movements. "I'm so sorry. If I'd known..."

"You would have let me die?" In saving her, he'd fundamentally altered the course of her life. Right now she wasn't certain whether she was better off alive. "Why didn't you? You could have easily left me in my car. As far as I can tell, the rest of your kind would've. Either that or made me into a meal."

Rafe lifted his shoulder in a vague shrug. "I couldn't." He met her eyes, sending another shiver through her. Even if her brain wasn't sure about the idea of souls bonding, her body obviously recognized him. More than that, wanted him. She was pretty sure she should be furious about this bonding thing, if only she could focus on the repercussions and not the strange-yet-familiar touch of his strong hands. "I...value life."

"Even human life?" It was either laugh or cry, and luckily she still felt capable of the former. "I'm nothing more than a piece of meat out here." Her levity quickly dissolved into tears. "Am I?"

"The full moon is tomorrow night. That's why it's so dangerous for you right now. More than it might normally be."

Katie wiped away a tear, not wanting to look weak. She refused to fall apart over this, no matter how dire the situation seemed. "What's so special about the full moon? It seems like you guys turn into wolves whenever you want."

Rafe nodded. "We can, but the moon forces us to shift. And for a day or two before and after, its energy gets us hyper-aroused. Puts us into hunting mode. For some of us that means going on longer runs than normal. For others, it's an excuse to engage in a little unchecked brutality."

"Terrific."

"As far as I know, I've never killed anyone on one of those nights." His jaw tightened. "But the reality is, I'm not in my head when the moon is full. None of us are. That's why Cooper was concerned that I could harm you." He flexed his fingers on her ankle, a gentle squeeze. "But I won't. I don't honestly believe I could."

"You don't believe you could," Katie echoed, stomach rolling. "And yet before you met me, you had no idea that this bonding thing could even happen the way it did. So what the hell do you know?"

"I know that I will die before I let anyone hurt you." Rafe couldn't even look at her, despite his heartfelt words. "And I know that tomorrow night, I'm locking you in this cabin with Shilah, a gun, and strict orders to shoot anything that comes inside." He paused. "Including me."

Great. She hadn't held a gun in years, let alone shot at a living creature with the intention of killing it. While she wouldn't hesitate to defend herself against the mouthy gray wolf who'd bitten her tonight and others like him, she was pretty sure there was no way she could ever knowingly hurt Rafe. The thought—errant, instinctive, true—pissed her off. "You said that if I hurt, you feel pain. If we're apart, we'll both feel the loss." She pinned him with a hard look. "So how, exactly, am I supposed to shoot you?"

He gently dabbed the last of the ointment on her calf. "It won't come to that."

"No, of course not. Because I'm your goddamn bond-mate."

His shoulders stiffened and he actively avoided making eye contact. "Yes."

The enormity of that concept flooded her with fresh panic. What did this mean? She couldn't exactly leave her life in San Francisco to be with a werewolf who lived in a cabin in the middle of scary, werewolf-infested woods. It wasn't like she loved him—no matter what her heart and body kept telling her. "Okay, I can see the advantage of our connection if you think it'll protect me from you tomorrow night. But after that, how do we undo it? How do we break the bond?"

"We don't." The words sounded hollow. "It's done."

Though she'd expected him to say as much, Katie's anger swelled. "So, what, I'm supposed to want to be with you now? You take off my clothes, cuddle with me in bed while I'm unconscious, and suddenly you're my soulmate? Without my consent?"

"I said I'm sorry." Rafe's voice turned gruff, as though he was holding back his own torrent of emotion. "I don't know what to tell you. I don't expect you to stay with me—in fact, I don't expect anything from you. What I said before still stands. Once the road clears, I'll take you to town. What you do after that is your choice. I'm not going to force you into something you don't want."

His kindness only stoked the fire of her fury. "Well, great. Except according to you, if I leave, it'll devastate both of us."

He stared at her with a blank expression. "I don't know what you want me to say."

She didn't either. All she knew was that she'd nearly died tonight, again, and she was apparently connected forever to a werewolf she barely knew. And according to him, leaving him would break both their hearts. That was if leaving was even an option, now that she had an entire forest full of werewolves out to get her. She dropped her head into her hands and exhaled. "I guess...I want you to say this is all a bad dream."

"I wish it were."

Katie sniffled, knowing she must seem pathetic but too overwhelmed to care. She wanted to scream at Rafe, maybe even hit him, but that required energy she didn't have. At least her legs didn't hurt anymore. Which seemed...odd. She peeked through her spread fingers at her calves, still cradled in Rafe's large hands. "The pain is gone."

"Good." Rafe released her and stood. "Let me know if it starts to bother you again."

She touched the area next to the more severe bite mark, confused by the lack of sensation. Just minutes ago she'd been in agony. All Rafe had done was flush her wounds and cover them with antibiotic lotion. He'd given her nothing for the discomfort. At least nothing she could see. "Why? What did you do?"

His shoulders tensed as he washed his hands. "I sent you some healing energy. Or at least I tried. I'm hoping it helped."

Healing energy. Wasn't that what had caused their predicament in the first place? "Don't do that again. What if you make it worse?"

"Your wounds? I won't."

"No, the...bond." Katie didn't want to admit how nice it was not to hurt anymore—not when the price was eternal devotion to a man she knew nothing about. A man whose friends wanted her dead. "You say we can't undo it, but maybe there's a way. And if there is, I'm pretty sure it starts with you keeping your damn hands off me."

Rafe flinched. "I apologize. I was only trying to help."

"Well, I've had enough of your help." She struggled to her feet, then shot out a hand to brace herself against the wall. She was so tired she could barely stand. "What was the deal before? I stay in the guest room, shut the door, and you won't bother me?"

Jaw tight, Rafe stared straight ahead. "Yup. That was the deal."

"Great." Katie moved to leave, then froze when Rafe caught her by the wrist. She jerked away from him, glaring. "I said don't touch me."

He stepped into her personal space but stopped short of making contact. "The other part of the deal is that you pull the curtains closed as soon as you get in there, you go straight to bed, and you let me know if you need to leave the room for any reason—even if it's only because you have to pee."

Katie deflated as the power of suggestion awakened her bladder. "Actually, I do. Need to pee."

Rafe edged past her and out the bathroom door. "I'll put Shilah in your room. He stays with you from now on. Always."

"Fine." Her problem wasn't with Shilah—and she didn't want to be alone, anyway.

"Good night." He didn't even look at her as he shut the door. When he left the room, it was as though all the air left with him.

Katie felt the loss.

CHAPTER ELEVEN

Lying in bed after washing up, Katie mused that the worst part about being mad at Rafe was how hard it was to stay mad. Once again warm beneath his comforter, surrounded by his masculine scent and protected by his faithful dog, she struggled not to succumb to the urge to go to him. The seductive pull of his comforting presence only a room away kept her from tumbling into much-needed sleep. Her body hummed with desire, a buzzing awareness that true peace and satisfaction was hers for the taking. All she had to do to find it was seek out her bond-mate and let him fill up all the emptiness inside her. Here, she was scared and lonely. With Rafe, she would be whole.

"Damn him," Katie whispered. She didn't want to need him. It wasn't fair that she did. Based on his dark good looks alone, she would date Rafe in a heartbeat. But love him? A werewolf? One who lived in the middle of nowhere, surrounded by other, murderous werewolves? He wasn't exactly her dream guy.

And yet she had to will herself not to crawl into bed with him. She was exhausted but every time she closed her eyes she saw those wolves—those naked men—and felt their teeth and hands all over her body. Unable to sleep, she had nothing to do except stare at the moon's glow creeping in beneath the curtain, and worry. How many more were out there? Did the rest of the pack know about the one Rafe had killed? Were they coming to exact revenge at this very moment?

She really would feel better with Rafe next to her.

No. Katie closed her eyes, determined to stay in her own bed. She was mad at Rafe, after all. He'd married their souls, for lack of a better term, while she was unconscious. He'd probably ruined her for any other man. That meant he'd also ruined her chance for a normal life, with kids and family vacations and 401k retirement plans. What was she supposed to do now? Move to the middle of nowhere? Or perhaps they could they find a little apartment in the city. One with enough room to build a giant cage to contain Rafe during his "time of the month". Katie smiled despite herself. How would she manage a relationship with a werewolf?

"Stop it." Katie kept her voice too low for anyone but Shilah to hear. "You won't. You can't." She took a deep, measured breath, then exhaled. "Besides, I hate him." She knew that was a lie—a huge lie, actually—but it helped fan the flames of her dwindling anger to say the words. "I hate him."

Beside her, Shilah sighed. She was pretty sure he didn't believe it, either.

03❧80

A low growl pulled Katie out of fitful sleep. Her eyes snapped open and she battled momentary disorientation before she remembered where she was. She sat up, then froze at the sight of Shilah crouched at the foot of the bed. His fur was raised in a line down his back, his tail held rigidly at attention. Holding her breath, she followed Shilah's gaze to the curtained window. It was still dark outside. She was beginning to feel like this night would never end.

Katie's heart pounded when Shilah growled again. The last thing she wanted to do was search for some sign of movement outside, but she couldn't look away. The curtain swayed lightly, caught in a subtle draft, revealing bare glimpses of moonlit sky and snow-covered trees. She could barely stand to watch, afraid that a shadow would pass across the window and literally frighten her to death. Just as the thought occurred to her, a muted howl arose from somewhere in the distance. Her breathing hitched as adrenaline surged through her body.

She needed to go to Rafe. Now.

Slipping out of bed, Katie nearly made it to the door before she stopped, conflicted. A howl outside didn't mean they were in danger. Of course there were more wolves in the woods—some of them were even Rafe's friends. If she went running to him now, it was as good as forgiving him. And she wasn't ready to do that. Not yet. Not unless she absolutely had to.

She turned and studied Shilah's body language. He was still on high alert, attention fixed on the window. Katie took a deep breath, then crossed the room to stand at his side. She put her hand on his head and stared at the window with him. As quietly as she could, she murmured, "What do you hear, boy?"

He uttered a soft half-bark and growled once more. Then he took a few cautious steps forward, planting himself squarely in front of the window. Before she could stop him, Shilah poked his nose beneath the curtain and peered outside. Time stood still as she waited for chaos to erupt. But nothing stirred, and at length she released a shaky breath. A lazy tail wag from Shilah relaxed her further, though she wasn't about to let her guard down. There was no way she was getting back to sleep now. All the exhaustion she'd felt earlier was gone. Her entire body crackled with nervous energy. Like any good prey animal, her fight or flight instincts were on high alert.

Rafe wouldn't be upset if she woke him. She knew that. He wanted to protect her and if she allowed him to do so, he would give his life for hers. She was certain of that not because of what he'd told her about their bond, but because she could feel it deep in her soul. He would die for her. All she had to do was ask.

"No." Katie straightened and took a tentative step closer to the window. She had some self-respect, didn't she? Even after what those wolves had done to her, she wasn't without dignity. She wasn't going to let the craziness of the past few days turn her into a weak little girl who needed a big, strong— gorgeous, her mind supplied—man to help her make it through the night. "Woman up, Katie. Go look out the stupid window."

Shilah turned his head at the sound of her voice. His soft, brown eyes gave her the courage she needed to close the distance between them. She knelt at his side and very carefully pushed the bottom corner of the curtain away from the glass, creating an opening just large enough for her to peer through.

Outside there was snow. And trees—lots of trees. Trees and snow surrounded them, stretching as far as Katie could see from her vantage point. Rafe's truck was on the other side of the cabin, as was the path she'd taken into the woods. The nearly full moon cast an eerie glow over the forest, illuminating the immediate area while creating impossibly dark, sinister shadows in which evil undoubtedly lurked. When one such shadow shifted, melting into the shape of a man, Katie's palms went damp. A second shadow moved close by—another man, standing beside the first.

Katie fell backward and landed hard on her ass. Then she scrambled to her feet, a single thought racing through her mind on endless loop.

Rafe. She needed Rafe.

CHAPTER TWELVE

Katie flung open the guest room door, slamming into Rafe as soon as she ran into the hallway. He caught her in impossibly strong arms and held her against his bare chest, and she buried her face in his neck before she could remind herself that she shouldn't. He tightened his embrace, then smoothed a hand over her hair and shushed her panicked breathing.

"Someone's outside." Katie clutched at Rafe's shoulders, battling a mixture of gratitude and embarrassment about how effortlessly his touch soothed her. "I saw two of them."

Rafe pulled her into his bedroom and closed the door after ushering Shilah inside. "I want you to hide in the closet. Do you know how to shoot?" Before she could process the question, he had pressed a large revolver into her grip. "Katie, do you know how to use this?"

"I..." The gun looked strange in her hand, and holding it made her feel like a child again. Her father had taught her to shoot a .22 when she was eight years old, but this was the first time she'd handled a weapon since high school. "Yes."

"Good."

Of course, taking out soda bottles perched on fence posts hadn't exactly prepared her to face murderous werewolves. Frightened and years past her last round of target practice, she had no faith in her ability to protect herself. Rafe, on the other hand, seemed calm and in control. He was probably a good shot, too. "Don't go. Please."

"I have to check it out." He nudged her toward the closet. "Get in there. Be quiet, no matter what you hear. Shilah will stay in the bedroom with you, and I promise he'll give you plenty of warning if anyone comes in who isn't me. If they manage to open the closet door, I want you to shoot them. In the head."

The thought made her sick to her stomach. "You've got silver bullets in this thing, right?"

"What?" Rafe paused, then chuckled. "No."

Feeling a little stupid, Katie stumbled on her way through the closet door. "Another myth?"

"Yeah. Katie, hey." He took her by the shoulders and turned her around. "I'm not going to let anything happen to you. I promise."

Tears welled and threatened to spill over. She didn't want anything to happen to Rafe, either. There was no reason why she should care so much about a man she just met—no reason except the bond he'd created between them. The pain in her chest at the thought of letting him walk into danger was so staggering it convinced her to set aside the anger that wasn't doing her any good, anyway. Katie wrapped her arms around Rafe's shoulders and brushed her lips over his in a quick but intimate kiss. "You come back to me. Okay?"

He gave her a gentle squeeze. "I will." Startled by something she couldn't hear, Rafe cocked his head. Shilah mirrored the pose beside him, eliciting an unthinking smile. It faded when Rafe walked her backwards into the closet, tension written all over his face. "Hide, Katie. Now." He reached for the gun as he guided her into the back corner. "Safety's off." Ready to fire, he pointed the gun at the floor and handed it back to her. "We'll both be fine."

He shut the door and left her in the dark. Katie blinked, waiting for her eyes to adjust, and leaned back against the row of shirts that hung behind her. She held the gun in both hands, ready to bring it up and pull the trigger the moment Shilah alerted her to an intruder. She said a quick prayer that she would be able to aim and fire under pressure. Despite being a Civil War buff and battle reenactment aficionado, her father had never prepared her for an actual life-or-death situation.

At first there was only silence. She couldn't hear anything outside her hiding place—not Rafe, not their enemies, not even the sound of Shilah's breathing as he stood guard. The darkness was oppressive and heavy like a thick, woolen blanket, making it hard to breathe. She fought against a wave of claustrophobia that urged her to throw open the closet door for just one whiff of fresh air. It would be a mistake and she knew it. Rafe had told her to stay hidden and shoot to kill if discovered. She sensed that her survival depended upon doing exactly as he said. Perhaps even more than that, she wanted to prove to him that she was trustworthy. That she wasn't the type of person to run off and get herself killed by being stupid.

Even if recent events suggested otherwise.

A muffled shout raised the hair on Katie's arms. She held her breath and strained to hear, uncertain whether it had been Rafe's voice or someone else. Shilah whined anxiously, drowning out everything else for long, tense seconds. After Shilah quieted, the same voice was audible but he spoke too softly for her to make out any words—yet somehow she knew it was Rafe. Another voice answered, deeper and booming. She couldn't understand anything the newcomer said before a loud crash shook the walls around her. Her mind conjured up a vision of a body falling heavily against furniture. Without knowing who had been attacked, Katie wasn't sure if she should be horrified or relieved. A wave of nausea rolled over her, then a dull pain throbbed in her stomach.

When you hurt, I feel pain. Oh, God. Katie clapped her hand over her mouth and fought not to vomit. Deep in her soul, she knew that Rafe was the one who'd been hit. She put her hand on the door without thinking, but stopped herself from turning the knob. Though her body urged her to go to Rafe, she knew that wasn't what he wanted. She also knew that she was no match against someone who could knock down a man of Rafe's size.

The man with the deep voice spoke again, and Rafe answered. Katie sagged in relief at the knowledge that he was conscious. Maybe there was still hope. Maybe he would gain the upper hand. She raised the gun and pointed it at the closet door, in case he didn't.

The bedroom door opened and Katie's legs turned to jelly at the sound of Rafe's tense voice. "Katie, it's me. Put down the gun and come on out."

She hesitated. Something wasn't right. Nothing about what Rafe had said before he left the bedroom had prepared her for the possibility that he would return and ask her to put down her weapon. She wasn't sure whether she should do as he said, continue hiding, or come out with her gun blazing.

As though sensing her internal debate, Rafe said, "It's okay. A couple of my pack mates dropped by for a chat. That's all." He hesitated, then said, "Nobody will hurt you. I promise."

Aware that staying in the closet forever wasn't exactly an option, and too afraid to emerge shooting, Katie slowly opened the door and poked her head out. Rafe stood between two men, both of them bigger than him, with blood running from a cut below his eye. The man to his left, powerfully built yet smaller than his companion, boldly appraised her T-shirt clad body as she emerged from her hiding place. Then he smirked. "You heard him, little girl. Drop the gun."

She would recognize that voice anywhere. Cooper. Confused, she glanced at Rafe, who gave her a subtle nod. Putting all her trust into her bond-mate, Katie set the gun on the nightstand beside the bed. The man who hadn't yet spoken, who was bigger and older and somehow more primal than either Rafe or Cooper, pointed at the bed. "Sit."

There was the deep, booming voice she'd heard before. She assumed that meant he was the one who'd hit Rafe. Too afraid to push her luck in a room full of seemingly hostile werewolves, Katie sat on the edge of the mattress without argument. The big man gestured for Rafe to join her on the bed and, to her surprise, he obeyed with a silent nod. He sat close enough that their thighs touched, calming her racing heart without even seeming to try.

Cooper greeted Shilah with a pat on the head while the deep-voiced man stared at her and Rafe for the span of several anxious breaths. Katie sat ramrod straight, unsure whether to let down her guard. As far as she knew, these were Rafe's friends. But despite the expressionless look on Rafe's face, he radiated uneasy fear. Acting on instinct, Katie took Rafe's hand and placed it in her lap, lacing their fingers together. If they were going to die, neither of them should feel alone.

The deep-voiced man's gaze fell on their joined hands. He frowned. Then he stared hard into Katie's eyes. "So I hear we've got ourselves a human problem."

CHAPTER THIRTEEN

"Katie is not a problem." Rafe's tone made it clear that despite this man's clear authority over him, she remained his priority. The realization shocked her as much as it appeared to irritate their visitor.

"Not a problem?" The intimidating stranger stepped closer, causing Rafe to angle his upper body in front of Katie's like a shield. "I got a call from Jack Devereaux at three o'clock this goddamn morning. To tell me that one of my wolves had murdered one of his. Over some human piece of ass."

Rafe squeezed Katie's hand, soothing her bruised feelings almost as soon as they arose. "She's my bond-mate. Don't call her that again."

The man glowered at Rafe and puffed up his chest. "You forget who you're talking to, dog."

"I haven't forgotten, Alpha. But you need to know that this woman is not just some piece of ass. We're bonded—and you know what that means." Rafe rubbed his thumb over her knuckle. "Two of Jack's wolves attacked her tonight. She was bitten and nearly raped. If I hadn't intervened, they would have killed and eaten her."

Visible disgust passed over Alpha's face. "I won't deny that they're savages. But killing him makes you no better."

"Katie is my bond-mate. I had to protect her. It was self-defense." Rafe's jaw bunched and he sat forward, as though challenging Alpha to disagree. "You know better than anyone what it means to lose one's bond-mate."

Alpha stiffened. Clearly Rafe had hit upon a sensitive subject. "The alpha wolf of a larger, dangerously sociopathic pack of werewolves just spent twenty minutes yelling at me about a murder I had no idea you committed. Can you appreciate how embarrassing it was that I didn't have a clue what—or who—he was talking about?"

Rafe lowered his head. "I apologize, Alpha. My radio was lost in the scuffle. I didn't realize I didn't have it until after I'd finished treating Katie's wounds. Then I didn't want to leave her alone to go find it. Not after what happened."

Katie's shoulders dropped and her stomach turned over. She'd lost Rafe's radio in the snow and prevented him from reporting to his alpha wolf. She had no idea what the penalty for Rafe's actions would be, but the entire thing was her fault. If she hadn't tried to escape from the man who had sworn to protect her, she wouldn't have gotten injured. Rafe wouldn't be in trouble. The thought that he might be punished for her own impulsive stupidity made her feel sick.

"Sir?" Katie's voice came out a bare whisper. She cleared her throat and tried again. "Sir, it wasn't Rafe's fault. He told me to stay inside and I didn't. If I hadn't disobeyed him, those wolves would never have had an opportunity to attack me. Rafe wouldn't have been forced to kill to protect me."

Her defense earned her a withering stare. "You will call me Alpha."

Katie swallowed. "Yes, Alpha."

"Good." He bent at the waist to bring his face to her level. "You're right, Katie. It is your fault...but only to an extent. After all, you're just human—which means you don't know any better." Alpha shifted his focus to Rafe. "You do."

"I didn't know we would bond. I was only trying to save her life. For that I'm sorry. To Katie, to you, and to the pack." Rafe straightened and threw back his shoulders. "But we are bonded now. As soon as that happened, Katie became my

78

number one priority. I won't apologize for that. I would kill that asshole again for what he tried to do to her. I wish I'd killed the other one."

Alpha moved to backhand Rafe across the face with his closed fist. Katie flinched, but Rafe stayed perfectly still. The veins in Alpha's neck stood out as he lowered his arm and exhaled. "There's no point in punishing you for something you'll do again. I know that. And I know why you did what you did...I do understand." He glanced at Cooper, who crouched on the floor beside Shilah, rubbing the dog's chest like a doting uncle. "I like you, Rafe. Despite what you did tonight, despite the fact that you've always been a bit of a lone wolf, you know I like you. That's why I'm so glad I managed to talk Jack down from his insinuations that pack wars have broken out over lesser offenses than you committed tonight. I would have hated needing to kill both of you myself to prevent even worse bloodshed."

Rafe's fingers tightened on hers. "I'm glad it didn't come to that, Alpha."

"We've shared this land with our friends across the river for over a generation now. Despite our polar opposite views on human interaction, we've managed not to step on their toes, and they've mostly stayed out of our way. That's the only reason Jack is willing to stop short of ordering a full-out assault on our pack. Which means this better never happen again." Alpha folded his arms over his chest and glared at Rafe, whose expression was tight. "What are your plans for Katie? Do you intend to keep her here? A human bond-mate among hungry wolves?"

"She's leaving as soon as the roads clear." Rafe didn't look at her as he delivered the news. "This won't happen again."

Katie's stomach dropped at Rafe's pronouncement. Her imminent departure wasn't a new concept—she'd wanted to leave this place for as long as she'd been conscious and had nearly killed herself to escape. Yet somehow one brief, heartfelt moment with Rafe had thrown all her earlier convictions into doubt. The comforting press of his fingers entangled with hers made it hard to remember what it was about her life that she was so eager to return to. It wasn't that her career, her apartment, and her parents, sister, and few close friends weren't important. Just that Rafe was too, to a degree that defied all logic.

Alpha must have noticed her ambivalence, because he smiled cruelly. "Is that what you want, Katie? To leave your beloved bond-mate?"

She gave Rafe a sidelong glance. No matter how strongly her soul responded to him, he wasn't her beloved. He couldn't be. They would need to have more than just a handful of conversations and a quick kiss for her to call what she was feeling love. Right now it felt more like a craving or an addiction. An itch she was desperate to scratch, because he made her feel so damn good.

Not that she was going to admit that much aloud.

Katie chose her words carefully. "I want to be safe. And I don't feel safe out here right now."

"Nor should you." Alpha bared his teeth in a vaguely menacing grin. "Jack promised me that none of his wolves would seek vengeance for the one you killed tonight. He's ordering them to stand down in the interest of not shedding a lot of wolf blood over a..." He paused, then smirked. "A woman."

"Good. We need to make sure he understands—that everyone understands—Katie is my bond-mate." Rafe's voice took on a dangerous edge. "She's off-limits, full stop. She's mine."

Rafe's possessive tone triggered a rush of arousal that left Katie hoping that werewolves didn't have a heightened sense of smell. Otherwise everyone in the room would know she was soaking wet. That she was even capable of feeling desire after the night she'd had was almost impossible to believe. It had to be their bond. There was no other explanation.

"She's yours, but she's leaving." Alpha kept his gaze locked on Katie's face as he spoke. "Well, I hope for your sake, dear Katie, that the roads clear before tomorrow night. Because although Jack is a wolf of his word and he's commanded his pack not to seek vengeance, we all know that there's no controlling a werewolf during his time of the month." His expression became deadly serious. "So I suspect that you'll have at least one visitor tomorrow night. Probably more. And Rafe will be...out of commission."

"No, I'll be protecting my mate." Rafe reassured her with a single look. "The moon won't stop me."

"I hope not, for both your sakes." Alpha finally backed away, crossing the room to stand at Rafe's bedroom door. "If you make it through tomorrow night, come see me. We'll talk about how you can start making reparations for the damage you caused to this pack."

"Yes, Alpha." Rafe's jaw tightened. "I apologize for the trouble. I'll do everything in my power to make sure no more blood is spilled." He hesitated, then threw back his shoulders and said, "But if they come after us tomorrow night, I'm afraid that will be impossible. Like you said...there's no controlling a werewolf during his time of the month."

"Indeed." Alpha gestured to Cooper, who came to him like an obedient pet. Shilah looked sorry to see him go. Pinning Rafe with a hard look, Alpha said, "Keep her inside. Even if you have to tie her to the bed. Don't let them catch a whiff of her. Find a place for her to hide during the transformation. I have no idea what will happen, but I know it's going to be a long night for both of you." His features softened slightly and he grimaced at Katie. "Especially you."

She didn't even want to imagine the terror of hiding for hours in the dark with bloodthirsty werewolves roaming around outside, determined to hunt her down. The thought alone was enough to nearly drive her mad—until Rafe wrapped his arm around her waist and eased her fear with his calm strength. "We'll be fine. Thank you."

"We'll see." Alpha left the bedroom and Cooper followed. "Make sure to lock up after us."

Rafe grumbled as he released her and stood. "Of course."

Katie didn't move to follow Rafe when he left the room. She wasn't entirely sure her legs even worked after the scare Alpha and Cooper had given her. She was desperate to talk to Rafe—about what was happening between them, their plan for tomorrow night, and then what they were supposed to do beyond that—but she was content to wait for him to return. She knew he wouldn't stay away long. That he couldn't.

As though he'd heard her thoughts, Rafe reappeared at the door. "They're gone. If Jack Devereaux is telling the truth, we shouldn't have to worry about any other visitors tonight."

"And what about tomorrow night?" For the first time since she'd woken up in his cabin, Katie looked directly into his eyes and he stared back into hers. "Rafe, what are we going to do?"

CHAPTER FOURTEEN

"Let's worry about that after we get some sleep." Rafe walked closer to the bed, but stopped a respectable distance away. He folded his arms over his bare chest, looking far more relaxed than she could understand. If he was worried about his impending transformation or her ill-preparedness when it came to defending herself from werewolves, he sure wasn't showing it. "There's literally nothing we can do tonight. It's still snowing and we're stuck here until it stops. We'll function better if we rest now and figure out a plan later this morning."

"I don't think I'll be able to sleep." The prospect of returning to the guest room alone—or even with Shilah—was chilling. How could she lie in bed and listen to the wind howling outside without going mad from anticipation? She was certain they would be attacked. The only question was when. Despite Alpha's confidence that Jack's promise to stand down was genuine, she wasn't convinced that they wouldn't be ambushed in the next few hours. Which was why she would feel better if she stayed with Rafe. "Not alone."

"You can take Shilah."

"I don't want Shilah." Katie hated the mild panic in her voice, a mere echo of her very real anxiety. "Do you think I could just stay in here?"

Rafe broke their eye contact with an uncomfortable smile.

"Of course."

It was obvious that he wasn't happy about her request, but was willing to comply anyway. Katie frowned. She didn't want to feel like she was forcing him to share his bed. Only hours ago she was frightened of the man and now she wanted nothing more than to soak up his strength and calm. But that was only if he wanted to hold her as much as she wanted to be held. She tried and failed to catch his gaze. "Unless that's a problem."

"It's not a problem. Not at all." Clad only in sweatpants—and still visibly aroused—Rafe laced his hands in front of his crotch and half-turned away from her. "If you'd like, I can stand guard in the hallway while you try to sleep."

"No, I want you to stay with me." Embarrassed by how forward that sounded, Katie lowered her gaze. "Besides, you need the rest, too."

"All right." He walked to the opposite side of the bed, hesitated, then sat on the edge of the mattress with his back to hers. She didn't turn to face him, sensing that this conversation would be easier if she wasn't staring into his intense green eyes. Rafe exhaled, then reached back to cover her hand with his. "Are you okay?"

She smiled at the absurdity of the question. "I'm tired, scared out of my mind, confused…at this precise moment, mostly about why holding your hand feels so good. But other than that, I'm fine."

He gave her a gentle squeeze. "I like holding your hand, too."

"Then why don't you want to stay in here with me?"

"I never said I didn't."

She vocalized what they both already knew. "You don't have to say something for me to know it."

Rafe was quiet for a long time. "So you feel our bond, too? I didn't know if it would be the same for a human."

"I feel it." Frightened by the admission, Katie circled back to her earlier question. "Why don't you want to be around

84

me?"

The nearly imperceptible hitch in Rafe's breathing made her stomach flutter. "I do. It's just...a little uncomfortable."

Shocked by the subtle anguish in his voice, she succumbed to the desire to turn and look at him. "Uncomfortable how?"

He grimaced. "Slightly, you know...painful."

At this point, Rafe's presence provided her with endless peace and comfort. The thought that it was unpleasant for him to be around her made her heart ache. She reached for his shoulder, then startled when he flinched away. "I don't want to hurt you."

"It's the moon." He rubbed his hands on his thighs, studiously avoiding her gaze. "That and our bond. My senses are heightened right now. The animal is coming out. Being around you isn't exactly helping." Red-faced, he gestured at his lap. "I know you've noticed. Though I appreciate that you've had the grace not to mention it."

"It didn't seem like the sort of thing that ought to be mentioned." Struck by the absurdity of the entire situation, Katie let slip an exhausted giggle. "At least not until we've had a few more dates."

Rafe smiled with her, then sobered. "Obviously I would never take you without your consent, but I want you so badly it literally hurts. And I'm afraid of offending you with..." He gestured helplessly at himself. "This."

"I'm not offended." On the contrary, she was strangely flattered. She was pretty sure no man had ever sported an hours-long hard-on for her before. Certainly not one so attractive. Somehow, despite everything she'd been through tonight and the past week, she would be lying if she said she wasn't at all pleased—and interested. She'd never been one to jump into bed too quickly and she was pretty sure sex should be the very last thing on her mind, but the intensity of their connection overrode any trauma she'd experienced or reservations she might have. If Rafe asked, she would probably let him have her.

Judging by his Herculean effort not to initiate more intimate contact, she doubted that was going to happen.

Katie drew back the covers on her side of the bed and crawled beneath. "I don't want to torment you, but it would be nice to get to know you better. Considering that our souls are basically married now."

He nodded and lay back, staying on top of the comforter. "That's fair." He rolled onto his side and looked into her eyes. "Ask me anything."

Where to start? There was so much she wanted to know—about Rafe, his pack, werewolves in general. She opened her mouth to speak, then paused, considering. Though it was hardly at the top of her list, she burned with curiosity over one topic in particular. "Why don't you have a girlfriend already?"

"There was someone when I was younger." Rafe's eyes darkened. "She was supposed to be my mate, but she went missing one day. I tracked her scent through the woods to a spot not far from here, but then it just...disappeared. I never saw her again. A few times after that, I'd catch a whiff of her on the breeze, but it never led anywhere. She was gone."

Shit. "I didn't mean to bring up a sad memory."

He shook his head, the corner of his mouth quirking slightly. "Susan isn't a sad memory. Her disappearance is, but it was a long time ago." He paused. "To be honest, I've always suspected that one of our 'friends from across the river' was responsible. I couldn't prove anything, though, and Alpha wasn't willing to listen to my suspicions. As you just saw, he would do almost anything to avoid confrontation with that pack."

"Why do you think it was them?"

"I don't believe Susan would have run away like that. The pack was her family. She wouldn't have left because she had nowhere to go. Something happened to her." He fingered a lock of her hair, seemingly riveted by its texture. "Besides, when you live next to monsters, it's natural to look to them when things go wrong."

"So Alpha's assessment that you've all co-existed peacefully until now..."

Rafe scoffed. "They've never done anything blatant enough to encourage Alpha to push back. He tells us to stay out of their way in the hope that they'll stay out of ours. At first that just meant turning a blind eye to the humans they killed. After Susan vanished, it became clear to me that Alpha is more concerned about avoiding war than taking a stand. Frankly, I'm surprised he didn't just kill us tonight if that's what he thought Jack Devereaux wanted."

"I'm so sorry, Rafe. Really." While the thought of Rafe being with another woman made her stupidly jealous, she hated knowing that he'd suffered that kind of heartache. "Did you love her?"

"Yes." He cupped her cheek and traced her lower lip with his thumb. "But we weren't bonded. Very few of us ever find a bond-mate."

"So you're saying that what you feel for me is different than what you felt for her?"

"Very different." Rafe rolled onto his back and stared at the ceiling. "But you're right. We barely know each other."

Katie propped herself up on her elbow. "Is your Alpha bonded to his mate? You said he should know what this means."

"No, his parents were bonded. And his father was never the same after his mother passed away." He covered his face with his arm, no longer looking at her. "Damn it, Katie. I really am so, so sorry."

"Because you've ruined me for other men?" Emboldened by the knowledge that she wasn't being observed, Katie allowed her attention to drift lower, to Rafe's tented sweatpants. If she really was ruined for anyone else, then wanting him was only natural. Even if it seemed really, really messed up.

87

"To start." Rafe dropped his arm and caught her looking. She appreciated his grace in not mentioning it. "I'm sorry I got you into this mess. That we bonded. That I didn't explain things to you and that you felt like you were better off running away into the night. If I'd handled any number of things differently—"

"If you hadn't done exactly what you did, I'd be dead. So no more apologies," Katie said. "You're forgiven. And that's that."

"I appreciate that." He entangled their fingers and looked up at the ceiling again. "But I'm not sure you should forgive me before you understand the full scope of what it means to be bonded."

"It means that you're my other half now. For better or worse. It means that without you, I'll never be whole again." She paused, watching turbulent emotion play over Rafe's handsome face. "Did I get that right?"

"Yeah." He lifted their joined hands to his face and kissed her knuckles. Then he closed his eyes. "They say that when one half of a bonded pair dies, often the other follows shortly after. Why, I don't know. Maybe it's a physical consequence of such an intense, soul-deep connection being severed."

Katie digested that news. So if Rafe died, she would either drown in sadness or join him. Excellent. "Is that the worst of it? Our bond?"

"Yeah, I think so." Rafe lowered their hands to rest between their bodies. "Having a bond-mate is an incredible gift, but it's also a burden. Especially for a human, I have to imagine." Self-loathing flickered across his face. "You didn't ask to get hooked up with a werewolf. We have nothing in common. You don't belong in my world. And I sure as hell don't belong in yours."

"Honestly? Right now I'm a lot more worried about getting attacked by angry werewolves than I am about whether or not we're compatible." Taking a chance, she rested her hand above his heart. The heat from his skin was scorching and his chest hair tickled her palm. Her rising desire made it hard to breathe. "As far as our bond goes, it is what it is. I feel it. I do. Which means that hating you—or even staying mad at you— is impossible. Trust me, I tried earlier and failed miserably."

Rafe chuckled, relaxing under her touch. "That's actually reassuring."

"Good." She scooted closer and rested her head on his shoulder. His body tensed right back up. Sighing, she wrapped her arm around his middle and cuddled closer. "Will you please hold me now?"

Rather than answer, Rafe eased his arm around her back. Katie closed her eyes and soaked up the intimacy of their embrace. She couldn't remember ever feeling so comfortable with a man. It really did defy all logic. In a way, that made it easier to just go with this situation. Clearly their connection was bigger than both of them. There was no point in fighting it.

He rubbed his fingers over his arm. "How about you? You don't have a boyfriend back in the city, do you?"

"God, no." That was a good thing, as it turned out. What if this had happened while she was in love with someone else? That would have been tragic. "No, my ex-boyfriend broke up with me almost eight months ago. Haven't dated anyone since. I decided to take a break from the whole relationship thing."

"How's that working out for you?"

She smiled at the trace of humor that had crept into his voice. "I'll tell you in a couple days."

"Deal." Rafe traced nonsense patterns on her skin with his fingertips. "So...tell me what your life is like. How do you spend your time?"

"Working, mostly. I'm a graphic designer for web, mostly, but also some print. I've been doing contract work lately and have had some luck building a pretty impressive list of clients." When Rafe didn't respond, Katie raised her head and looked at him. "It allows me to work remotely from home, make my own hours. I like it."

"I'm not sure what all of that means, but it sounds great." He gave her a sheepish shrug. "I don't completely cut myself off from human culture, but my knowledge is definitely limited. Computers are beyond me."

Apparently they really didn't have much in common. At least beyond the fact that they were attracted to each other. "How do you earn money?"

"I don't, for the most part. I live off the land as much as possible. When I do need tools or supplies from the outside world, I barter and work odd jobs...carpentry and construction, mostly. But I don't need much. I live a very simple life. I have a little in the way of clothing, but most of that came from Alpha." Rafe raised an eyebrow. "I don't wear them very often. Not unless I have guests."

"Probably easier to change into a wolf when you're naked," Katie said lightly. She sobered when her words registered. Rafe was a werewolf. Just like every other man she'd met over the past twenty-four hours, each of whom scared her silly. She placed her hand flat on Rafe's chest, amazed by how firm and muscular he was. She had to force herself not to look at his crotch again. The man was a wild animal and here she was snuggled up to his side. Yet she'd never felt safer in her life. "So...do you like it? Being a wolf?"

"It's all I've ever known," Rafe murmured. "But...yeah, I like it fine. I love running and playing with Shilah, both of us on the same level. I love being part of nature in a way that no human ever could. I love that I rarely get sick, that I'm stronger than your average man, that I heal quickly when I'm wounded. I don't particularly love the full moon, but everything comes at a price." He caressed her shoulder. "Right?"

"Apparently so." Like the way she'd finally found the companionship she'd craved with a man, at the expense of her autonomy and maybe even her life. Without thinking, Katie pressed her lips to Rafe's chest and planted a gentle kiss only inches from his nipple. He froze beneath her. "Have you ever been with a human woman before?"

"I'd never even touched one before the night I rescued you." Rafe's voice was strained. "Katie—"

She raised up and placed a finger against his lips. "Please don't say whatever you're about to say."

He spoke anyway. "We should sleep."

"I know." Katie let her hand slide down to his hard belly. She had no idea what she was doing or why she felt so powerless against her hormones. This wasn't like her. "But I'd rather keep getting to know each other."

He caught her wrist before she could go any lower. "You had an incredibly traumatic night. You're injured."

"You're right, I did. And I am." She searched his face, hoping for some sign that he was just as swept away by their connection as she was. "There's not one reason I should want you right now. But my body doesn't seem to know that."

Rafe's throat bobbed as he swallowed. He inhaled, nostrils flaring, and closed his eyes. "You're not making this easy, sweetheart."

Her heart melted at the endearment. "What are you afraid of?"

"Hurting you." He tightened his grip on her wrist. "Frightening you."

"Is that what werewolves do in bed?" Katie bent and kissed the nipple closest to her. "Hurt their mates?"

Rafe trembled. "I would never hurt you."

"Then show me." She couldn't believe she was goading him like this. She'd never been the aggressor in a physical encounter. She'd never even slept with a guy before the third date. "Show me what a wolf does with his bond-mate."

Growling, Rafe rolled so that he was on top of her. He dragged her hands above her head and pressed them against the mattress, lowering his face so it was only inches from hers. Katie's chest heaved as she reacted to the pleasure of his heavy weight pinning her down. She shouldn't enjoy it. Not after the biter and his blond friend from earlier. But she did. God help her, she did.

"You're wet." Rafe kissed her neck and ground his hips into her.

Despite her assertiveness, Katie blushed. "Yes."

"I can smell it." He nipped at her earlobe. "Your scent has been driving me crazy for hours."

"Crazy enough to believe me when I say I want this?" She licked her lips as she stared up at him. "And that I might explode if you don't kiss me?"

Rafe's breathing grew ragged. "I thought you didn't want to make our bond any stronger."

"Does it really matter? Is there any undoing this?"

His gaze strayed to her mouth. "No, I don't think so."

"Then please. I feel so empty." She lifted her head, straining for a kiss. She felt wanton and desperate and needy and for whatever reason, she didn't care. It didn't matter. Nothing mattered except sating the hunger that was eating her alive. "Kiss me, Rafe. Please."

His mouth crashed down onto hers.

CHAPTER FIFTEEN

She'd never been kissed before. Not really. Not like this.

The moments of intimacy she'd had with men in the past simply couldn't compare. Those kisses had been practice, a pathetic shadow of what she was doing with Rafe now. His mouth tasted faintly of mint and his tongue stroked hers as though they'd been born to do this together. There was no trace of awkwardness, no uncertainty in their movements. She bucked and surged beneath him, desperate for friction. He maneuvered his hips between her spread legs and ground the hard length of his cock against her slick pussy, his sweatpants and her thin cotton panties the only barriers between them.

Rafe broke their kiss with a low grumble. "Damn it. We shouldn't do this."

"Why not?" Nothing else mattered except connecting with Rafe. Not what brought them to this point, not even what would happen after they consummated their bond. She needed him. Every cell in her body cried out for him to fill the emptiness inside her. "We should do this. Nothing has ever felt more right in my entire life."

He released her wrists and planted his hands beside her head, holding himself above her. She groaned in disappointment at the realization that she was no longer trapped beneath his delicious weight. Turbulent desire darkened his eyes as he stared down at her. "I want to make love to you so badly I can hardly contain myself."

"Then why don't you?" She curled her hand around the back of his neck. "I'm your bond-mate. According to you, that's irreversible. So why not do what we both want to do?"

Rafe gritted his teeth. It looked like it was taking all his effort not to ravish her. "We should wait."

That was the very last thing she wanted to hear. "For what?"

"Until we know each other better. Until you have a chance to think about what you want...what you really want, beyond the next couple days." Rafe pressed an almost platonic kiss on the corner of her mouth. "It would destroy me if you wound up regretting this. And after what they nearly did to you tonight—"

"After what they nearly did, all I want is to feel safe. You make me safe." Katie tickled the back of Rafe's neck with her fingernails, pleased when he shivered. "I trust you. I even love you, believe it or not. It may not make any logical sense, but my body recognizes that you're my other half." She paused to allow her words to sink in. "We could die tomorrow, Rafe. I don't want to die before we can be together."

He cut her off with another kiss. When he pulled away, he mumbled, "You're not going to die." She gasped when his mouth moved lower. He scraped his teeth over her throat, then sucked gently. "I won't let you."

Her thighs quivered as she struggled not to orgasm right then and there. She'd never come without direct clitoral stimulation before, but it felt like Rafe was about to get her off simply by kissing her neck. She traced her fingernails down his sides, eliciting a pleased grunt and a jerk of his hips. Moaning, Katie said, "Tell me you won't die, either."

"I won't." Rafe tugged at the hem of her T-shirt, dragging it over her head. Bare above the waist, she battled a split-second of modesty before Rafe latched onto her nipple and laved the tip with his tongue. Katie arched her back and cried out, pleasure rippling through her body. Rafe smiled around her breast. "I'm going to make you feel so good, Katie." He trailed a string of kisses over her chest to her other nipple. "So good."

She tightened her hand in his hair and struggled to answer. "It's so intense." Rafe slid down her body, pressing open-mouthed kisses along her stomach to her abdomen. "I've never felt anything—" Her toes curled when his hot mouth covered her pussy and he licked her through the damp cotton of her panties. "Oh."

He licked her again. "Does that feel good?"

She couldn't answer. Language eluded her. She simply nodded and lifted her hips, bumping Rafe's nose with her swollen clit.

He grabbed her hips and squeezed. "I'm going to take off your panties. Then I'm going to lick up all this wetness you've made."

That was the sexiest thing she'd ever heard. She managed a single word in response. "Please."

He brought his thumb up to rub over the sodden material. The sight of his dark eyes glittering at her from between her legs made her tremble with anticipation. "I love you, too. If I do anything you don't like, or if you get frightened—"

Katie put her hand over his, pressing his thumb against her labia. "Please." He stopped talking and kept his promise, tugging her panties down over her hips. He paused to examine her bite wound, but she threaded her fingers in his hair and guided his face between her legs. "I'm fine."

He allowed her to coax him back to where she wanted him, then bent to give her a long, slow kiss. She shuddered in relief when he dragged his tongue through her folds, grateful that he didn't seem interested in teasing her any longer. Tears leaked from her eyes as pleasure rippled through her belly and curled her toes. His mouth was hot and wet and the very best thing she'd ever felt between her legs or anywhere else on her body. She'd never been a big fan of oral sex, probably because she'd never slept with anyone she trusted completely and without reservation. With Rafe, the act was pure bliss with none of her usual self-consciousness. She never wanted him to stop.

Afraid he might, she tightened her fingers in his hair and rolled her hips against his mouth. He brought his hands to her inner thighs and pushed her legs apart as far as they could comfortably go, then used his thumbs to spread her labia and expose her clit. He teased her with the tip of his tongue, circling the distended flesh, then snaked a trail down to her opening. She held her breath as he only barely penetrated her, then gasped when he moved lower to lap at the tight circle of her anus.

He eased back. "You like that?"

"I like everything you're doing." Katie tugged at his head but he refused to be moved. She groaned. "You're going to make me come."

He shivered. "Yes, I am." Eyes sparkling, he shifted his weight and grinned up at her. "You taste so fucking good." His arm flexed, drawing her gaze to the motion of his hand inside his sweatpants. He lowered his face and licked around her clit, then sucked gently, all while stroking his cock.

The sight of his self-pleasuring was all it took to bring on her climax. Her knees locked and she arched her back, digging in with her heels as she cried out his name. He slid his free hand under her ass and squeezed her possessively, a show of dominance that took her orgasm to a different level. Shockwaves of pleasure rolled through her and she convulsed beneath his unrelenting tongue.

Finally she had to push him away. "Wait..."

He lifted his head, his concern evident. "Are you okay?"

Katie nodded, then smiled. Her entire body tingled in the most pleasant way. "I need a moment to breathe."

Rafe kissed a path up her body, lingering on her breasts for quite some time before planting an almost chaste kiss on her lips. "That was incredible." His breathing was labored and when he settled back between her thighs, she could feel that he was still rock hard. The soft hairs that covered his broad chest tickled her erect nipples, raising gooseflesh along her arms and legs. "I could lick you for hours. Happily."

"I'm not sure I'd survive that." Katie rested her hand against his cheek and really studied Rafe's features for the first time. She'd never been so attracted to anyone in her life. She didn't think it was solely their bond—he was legitimately gorgeous. He was spectacular to behold. The adoration in his eyes as he stared back made her feel like the most beautiful creature in the world. "That was incredible."

"Good." He moved to roll off to the side, but she grabbed his broad shoulders to stop him.

"Where are you going?"

"We really should get some rest. We'll need our strength." Rafe's entire body stiffened and, despite his words, he ground his hips against her.

"No, you need to come." Katie slid her hands down his back, to the waistband of his sweatpants. "And I know you want to be inside me just as badly as I want you there."

Shuddering, he said, "You could just use your hand." He rocked into her, dragging the length of his erection over her slit. "Or your mouth, if you wanted."

"If that's what you want, I'd love to suck you off." She blushed, amazed by how uninhibited she felt with Rafe. Not only was she not the type to talk dirty in bed, but she'd never enjoyed giving blow jobs before. Now the thought made her mouth water. But it wasn't what she craved most, and she suspected that she and Rafe needed the same thing. "But if you want my pussy, take it. I can't wait to feel you filling me up."

Rafe growled and got up onto his knees, pushing his sweatpants down over his hips. Katie sat up to help him, but stopped short when she realized that she was face-to-face with the biggest erection she'd ever personally encountered. He wasn't a monster by any means—just longer, thicker, and harder than any man she'd taken to bed before. And prettier.

Yes, indeed. Rafe had a beautiful cock.

Shocked by the aching hunger she felt at the sight of his arousal, Katie inched forward and kissed the tip of his cock. He groaned and jerked his hips forward slightly. She opened her mouth and took in the first few inches of his impressive length, fisting her hand around the base as she sucked languorously. Pleasure rolled through her body, coinciding with her firm suction—almost as though she could feel what Rafe must be feeling. She cupped his heavy testicles in her hand and applied the gentlest pressure, massaging him with a wanton groan.

He placed his hand on her head. "Keep doing that and I'll come."

It wasn't an unappealing idea. But she forced herself to stop, determined to end this horrific evening with Rafe inside of her. Releasing him with a wet kiss, she lie back and spread her legs. She'd never felt so desperate for penetration before. Like she'd go mad if he didn't fuck her this very instant. "Not before you're inside of me."

Rafe scrambled out of his pants and positioned his hips between her thighs. He gripped himself and rubbed the head of his cock over her sensitive labia. "I'll try and take it slow."

She pressed her hand against his chest as a sudden thought occurred to her. "Do you have a condom?"

He deflated. "No. I don't normally...do this." He shrugged and his cheeks flushed, triggering a wave of affection that started in Katie's heart and quickly spread to the tips of her fingers and toes. "Entertain women, I mean. I'm not exactly prepared."

That meant he was most likely in good health, sexually. So was she. And she couldn't imagine stopping this encounter over something as silly as a prophylactic. "It's okay. We don't need it."

"I'm not sure whether I can impregnate you or not." A twinge of regret passed over Rafe's face. "Technically we're different species, but I suppose I'm at least partially human—"

Katie shook her head. "I'm on birth control. It's okay." Never mind that she'd missed a week of pills.

Rafe jerked his hips, but stopped short of pushing inside. "We don't have to—"

"Rafe." She put a hand on each stubbled cheek and stared into his eyes. "Fuck me. Make love to me. Be with me tonight." Knowing she sounded like a broken record but too greedy for his touch to care, Katie said, "Please."

He put a large hand on the side of her face, ran his thumb along her bottom lip, and pressed the head of his cock against her slick opening. Her body yielded to the invasion immediately, allowing him to slide home in one smooth, torturously slow thrust. She tipped her head back and moaned, overcome by the intense bliss of being physically joined to her soulmate for the first time. Rafe eased his arm beneath her back and held her close, kissing her throat.

"You feel so good." Rafe's voice shook. The rest of his body followed suit, as though it was taking everything he had not to just plunder her mercilessly. "I'm not hurting you, am I?"

All she felt was ecstasy. "No." She tilted her hips, gasping when Rafe slid impossibly deeper. "It's so good."

He withdrew, then drove into her again. "Like that?"

She nodded and met his next thrust with enthusiasm, rocking her pelvis to increase the friction against her clit. "Just like that."

"I've never felt anything so goddamn hot and wet and tight." Rafe moved against her with increasing fervor. "And you're mine."

Her inner muscles clenched at his words. "I'm yours." The more he moved within her, the wetter she became. His strokes grew longer and deeper as she opened to him, his movements less careful. Sheer, decadent bliss rolled over her and settled in the pit of her stomach, sparking a delicious build of pressure that signaled another orgasm. "Don't stop."

"I won't stop." He wound his hand in her hair and tugged, somehow rough and tender at the same time. "Not when you feel so fucking good on my cock." He growled and nipped at her throat. "Tell me you like this."

"I like it." She dug her nails into his shoulders, matching his intensity with ease. She'd expected slow, tender lovemaking after Rafe's reluctance, but understood that he was under the sway of the moon. There was a reason he'd been concerned for her, even though he needn't have been. The sex was animalistic and passionate and it transcended every physical experience she'd ever had. Sensing that he enjoyed talking, she pressed her lips against his ear. "I love how you fill me up with your big, hard cock. Do you feel how wet I am for you?"

He shuddered. "Yeah."

"Is my wet pussy going to make you come?"

Rafe stopped suddenly, buried to the hilt, and ground his hips against her. His pelvis rubbed against her clit, causing her to tighten around him. She clawed at his back and rolled her own hips, desperate for release. He pumped into her once, twice more, and then she was coming apart in his arms. As her climax began to ebb, Rafe pulled out of her and came with a hoarse moan, spilling his seed onto her stomach. She reached for him and brought his full weight back down on top of her, already mourning his absence inside her body.

"You didn't have to pull out." She cradled the back of his head, holding him against her chest. "You could have come inside me."

He ran his tongue over her clavicle. "Did I hurt you?"

Katie chuckled. "How delicate do you think I am?"

Rafe wrapped his arms around her middle and buried his face in her breasts. "I'm not worried because I think you're delicate. It's that I know how I get during this time of the month."

"You mean sexy?"

He lifted his head, green eyes sparkling. "You think I'm sexy?"

She exhaled in a rush. "Are you kidding?"

He grinned and rolled off to the side, then gathered her in his arms, settling her against him. "I'm glad you approve. 'Cause you're stuck with me."

Katie rested her face against his solid chest and smiled. "I might actually be okay with that."

He ran his fingers along her spine, making her shiver. "That's easy to say in the afterglow. We'll talk again after tomorrow night."

She drew a circle around his navel with her fingernail. "I don't want to think about tomorrow right now."

"Okay." His cock, still half-erect, twitched when she trailed her fingers lower, onto the trail of dark hairs that led to his groin. "We should sleep."

Katie flattened her hand over Rafe's abdomen. "You're still hard."

"I'm pretty much always hard for a few days surrounding the full moon." He reached between his legs and gave himself an absent stroke. "It's not always like this."

"I'm not complaining." She licked her lips, turned on by the sight of his strong hand wrapped around his thick member. A fresh flood of arousal threatened to chase away her exhaustion. "I like you hard."

As though sensing her thoughts, he released his cock and pulled the comforter up to cover their lower bodies. "Sweet girl, we really do need our rest. You know we do."

She knew. But that didn't mean she had to like it. "Fine."

"We'll get up in a few hours, shower, then I'll make us breakfast. There will be plenty of time to keep getting to know each other then."

Katie smiled in anticipation. Her good humor faded quickly, when an unwelcome truth flitted through her head. We may never have another night like this. This could be the first and last time we fall asleep in each other's arms.

Rafe was right. She needed her rest. Tomorrow she would face the most important test of her life—and it was one she couldn't bear to fail.

CHAPTER SIXTEEN

shushed him by holding up her hand. Determined to make it a quick trip, she opened the bedroom door and tiptoed down the hallway to the bathroom. Once inside, she relieved her bladder and washed up. Then she soaked a fresh washcloth in warm water and made her way back to the bedroom.

She'd imagined Rafe would be a light sleeper, but apparently not. Whether it was the impending full moon or simply exhaustion brought on by the best sex she'd ever had, he was out cold. She crept back to bed and slipped beneath the comforter. Careful not to startle him, she brought the wet cloth between Rafe's thighs and used it to grip his cock. He moaned and twitched in her hand. She stroked him lightly, washing last night's passion away. He twisted his hips and pumped into her fist, but showed no sign of waking.

Not wanting to push her luck, Katie tossed the towel aside. His cock glistened with water and pre-ejaculate, triggering a Pavlovian surge of naughty, decadent hunger. Last night she'd tasted him for only a minute before asking him to fuck her. Now she wanted to return the favor for the incredible oral worship he'd given her. Single-minded in her desire to please him, she crawled down the bed and hovered over his erection, lips inches from the bulbous head. She bent and pressed a light kiss to the tip, then followed up with a slow lick.

Rafe stirred, then groaned.

Thrilled by his unconscious reaction to her touch, she wrapped her hand around the base of his cock and squeezed gently. His groan turned into a strangled noise of anticipation. Sensing that he was about to come crashing into consciousness, she abandoned the idea of teasing him any longer. She opened her mouth wide and brought it down on his thick shaft, taking in as much of him as she could.

Rafe awoke with a gasp. "Katie..."

She grinned and slid her hand down to cup his heavy balls. His hips bucked slightly, forcing her to swallow another inch or so of his cock. She took it willingly, and with a contented moan. He tangled his fingers in her hair and tried to push her away.

"Katie, I—" He cried out when she stroked her thumb over the sensitive skin of his testicles. "Wait."

She'd been optimistic to think that he'd gotten over his unnecessary concern for her virtue. Determined to make him understand that she was a grown woman who knew what she wanted, Katie drew back and let his cock slide from her mouth. The expression of sheer relief on his face quickly dissolved into a mixture of joy and panic when she licked a path down the underside of his shaft, then laved her tongue over his balls.

"Fuck." His fingers twined in her hair and pulled hard. The twinge of pain from his rough handling swiftly turned into ecstasy. "Katie—"

She sucked him, moaning, then dragged her tongue back up his shaft. Making eye contact for the first time since he woke, she murmured, "Good morning." Then she took him into her mouth again.

An almost inhuman growl rumbled up from deep in Rafe's chest, startling her. More jolting was the tug he gave her hair as he yanked her off his cock. She looked up at him, concerned, and then he was rolling her onto her belly and pinning her to the bed. His hands smoothed over her back and her sides, then gripped her buttocks and spread her open. With another growl, he lowered himself onto her body. He forced his erection between her thighs and positioned himself at her entrance.

"Tell me to stop," Rafe said in a rough whisper. She turned her face to the side, gasping at the intensity of her desire to be taken. His fingers curled around the back of her neck and pushed her down. He had her immobilized. "Unless you want me inside you, tell me to stop right now."

It took her a moment to remember how to speak. "Don't sto—"

Rafe didn't let her finish. He drove into her with one hard thrust, sliding home with a strangled groan. Katie cried out in surprise, then moaned as an overwhelming feeling of satisfaction rolled over her. She was soaking wet and accommodated him easily, despite the lingering ache from their first lovemaking session. Rafe snaked a hand beneath her chest and cupped her breast in his palm. He gave her a firm squeeze and withdrew from her pussy, then pounded into her again without restraint. Sharp teeth ghosted over her shoulder, hinting at the primal strength atop and inside her. A delicious shiver crawled up her spine, and her nipples tightened into painful points.

Another growl tore from Rafe's throat as he set a frantic pace, no longer the tender and vocal lover he was only hours ago. This morning there were no naughty, whispered words and gentle caresses—just primal, guttural noises amid relentless fucking. He'd become the animal he'd feared.

And yet she loved this Rafe every bit as much as the one who'd made love to her last night. This Rafe wasn't burdened with tentative, unnecessary concern for her virtue. He was sating his own needs—and she was enjoying every second of it. Each aggressive stroke caused her to tighten and contract around him. Unrelenting waves of pleasure exploded deep within her, stealing her breath and leaving her limp beneath his heavy weight. All she could do was lie there, completely at his mercy. She closed her eyes and bit her bottom lip, tears streaming down her cheeks as she contended with the most intense ecstasy she'd ever felt.

Rafe tightened his grip on the back of her neck and pumped harder. The sound of her ragged breathing, Rafe's animalistic grunting, and the slap of his lower body against hers filled the room, all of it pushing her closer to the edge. She fisted her hands in the sheets above her head, hanging on tight as her climax crescendoed. Overwhelmed by the riot of sensation that lit up her body, she stiffened and sobbed quietly into her pillow. Rafe released her neck and planted his hands beside her head, rocking against her in a final series of short, hard thrusts. He gave a hoarse shout as he emptied himself into her, then collapsed heavily onto her back.

Stunned, Katie could only lie boneless beneath him. She knew she ought to say something, but spoken language eluded her.

"Shit," Rafe croaked in a broken whisper. "Katie..." He withdrew from her with excruciating slowness, inhaling audibly when she whimpered. "Oh, no. No."

She didn't want him to regret what had just happened. Not when he'd given her the most intensely gratifying ride of her life. "Please don't—"

He scrambled off her, choking back a sob. "Oh, fuck."

Clearly he misunderstood her reaction. With effort, she rolled over and sat up. "No, Rafe—"

He knelt at the foot of the bed, pale and stricken and still erect, and stared aghast at the blood-stained sheets beneath her legs. "You're bleeding."

Confused, she looked down at her calves. The larger bite wound had reopened and was trickling a steady flow of fresh blood. "It's no big deal. I didn't even feel it." She raised her knee to examine the area, then frowned at the mess she'd made. "I'm sorry about your sheets."

"I don't care about the fucking sheets." Rafe grabbed the comforter and wrapped it around his hips, covering himself. "Fuck." He closed his eyes briefly, then opened them and regarded her soberly. "I hurt you."

Damn it. "No, you didn't. We just aggravated the wound. It happens."

"You're crying." He swallowed hard.

"These aren't tears of pain. I promise."

Rafe dismissed her words with a shake of his head. "I held you down. Like you were an animal." He deflated, suddenly looking so very small. "I raped you."

"Whoa." She put her hand on his arm and gave him a reassuring squeeze. "You definitely did not do that. I didn't say no."

"You said, 'Don't.'"

"I said, 'Don't stop.'"

"Did you?" He stared at her with haunted eyes. "I don't remember giving you a chance to say that much."

"You knew I wanted it," Katie said. "I refuse to believe that you would have done that if you hadn't."

"Why are you defending me?" Rafe looked totally disgusted—with himself or with her, she wasn't sure. "Don't."

"I'm telling you that you just gave me the most intense sexual experience of my life. I've never come like that before." She rubbed her thumb over his arm, playing with the fine hairs that covered his skin. "It may have been rough, but it was completely consensual."

Rafe shrugged away from her touch and stood up. He brushed past Shilah, who had jumped up to greet him, and hurried to his dresser. "It was disrespectful and degrading and it will never happen again. I promise you that."

Katie got off the bed and crossed the room to stand at Rafe's side. He pulled on a pair of loose linen pants without meeting her eyes, his movements stiff and controlled. She wanted so badly to touch him, but his body language made it clear that the contact wouldn't be welcome. "Please don't do this. Not after we just found each other. Not today."

He handed her a T-shirt without looking at her. "Put this on. You need to get cleaned up."

She took the shirt but didn't cover her nudity. Instead she inhaled deeply and stepped closer to him. "If you'd raped me, do you think I'd be standing here telling you that I love you?"

"What choice do you have?" Self-loathing twisted his handsome features. "We're bonded."

"Rafe—"

He edged around her and walked to his bedroom door. Opening it, he paused and stood with his back to her. "Put on the shirt and go take a shower. I'm going to let Shilah outside for a minute and then I'll clean your wounds again." He hesitated. "If you want me to."

Clearly he wasn't going to be talked out of his self-flagellation so easily. Fine. She would just have to be persistent. "I was hoping you'd shower with me."

His shoulders tensed. "I can't."

A nauseating wave of sadness rolled over her. "I hope you don't mean what you said. About it never happening again." Her voice wavered. "I need you, Rafe. I sure as hell need you today, but I need you after today, too. I need you."

"You need to get cleaned up." Rafe glanced over his shoulder. "We'll talk about it later. Okay?" He fled the room before she had a chance to answer.

Numb, Katie pulled the shirt she was holding over her head. The familiar smell of Rafe shattered her tenuous hold on her control, and she sat down on the bed and cried.

CHAPTER SEVENTEEN

Katie forced herself to take a long, hot shower. As much as she ached to be with Rafe, she sensed he needed space right now. He needed to calm down and collect himself so he could listen to her instead of drawing his own conclusions about what had just transpired between them. That he was convinced he'd taken her against her will was disturbing, to say the least. Just yesterday he'd sworn that he was incapable of hurting her. Now, hours later, he'd decided that he was a rapist—regardless of what she said. It made her wonder about his state of mind during the act. She simply couldn't imagine that he'd tried to hurt her. But then why did he feel so guilty?

"Shit." Fresh tears streamed down her cheeks only to be washed away by the spray from the shower head. It was good to have this time alone. She didn't want Rafe to see her upset. He would just take it as evidence that he'd traumatized her in some way. The terrible irony, of course, was that the only harmful thing he'd done was to dismiss the most exciting sex of her life as an act of violence.

Glad for the opportunity to work through her own emotions, Katie made sure to be thorough as she washed. Her biggest worry was the possibility of infection from the bite wounds on her calves, though truthfully, she hadn't felt any pain since Rafe had performed his magic healing trick the night before. His horror over her spilled blood was sweet but misplaced. She didn't care that the wound had reopened. It was a small price to pay to be the object of Rafe's wild, uninhibited lust. Never before had she felt so desired—or so powerful, strange as that might seem. She craved Rafe and he craved her back, and she could see nothing wrong with that.

By the time she'd dressed in Rafe's T-shirt and her panties, she was desperate for their separation to end. This distance between them was killing her—and they'd only been apart for thirty minutes. For her own sanity, she needed to convince him that he'd done nothing wrong and that her love and desire for him remained steadfast. After the emotional roller coaster of the past twenty-four hours, she needed Rafe by her side. He was the only thing keeping her sane right now.

She didn't even want to imagine what being separated from Rafe would do to her after thirty hours. Or thirty days. She shuddered, too afraid of the implications to pursue that train of thought any farther. She would worry about the future later. Right now she had to focus on the situation at hand. First they had to reestablish the trust and openness she'd thought they'd forged last night. She'd hoped that Rafe would knock on the bathroom door and initiate the conversation he'd promised they'd have, but she sensed that if she waited for him to approach her, she would be waiting a long time. So she made a decision: If Rafe wasn't going to come to her, she would go to him. They would hash things out and repair the damage the full moon had caused.

Katie opened the bathroom door and walked into the hallway. She looked toward the kitchen and caught Rafe staring out the window next to the front door. He'd dressed in a long-sleeved thermal shirt and his hair was wet as though he'd also showered—where, she wasn't sure. Eyes narrowed, he leaned forward so his face was only inches from the glass. Thoughts of the rift between them receded as the very real problem of vengeance-seeking werewolves came to the front.

"Do you see something?" she asked. Rafe jumped slightly, bumping into the window frame. Katie couldn't suppress a smile as he rubbed his forehead. "Sorry."

He barely glanced at her. "Nothing yet."

"When do you think they'll come?"

"I don't know." Rafe pulled the curtain back over the window and stepped away. He kept his eyes lowered, refusing to look at her. "I'm guessing before they transform. Question is whether they'll let us know they're here or not."

"How many do you think there'll be?" She hoped his estimate didn't freak her out too badly.

He shrugged. "Honestly, I'm not sure. We don't exactly have a werewolf census, so I don't know how big their pack is. Or how many of them will be interested in initiating a fight over that wolf I killed." Rafe peered out the window again. "I'll be outnumbered, but hopefully my protective instinct toward you will work to my advantage."

"Hopefully," she echoed. Praying she wasn't making a mistake to bring up their encounter so soon, she said, "Although I think that protective instinct is working to your disadvantage this morning."

Rafe's entire body tensed. "This isn't about me being overprotective."

"Sure it is. Why else would you insist that you'd hurt me even when I keep saying you didn't?" Katie joined him at the window. She touched his arm as she peered outside. "By the way, coping with the thought of an army of pissed-off werewolves would be a lot easier if I knew that you and I were okay."

He pulled her away from the window and closed the curtain. "Stay out of sight." She raised an eyebrow, irritated by his brusque manner. He surprised her by giving her an apologetic shrug. "Please."

Katie nodded and sat at the kitchen table. Her stomach growled at the mere thought of food. "Will you at least eat breakfast with me?"

Rafe walked to the icebox without meeting her eyes. "Do you like sausage?"

"That sounds wonderful. Any chance you could whip up some eggs, too?" It might be a long shot, but she was desperate for sustenance.

"Sure thing." He gathered a handful of items from the icebox, then walked to the counter.

The man was a mystery. He lived in the middle of nowhere without an obvious income or access to technology, and yet he had a fully stocked kitchen in the middle of winter. "Do they have a grocery store out here?"

"There is a general store a few miles down the road. I go on occasion and stock up on what I can. But most of my food comes from hunting. And trade, with other members of the pack."

Her last boyfriend hadn't been able to grill a decent steak, let alone go out and kill one. To say that Rafe wasn't her usual type was the understatement of the century. She found his self-sufficiency incredibly attractive. "A man of many talents."

Color rose on his face as he lit the burner on the stove. "Not sure I'd go that far."

"Well, you're damn sure the best lover I've ever had. So that's one talent. Pretty amazing kisser, too."

Rafe closed his eyes. "Don't." He paused. "Just...don't."

"Why?" Katie stared at Rafe's profile, willing him to look at her. "You are."

His jaw twitched. "We shouldn't have slept in the same bed. I knew what I would be like when I woke up this morning. I knew I'd want you again—and that it would be rough. It always is."

"During the full moon, you mean?"

Rafe nodded, his mouth a grim line. "When werewolves fuck close to the full moon, it's primal and aggressive and...it's not something I should have ever subjected you to.

112

I'm ashamed that I did."

"Even if I liked it?"

His lip curled in disgust. "How could you? I treated you like a piece of meat. Like a tight, wet hole for me to stick my dick inside."

Katie tried to ignore the twinge of arousal between her legs. If not for the tortured look on his face, his words would serve as tantalizing foreplay. "When I woke up, I wanted sex. That's why I put your cock in my mouth. That's why I ignored you when you told me to wait. That was my choice. I wanted sex and you gave it to me. Fantastic sex."

The sausage sizzled in the frying pan, making Katie's stomach growl. Rafe prodded at it with a spatula, angrily. "You didn't know what you were getting into when you decided to wake me up like that."

"I knew the full moon was tonight and that you were worried about being too rough with me." Katie got up and crossed the kitchen to stand beside him. He stiffened. "Rafe, you gave me a chance to say no. I didn't. I didn't want to." She caressed his arm, ignoring the way he flinched at her touch. "So unless you were trying to hurt me—or wanted to hurt me, in that moment—you did nothing wrong. You did nothing that I didn't want you to do."

Rafe didn't take his eyes off the skillet, silent for the span of several breaths. She'd almost decided he was going to ignore her, but then his shoulders dropped and he said, "Seeing you with your mouth on me, so beautiful and playful and sexy…I just lost control." He stopped what he was doing and leaned heavily on the counter, exhaling. "I lost control. But I never wanted to hurt you. I would never intentionally cause you harm."

Her chest constricted at the guilt that poured from him, so overpowering she almost couldn't breathe. "Losing control isn't always a bad thing. Not when you're with someone you trust." She curled her fingers around his. "You told me that if I hurt, you feel pain." Ducking her head to force eye contact,

113

she said, "Did you feel pain when you were fucking me?"

His throat bobbed. "No."

"What did you feel?"

Rafe finally met her gaze. "Pleasure."

"How about now?" She let the agony she felt at his torment come to the front. "What do you feel now?"

He blinked rapidly, then pulled away from her to swipe his arm over his eyes. "I ache."

"So do I. It's this distance between us." Katie pulled on his shoulder so that he faced her. "If you and I are going to work, you can't see me as this fragile, helpless human who's going to get broken by the big, bad wolf. I'm your bond-mate. I still don't believe that you would ever intentionally cause me pain or discomfort. Yesterday you believed the same thing." She waited for him to relax, to understand, to accept what she was saying, but he stood rigid and stared at the floor. "Trust our bond, Rafe. Listen to what it's telling you. Listen to me." She took a breath. "Trust me."

He surprised her by curling an arm around her waist to draw her into a tentative hug. When his erection bumped against her thigh, he jerked away quickly. Katie snugged in closer and returned his embrace, but Rafe remained guarded. "I just wish I'd given you the chance to actually consent."

"You did. I consented and you knew it. Deep down, you knew."

He set down the spatula and put his other arm around her, splaying his fingers against her lower back. "I don't understand how you can be okay with the way I treated you this morning, especially after what those animals put you through last night. But I am listening to you, I do trust you, and I know you're telling me the truth." He released her with a gentle squeeze. "Doesn't mean I want to do that to you again, though."

Katie ran her hand down Rafe's chest to his stomach. "I hope you don't mean that. I'm not saying I want it to be like that every time, but once a month or so might be nice…"

A strained smile played across Rafe's face as he turned his attention back to breakfast. "I suppose if we establish boundaries and work out the terms of the encounter beforehand...and you promise not to surprise me with good-morning blow jobs during the full moon..."

Katie patted his stomach and stepped away. "Deal." Even now she could feel Rafe struggling to maintain an iron grip on his control. She sensed that being able to hang on to his humanity in the hours before his transformation meant everything to him, and she didn't want to jeopardize his ability to do so. Though she wouldn't exactly mind being bent over the counter and fucked, she wasn't sure their relationship could take it. "That sausage smells amazing."

"Yeah, it does. I'm starving." Rafe scraped the meat onto a plate, then cracked a few eggs into the pan. "How do you want your eggs?"

"Over medium, if you don't mind."

His shoulders relaxed. "I can do that."

The obvious affection in his voice washed away the lingering stain of the morning's misunderstanding. Warm all over, Katie murmured, "This is nice."

Rafe snorted. "Really?"

"Well, impending werewolf revenge attack aside...yes." Taking her seat, Katie propped her chin on her hand and watched Rafe flip an egg. "I've never dated a guy who made me breakfast the morning after."

"Seriously?" He scoffed. "Humans."

"Hey, watch it." She grinned so he'd know she wasn't really upset by his vaguely insulting dig. The look he shot back clued her in to the fact that he was actually trying to be playful. "Though to be fair, you're right. Now that I've experienced being with a werewolf, I'm not sure I'd ever be able to go back to a normal human boyfriend. Even if you and I weren't bonded."

"You say that now, but you've only been with a werewolf for less than twelve hours. Let's make it through our first full moon together and then you can decide how you feel about having a boyfriend like me." Rafe divvied up the sausage he'd just cooked between two plates, then followed up with the eggs. "After tonight you'll have seen the very worst aspects of being with someone like me. It may change your perspective."

"Or it may not."

Rafe set a plate of food in front of her, along with a glass of water. Then he brought his own food to the table and sank onto the chair to her left. "It'll only get worse the closer we are to sunset."

"What will?" Katie took a bite of sausage and moaned. She assumed the flavorful meat was the fruit of Rafe's hunting efforts, which somehow made it even more delicious. "Oh, this is yummy."

Rafe quickly took a bite of his own food. "I'll only get worse. Especially if you keep moaning like that."

"Oh." Katie popped a forkful of eggs in her mouth, careful to stay silent as she appreciated the flavor. She could practically feel Rafe's hunger for something more than food. It turned her insides to water. "I understand."

"The closer I get to my transformation, the more...primal I become." He shoveled another bite into his mouth and chewed voraciously. "I'm not really used to having a female around. Especially one I'm bonded to." Rafe kept his attention locked on his plate. "If it seems like I'm keeping my distance, that's why."

"It's not me, it's you. Pretty much."

He gave her a reluctant smile. "Pretty much."

"I get it." Katie caught his gaze. "Just don't be too distant, okay? It really isn't necessary." She paused to chew, too hungry to slow down for conversation. "I'm not as delicate as you think I am."

"Glad to hear it." Polishing off the rest of his plate with astonishing speed, Rafe set down his fork and folded his hands on the table. "Because you'll need not to be delicate tonight."

CHAPTER EIGHTEEN

Katie sighed. She really didn't want to think about what lie ahead. Unfortunately, ignoring the fact that there were vicious creatures coming to kill them wouldn't delay their inevitable appearance. "What time will you transform?"

"After dark. Around eight o'clock, most likely." Rafe pushed away from the table and turned his chair to face her. "I'll go outside as soon as the sun goes down. I don't want you anywhere near me when I turn."

"What if the others are out there?"

"I assume they will be." He shrugged. "They'll listen to Jack. If he told them not to retaliate while they're in control of their actions, they won't. But once we all transform, it's going to be a bloodbath." Gathering both their plates, Rafe stood, but not before planting a gentle kiss on top of her head. "The important thing is that you stay locked inside the cabin, no matter what happens. And that you shoot anyone who comes in after you."

Katie shuddered. It all sounded so much like a bad dream that she could hardly believe it was really going to happen. If not for the memory of being trapped beneath the heavy weight of a werewolf whose mouth dripped with her blood, she probably wouldn't. "I understand." She watched Rafe rinse off their plates, overwhelmed by the myriad of emotions washing over her. Despite the ominous cloud hanging over them, there was a part of her that was happier than she'd been in a long time. Stupidly, improbably happier. If only they were a normal pair of new lovers, she'd suggest they head back to bed. Instead she had to face the very real possibility that one or both of them wouldn't make it through the night. "Do you think any of your pack-mates will come help?"

Rafe's expression hardened. "I don't know. Even if they wanted to risk angering Alpha by involving themselves, they won't have conscious control over their actions. Some may show up. It's likely nobody will." Rafe dried his hands on a dish towel, affecting a casual air that Katie didn't believe. "I'll protect you with or without them."

"How? You'll be outnumbered."

"But I'll have the strength that our bond gives me." He walked back to the table and dropped into his chair. If not for the trace of uncertainty she sensed in his voice, she'd think he was all confidence. "I'll be fine."

Katie glanced toward the curtained window. Muted light filtered through the material, evidence that the sun had risen. "What if we try to make a break for it? Maybe the roads are clear."

"Unfortunately, I'm not able to radio Cooper and ask about the roads. I may have to leave you for a few minutes to scout ahead and see if they're open. I don't want to take you away from the cabin unless it's a one-way trip into town."

It was her idiotic escape attempt had led to the loss of Rafe's radio. She wanted to kick herself for not remembering to grab it after Rafe stopped her assault. The idea of being separated for even a few minutes panicked her. "I don't want you to go."

"I shouldn't have to run very far to see whether the route is passable. Unless the roads are safe to drive on before three o'clock at the very latest, I think trying to leave will be more dangerous than staying. If we got stranded out there, we'd have to try and fend them off in the open woods. I'd also have to transform in your presence, which is not something

I'm keen to do." Rafe shook his head as though shrugging off a bad memory. "That said, if by some miracle the road is open, I do think that getting you to town is the best possible option. Even if they can't evacuate you tonight, the others aren't likely to follow you into civilization."

Katie's heart sank as she interpreted Rafe's meaning. "You sound like you're not planning to go with me."

"Because I can't." Shame radiated from his every pore. "Tonight I'll become a murderous, bloodthirsty wolf. I have no business being around human beings when I'm like that."

"Then I'm staying with you." She folded her arms over her chest and put on her most defiant expression. He could try to talk her out of it, but she wasn't going to be swayed. Insane as it sounded even to her, Rafe's life had somehow become as precious to her as her own. She couldn't flee to safety knowing that he was going to spend the night fighting a war on her behalf. "I won't leave you here."

"I'll be fine. If we can get you out, that's what we need to do."

Katie rejected his bravado with a dismissive wave. "They're going to come for you whether I'm here or not. And if I'm not, you won't have that protective instinct working in your favor. Considering that the best-case scenario in the event of your death is that a part of me will die along with you, and the worst-case scenario is that all of me will die, abandoning you doesn't really work for me. So you don't need to bother checking on the roads. I'm staying."

Rafe leaned back in his chair. "You're strong-willed, aren't you?"

Her ex-boyfriend Dylan had made a similar observation— albeit in cruder terms—right before ending their relationship. In the months since he'd left, she'd tried to embrace her willful nature but secretly worried that she would never find a man who could love that about her. She sincerely hoped that Rafe wasn't put off by spirited women—that would spell disaster for any relationship they might have. "So I've been told."

"Good." He raked his eyes over her body, yet again visibly aroused. His desire was palpable, hanging heavily between them. "It'll help."

When his nostrils flared and he looked away to take a deep, steadying breath, Katie said, "Is this why your pack stays away from humans? Because it's too difficult to control your primal urges?"

"Among other reasons." Rafe licked his lips and met her gaze with effort. "Threat of discovery is also a concern. My pack operates on the assumption that if humans realize we're out here, sooner or later they'll try to hunt us down. And that would get ugly, fast."

"So then why are the others so cavalier about revealing themselves? Don't they stand to lose just as much?"

The grim expression on Rafe's face raised the hairs on the back of Katie's neck. "They consider themselves more evolved than humans. Werewolves have superior speed and strength, plus the ability to heal ourselves at an accelerated rate. So they don't see humans as equals—they see you as easy and honorable prey for their animalistic urges. As toys to beat and violate and devour after they're all used up. They don't worry about discovery because they don't leave witnesses alive." He curled his lip in disgust. "And they don't much care about getting ugly, anyway."

All the warmth in her body drained away. "Do you think I'm the first human to escape one of their hunts?"

"It's possible." Her worry seemed to take the edge off his unrelenting desire, because he softened and took her hands between his. "No one in my pack has ever claimed a human before. The idea of allowing one inside our society is absolutely unheard of—for the others and for my own pack. I'm not sure whether anyone could ever accept it. Or us. Make no mistake...we're breaking new ground here."

Katie managed a smile she didn't really feel. "Guess it's a good thing you were already a lone wolf."

Snorting, Rafe murmured, "Guess so."

Hoping he wouldn't take the gesture as a tease, Katie put her hand on his arm. "But you know you're not alone anymore. Right?"

Rafe shifted his gaze to the tabletop. "Like I said, let's just make it through tonight. Then we'll talk about the future."

Tonight. Katie curled her hands into fists and pressed down hard on her thighs. Like it or not, it was time to start getting serious about survival. She wanted the chance to talk about a future with Rafe more than she could logically explain. "On that note, last night I told you I knew how to use a gun. And I do. My dad taught me to shoot as a kid...but I haven't actually fired a round in years. So I'd be lying if I said I felt totally confident about taking out an angry, snarling, moving wolf."

Rafe failed to hide his mild alarm at her disclosure. "Then it sounds like it's time for a little target practice."

CHAPTER NINETEEN

Rafe insisted that she bundle up in a pair of his sweatpants and a heavy coat, but only after he'd checked her legs one last time. This examination was quick and efficient and he didn't touch or even look at her any more than necessary. Throughout, his struggle to keep his libido in check was plain to see. When he deemed her fit for target practice and she finally pulled his baggy clothing on over her T-shirt and panties, the palpable relief on his face made her feel genuinely bad about having traipsed around in her underwear all morning. That he wanted her with such ferocity was undeniably exciting, even if the intensity of his desire clearly frightened him. Despite his unease, her gut remained convinced that there was no reason to be afraid of him. She just wished that he was ready to believe in his inability to hurt her, as he had only hours ago.

When Rafe led her to the front door, revolver and box of shells in hand, Katie battled a jolt of anxiety. "Do you think it's safe for us to go outdoors?"

"Yes, as long as you do exactly as I say. You aren't to step off the porch. I want you standing next to the front door and paying attention to me at all times. If something happens, you're to run inside and close the door when I tell you. Just do exactly as I tell you, when I tell you." Suddenly looking like he was aware that he was barking orders at her like a drill sergeant, he modulated his tone. "Got it?"

"Yes."

"And if anyone approaches, let me do the talking."

"With pleasure." So far none of Rafe's associates had struck her as having particularly worthwhile conversational skills. She was more than happy to let him take the lead. "I doubt any of them wants to lower themselves by talking to a human anyway."

Rafe stopped with his hand on the door knob and looked at her sadly. "You know I don't think of you that way, right? As inferior." He curled an arm around her waist and gave her a slightly awkward hug. "You're not."

"I appreciate that." She hugged him back. "Just like I don't think of you the way I think of the others. As an animal."

Rafe released her with a weary chuckle. "Except that's exactly what I am, Katie. It would be a mistake to forget it. I just control the animal inside of me a little better than some of others."

"I know what you are. And I still can't help but love every part of you." She bumped his shoulder and gestured at the door. "Let's go shoot something."

A chilly blast of winter air took her breath away when Rafe pulled the door open. At his silent command, she lingered within the warmth of the cabin as he strolled down the length of the porch and checked their surroundings. His movements were sure-footed and powerful, predatory in the extreme. The way he surveyed his environment reminded her of a wolf on the hunt. She knew he could see, hear, and smell so much that she couldn't. Nothing about his abilities frightened or disgusted her. Rather, he intrigued her in a way that no mere mortal could.

"Come outside." Rafe kept his voice low, clearly concerned about being overheard. "Leave the door cracked behind you."

Katie stepped out into the cold, studying the trees beyond the porch. Seeing nothing out of the ordinary, she turned her attention to Rafe. He walked to her side and placed the revolver in her hand. She leaned into him unconsciously, glad for his heat. Already the chill had permeated Rafe's thick winter coat and settled into her bones. "So what should I aim for?"

He pointed at a tree not far from the corner of the porch. The trunk split about six feet off the ground, each thick segment exploding into a riot of smaller branches. "See where that one forks?"

She raised the gun and lined up the sight, aiming directly at the juncture of the two branches. The revolver felt odd in her grip, quite unlike the rifles her father had encouraged her to master. Rafe reached for her free hand and guided it into a supportive position on the grip. She nodded in acknowledgment and set her feet apart, bending her knees ever so slightly. "Should I just shoot?"

"Whenever you're ready."

Katie narrowed her gaze, exhaled, and squeezed the trigger. Nothing happened.

Rafe reached past her to flick off the safety. "There's the most important thing to remember for tonight."

"Safety off. Got it." Her face heated despite the cold air. "Clearly this practice was a good idea."

"It's not like you go running around shooting things in your daily life." He nuzzled her flushed cheek with his warm nose, then moved his lips to brush against her ear lobe. "It's okay. That's why we're going over this now."

Exhaling, Katie leveled the gun and focused in on her target once again. Rafe backed away a step and stood to the side, watching without speaking. She aligned her stance, set her sight picture, and carefully squeezed the trigger. A loud crack echoed through the forest as a chunk of wood flew through the air from a couple inches left of the split in the trunk. Rafe whooped and clapped her on the back.

"That's my girl." He folded his arms over his chest and set his own bare feet apart on the deck. Still clad in only a long-sleeved shirt and thin linen pants, he looked like he should be shivering. But instead he grinned broadly at her, rocking on his heels. "Can you do that again?"

"I think so." Katie aimed once more, not giving herself as much time to line up her shot. After all, she wasn't going to have the luxury to plan everything out tonight. Despite her rush to fire, the second shot hit the tree directly in the juncture where she'd aimed, sending another shower of splinters into the snow.

"May I just say that I find this very attractive?" Rafe shot her what was truly a wolfish smile. "The city girl knows how to shoot."

As pleased as she was by his approval, she wished her ability to fire at a stationary target while her emotional rock cheered her on made her feel better about the night ahead. Unfortunately, a rampaging wolf wasn't going to do her the courtesy of standing still and letting her aim. "I picked off a lot of bottles on fences with my dad. Can't say I've ever tried to hit a moving target, though. Let alone a living one."

"Hold that thought." Rafe jogged to the porch steps and descended them in one giant leap. "You stay right there. I'll be back."

Her stomach dropped when he disappeared around the side of the cabin. "Rafe..."

She heard a door close in the distance. "I'm right here. I'm coming back."

Convinced that she would be ambushed before he could return, Katie searched the trees for monsters. She saw no signs of life, but two gunshots had to have drawn someone's attention. Whether they would take the shots as a warning or an invitation was the question. She told herself nothing would happen. Not until tonight. Surely she'd feel more ready by then.

"I'm back."

Katie yelped at the sudden realization that Rafe had snuck up behind her. She set the gun on the flat porch rail and fell into his arms with a hoarse cry, unashamed by how badly she wanted to be held. "I'm freaking out."

"I know." He rubbed his hands over her back, warming her through the coat. "Everything is going to be okay. It really will."

He couldn't know that, but it was sweet of him to try and make her feel better. She pressed her body against his, unconsciously drawn to the heat that emanated from his solid form. It floored her that this man would give his life for her. She wished she could do something more than hide inside while he fought for both of them. "I don't want to let you down tonight."

His heart pounded against hers. Its vibrant rhythm thrummed through the thick layers of fabric covering their chests, in perfect synchronicity with her own. Rafe threaded his fingers through her hair. "I don't want to let you down, either." He pressed his mouth to hers in a brief but passionate kiss. "But I'm not worried about you. You're going to be great."

She looked down and noticed what he'd fetched for the first time. "A log. And rope."

"Yeah." He shouldered the log like it weighed nothing. It was nearly as tall as she was. Twin lengths of rope joined the load, balanced in his arms with negligent ease. "I'm going to go right over there to rig this up." He nodded at the tree she'd been shooting at. "Keep your eyes peeled and the safety off."

She swallowed. "All right."

"It won't take long." He ran two steps then planted his hand on the railing of the deck, vaulting over with an athletic prowess that set Katie's pulse racing. He landed with a muffled thump in calf-deep snow, perfectly stable despite the heavy burden he carried. He turned and raised his eyebrow. "You liked that."

Katie cleared her throat, both amused and embarrassed that he was so in tune with her body's reactions. "I found it very attractive."

Rafe grinned and swaggered over to a pair of trees close

127

to the one with the split trunk. He tied a length of rope to one end of the log, then did the same thing at the other end. Katie divided her attention between Rafe's activities and the forest surrounding them, which seemed almost suspiciously quiet. She kept the revolver pointed safely at the ground in front of her, but stayed ready to raise her weapon and fire at the first sign of trouble.

"Katie."

She snapped her focus back to Rafe. "Yeah?"

He pulled a canister from his pocket and drew a crude, bright-orange circle on the middle of the log, which now hung horizontally between the two trees. After pocketing the spray paint, Rafe gave the log a hard shove. It swung back and forth, a perfect moving target. "Try it now."

She waited until he was back on the porch before bringing the gun up to aim at the painted circle. The log's movement had barely slowed at all, and she honed in on its lazy cadence fairly quickly. She kept the gun still and waited for the target to pass in front of her sights. On the return pass, she slowly squeezed the trigger. The bullet glanced off the top of the log, inches high and to the left of the bullseye. Katie cursed under her breath, frustrated by her lack of precision.

"That was pretty damn good for your first try." Rafe vaulted over the railing, gave the log another shove, then raced back to her side before she had a chance to register his absence. Stepping behind her, he wrapped an arm around her stomach and pressed his cheek to hers as she sighted the painted circle again. "Shoot ahead of the target. Not where the bullseye is, but where it will be. Lead the target, if you know what I mean."

She relaxed into his embrace, and he reacted by tightening his fingers on her belly and bumping his hips against her bottom. The sensation of his hard cock pressed against her ass wreaked havoc on her concentration. "Are you trying to distract me?"

He growled, a low rumble that bubbled up from his throat

and vibrated against her back. "Just trying to engineer an appropriately challenging training scenario." His hand trembled on her stomach before he abruptly let her go. "I'm sorry. Just take the shot."

She bent at the waist slightly, pushing her bottom into his crotch. He grabbed her hips and uttered a strangled grunt. Smiling, she murmured, "Distraction is good." Straightening, she took aim and fired a single shot that landed just outside the orange circle. Dissatisfied, she followed up with another shot on the return swing. This time she landed within the target circle, only an inch off-center.

Rafe touched her lower back. "Nice job."

His praise made her whole body sing with happiness. "Thank you."

"Try again. Faster this time."

Katie lowered her weapon, took a breath, then lifted the gun and took two more shots, adjusting her aim for the second. The first landed fairly accurately, and the second was only a couple inches off target. Not at all bad for less than a clip of practice rounds.

"Reload." Rafe snarled next to her ear, sending an unpleasant chill down her spine. "Now."

She knew without asking what Rafe was trying to do. Tonight she would be operating from a place of true, stark fear. Rafe could never truly frighten her like the other wolves did, but his sudden aggression instinctively triggered a rush of adrenaline similar to what she'd felt during her assault. Her hands trembled as she tried to release the cylinder hatch so she could reload. She couldn't remember feeling so clumsy in her entire life.

Rafe grabbed the gun and demonstrated in silence. Then he snapped the cylinder back into place. "Now you do it."

She mimicked his action, finally pushing the cylinder through the frame. He handed her a box of shells and she fumbled five rounds into their individual chambers. Rafe stalked around to her side and bent to whisper in her ear.

"You smell delicious, bitch."

Katie jolted at the ugly words and nearly dropped the box of shells. Rafe snatched the box from her hand with another fierce grumble. As soon as her hand was free, she brought the gun up and aimed at the still-swaying log. Blocking out her warring sensations of fear and arousal, Katie hesitated only an instant before firing two shots in quick succession. The first landed within the bullseye, the second just outside the painted circle. She took a breath and squeezed off a third shot, gratified to see that she could correct her aim at a moment's notice.

She startled when Rafe touched her waist again. "Darling, you're going to be just fine." He gave her a reassuring squeeze. "You're a natural."

Katie tried to relax at Rafe's murmured encouragement, but couldn't. After spending all morning insistent that Rafe could never hurt her and that she wasn't afraid of him, she was surprised by how intimidating she'd found his playacting. "Thank you."

"Hey." Rafe captured her chin between his thumb and forefinger and gently forced eye contact. "You okay?"

She nodded quickly. "I'm fine."

"But I frightened you. I'm sorry."

"Well, that was the point. Right?"

He looked almost ashamed. "Yeah."

"It was good. God knows I could practice like this for weeks and still not feel ready to defend myself against werewolves." Katie conjured up her bravest smile. "You wouldn't be doing me any favors by holding back. So throw everything you've got at me. I can handle it."

Rafe regarded her with a look of half-hunger, half-respect that sent a pleasant flutter through her belly. "Ready for the good news?"

"Very ready."

He stepped into the cabin and emerged a moment later with a shotgun in hand. "Cooper left this here last night. He didn't say anything to me but I assume it's meant for you." He held up a battered cardboard box. "You've got ten shells. I don't want to use any to practice right now because this is the weapon I want you to rely on tonight. You're great with the revolver, but there's no way you'll miss with a shotgun. You'll have the handgun as backup if you run out of ammo. And I'm sure you'll kick ass with it. But at least you can take ten shots with this bad boy first."

Katie's heart lifted. She took the shotgun and turned toward the still-swinging target, then lifted the weapon and adjusted to its weight. "Why didn't you tell me we had this?"

"I wanted to train for the worst-case scenario first." Rafe curled his arm around her waist and she leaned into him on instinct. The shotgun was more awkward to handle than the revolver, but it made her feel powerful. Rafe pressed his lips to her temple and inhaled deeply. "Feel better now?"

"I do." She lifted her face and planted a grateful kiss on his mouth. "Thank you."

"You're very welcome." Rafe started to say something else, then froze. His entire body went on high alert, not unlike Shilah's when he'd heard Cooper and Alpha lurking around outside the night before.

"What is it?" Katie whispered. She swung the shotgun to the left, then the right, scanning the tree line for any sight of a threat. She saw nothing.

Moving with deliberate care, Rafe put his mouth against Katie's ear and whispered, "Keep the safety off. We've got company."

CHAPTER TWENTY

Katie's first instinct was to retreat indoors, but Rafe caught her by the elbow before she could flee. "Stand behind me and don't run. Just be ready to go inside when I tell you." He kissed her cheek, then murmured, "They've already seen us. We don't want them to think we're intimidated. They get off on the smell of human fear. Don't give them the satisfaction." He released her so she could step behind him. "I won't let anyone hurt you."

She clutched the shotgun closer to her chest and nodded. She fought to put on her bravest face, a losing battle. "I know."

Rafe reassured her with a subtle smile, then turned and shouted in the direction of the trees. "Show yourselves!"

A peal of feminine laughter floated to them on the frigid breeze. Heart hammering, Katie scanned the forest for some sign of their visitors. She didn't understand how they stayed so hidden. Male chuckles joined in from all around. It was as though the barren forest was mocking them.

"That's her?" A lithe, athletic brunette slinked out from behind a redwood tree about thirty feet from the deck. Dressed all in black, she reminded Katie of the goth chicks who used to scare the shit out of her in high school. Her eyes glittered with malevolent disdain as she looked Katie up and down. "That's why you killed my mate?"

"Your mate was trying to rape mine," Rafe called out. "He

would've killed her when he was done. I only stopped him. I had every right to do that."

"Your mate? That's just a worthless human cunt." The woman stopped about fifteen feet away from the porch and folded her arms over her chest. Behind her, seven men and two more women emerged from the cover of the forest. They all wore similar expressions of enraged disgust. The man who'd bitten her the night before loped to stand at the woman's back, eyeing Katie with unwavering aggression. The hunger in his gaze made her shudder and took her right back to the sensation of being trapped on her back in the snow.

Forming a semi-circle behind their widowed friend, the rival pack put on an intimidating display. The brunette snarled, laughing when Katie visibly startled. "And you're a fucking disgrace. You murdered a wolf for being a wolf."

"I'm not the one who attacked someone's bond-mate." Unlike the others, Rafe maintained a facade of placid strength. Where they literally seethed with anger, he didn't even raise his voice. "I had every right to defend her, and myself."

"Did he know she was your bond-mate before you killed him?" The brunette's lip curled into a dangerous sneer when Rafe didn't answer. "Why would he have thought that was a possibility? As far as I know, you're the first werewolf to ever stoop so fucking low."

Her cohorts snickered, but Rafe didn't react. He just returned her cold stare. "Even if she weren't my bond-mate, she's a human being. Wolves being wolves aside, it's not right to hunt and slaughter them like animals."

"Why not?" The dead wolf's widow grinned. "That's what they are. Weak, pathetic, inferior animals."

The wolf who'd bitten her finally spoke up. "And in the case of yours, a hot, tight, tasty animal."

His friends laughed and the woman in black tossed a smile over her shoulder. "You'll get your chance. Just remember that I have first dibs."

"Of course." The biter bent at the waist in a jaunty little bow. "I'll make sure to let my wolf know to wait until you've had your fill." The group chuckled again.

Rafe tugged lightly on Katie's arm, encouraging her to step forward and stand at his side. She noticed that he was careful to keep her between him and the front door. He curled his arm around her waist and held her close to his body. "I know that Jack Devereaux ordered you not to retaliate. He wants to avoid more bloodshed, as my Alpha does." He tightened his jaw and ground out his next words. "I'm sorry that things went down the way they did. I wish your mate hadn't died. I wish he hadn't attacked Katie at all."

"Katie." The woman spat out the word as though disgusted by the way the syllables tasted in her mouth. "How cute. It has a name." She advanced until she stood at the bottom of the porch stairs. "Want to know my mate's name? It was Zeke. Our son is Ben." Her voice caught, revealing a glimmer of vulnerability completely at odds with her gruff demeanor. "He doesn't understand why his daddy isn't coming home. Seven years old. That's on you." She bared her teeth at Katie. "Both of you."

"I'm sorry for your son," Rafe said quietly. "Honestly, I am. That's why I suggest that his mama do whatever it takes to get home to him safely tomorrow morning. I understand your desire to avenge your mate's death, but you and I both know that your boy needs you more than you need revenge."

The woman stared at him for so long that Katie almost screamed from the uncertainty of what would happen next. When the brunette finally spoke, her voice dripped with vitriol. "My name is Lisa, and don't you tell me what I fucking need. I'm going to spend the day sitting out here remembering my mate and fantasizing about all the ways I'd like to savage yours. When I transform tonight, the fucking hatred I feel toward both of you will ensure that I get home to my boy tomorrow—but only after I eat your hearts."

"Well, I'm sorry to hear that, Lisa." Rafe kept his tone

even. "When Ben wakes up an orphan tomorrow morning, it's on you. Only you."

Lisa snarled and leapt up the first two porch steps. Adrenaline surging, Katie brought up the shotgun and leveled it at Lisa's chest. The rest of her pack surged forward even as she froze in place and pinned Katie with a murderous glare.

"Everyone calm down." Still outwardly calm, Rafe spoke in an authoritative tone that commanded everyone's attention. Lowering his voice to a murmur, he said, "Katie, may I have the gun?" He took the weapon while staring Lisa down.

One of the other women in the pack, a hardened blonde, called out. "You better get your bitch under control."

Not rising to the bait, Rafe said, "You have all afternoon to change your mind. I hope you do, for your son's sake." He handed Katie the revolver with a look that Katie interpreted as, Don't kill anyone. She nodded and held the gun with the barrel pointed at the ground. Rafe turned back to Lisa. "Katie is one hell of a shot. And I'll die to make sure she doesn't have to prove it to you. So you don't stand a chance."

Lisa grinned. "We'll see." She regarded Katie coldly, then chuckled with pure malice. "How do you like being a wolf's bitch, Katie? I always figured humans would be too delicate for that sort of thing."

Rafe put his hand on her lower back and moved to shield her from Lisa's vicious gaze. "Let's go inside."

Lisa backed away from the porch wearing an evil smirk. "How are you holding up today, sweetie? Full moon and all, I'm surprised you can even walk."

Rafe stiffened at her comment and Katie knew exactly where his mind had gone. Lisa's provocations triggered her own protective instincts to come to the front. Without flinching, she met Lisa's derisive smile with one of her own. "Don't worry about me. I can handle Rafe."

"Oh, I'm sure you can. Nasty little bitch." She lunged forward, laughing when Katie scrambled to raise the revolver and held it with a shaking hand. "We'll see how you feel the first time your new boyfriend makes you bleed."

The color drained from Rafe's face, a clear indication that Lisa's comment had struck the intended nerve. Katie lowered her free hand to Rafe's ass and patted him carefully. "Come on."

Rafe's throat jumped. He seemed to be genuinely struggling not to leap over the railing and attack Lisa. "Get the fuck off my property. All of you."

Movement among the pack caught Katie's attention. The woman who hadn't yet spoken, a stocky brunette, shocked the hell out of her by pulling off her long-sleeved shirt. She was bare beneath, as though the temperature wasn't below freezing. Her companion, a tattooed man with dark, tangled hair, unbuttoned his jeans and pushed them down over his hips to reveal his naked, engorged cock.

The tattooed man stared at Katie as he stroked himself. "Has your new mate shown you how wolves fuck yet? Or is he softening his rough edges until you get more comfortable?"

"I don't think he's truly broken her in yet," his now naked partner said as she got onto her hands and knees in the snow. "So let's show her."

The tattooed man dropped to his knees behind the brunette and grabbed her hair in his fist, yanking hard. She growled but arched her back to offer him easier access. "Just remember, fighting back will only excite him more." He slammed into his lover, who reacted by howling and twisting around to claw at his face. He grinned as her nails sliced into his skin, then pounded into her again with a guttural grunt.

"Inside," Rafe said. "Now." He dragged her into the house as the half-naked werewolves rutted on the ground like wild animals, panting and moaning and spilling blood onto the snow around them.

Katie didn't argue. She let Rafe usher her inside, jumping when he slammed the door shut behind them. Sensing his distress, she said, "Rafe, it's okay."

He brushed past her after locking the door. It was clear that their taunting had affected him, no doubt undoing some of the progress they'd made over breakfast. Katie sighed as he stormed into the kitchen and laid the shotgun on the table.

"Don't let them upset you. That's what they want." She followed him and put her hand on his tense back. "I know you're not like them."

"Do you?" Rafe squirmed away from her touch. "Stop it. For fuck's sake, Katie."

Katie backed away. Until that moment, she'd assumed he was simply reacting to Lisa's unfortunate insinuations. Now she sensed the conflicted arousal behind his discomfort. "Sorry. But…it's all right to feel this way. Really."

"Like hell it is." Rafe banged his fist on the table, making her jump again. "I'm a hypocrite to judge them when I can't even let you touch me because I might tear your clothes off and take you."

"Struggling with urges and relishing in the act of indulging them are very different things." Aware that she might set him off by pointing out that he wasn't the only one who wanted to connect physically, she murmured, "You're not wrong to feel this way. We just found each other. There's a crazy, supernatural connection drawing us together. Believe me, I want you just as much as you want me. If you weren't so scared to get near me, I'd be all over you right now. And that's despite the fact that I'm still shaking from talking to that crazy bitch outside."

Rafe turned around. "I counted ten of them."

Normally she hated it when boyfriends changed the subject in the midst of conflict, but she knew it was the only way for Rafe to regain his emotional footing. Because she needed him to recover as quickly as possible, she went with the flow. "So did I. Three women, including Lisa, and seven men."

Rafe inhaled deeply, then offered his hand. His eyes had gone dark and slightly unfocused. His chest heaved. She laced her fingers with his, unsure what he planned to do with her. From the way he drank her in with ravenous eyes, she half-expected him to drag her to bed. She wouldn't fight him if he did.

But he didn't. Instead, he walked them to the couch in the den right next to where she'd found his radio. He gestured for her to sit, so she placed the revolver on the coffee table and settled at one end of the sofa. She wasn't surprised when he chose to keep his distance by sitting as far away from her as he could. Fisting his hands in his lap, he said, "I'm not worried about your shooting skills. You'll be great."

"The shotgun definitely makes me feel better." Suddenly very aware of her bulky outerwear, Katie bent to unlace her boots. "Unless more show up later, I should have enough ammo to take them all out."

"Hopefully you won't have to. My goal is for you to ride out tonight in peace with Shilah. I figure we'll board up the windows from the inside. That way if anyone does get past me, they won't have as easy a time getting in. You'll have some warning, at least." Rafe's voice faltered as Katie kicked off her last boot and shrugged out of the bulky coat. "After I go outside to transform, I don't want you to open the door until tomorrow morning—wait until at least eight o'clock. If all goes well, I should be back before then. If I'm not, take my truck and drive into town as soon as the weather lifts."

"Don't be silly. You'll be fine." She clung to the simple truth that Rafe had to be fine. He was her lifeline. Literally. Stomach sinking, Katie assessed the situation with a clear head. It was going to be ten against one. Protective instincts or not, Rafe wasn't nearly as brutal as the werewolves she'd just met. It was hard to picture him fighting off so many angry wolves, what with their unholy bloodlust and thirst for vengeance. She scooted closer to Rafe but didn't touch him. It was enough to feel the heat emanating from his body. "Tell me you'll be okay. Please."

Rafe surprised her by taking her hand between his. "I'll be

okay." His expression grew deadly serious. "Now promise me that on the off chance something does happen to me, you won't stop fighting. You'll never give up."

That was an easy promise to make. "I don't want them to take me. I'll never give up."

Rafe cleared his throat. Gruffly, he said, "Neither will I."

Yearning swelled in her chest, an ache that felt just as good as it hurt. It was torture to know her affection wouldn't be welcome, because she wanted to kiss and touch Rafe so badly she could hardly breathe. Connecting like that would be a way to reaffirm that they were still alive, and it would be a memory to hang onto if the unthinkable happened.

But she couldn't do that to Rafe. Not when he was barely in control. Not when they only had hours left together before nightfall, and she didn't want to risk spending them apart in any way. Katie forced a brave smile and stretched out her legs so she could relax against the couch cushions. "Thank you for protecting me."

His willpower melted away before her eyes. Before she could register what was happening, Rafe's mouth covered hers, more intensely pleasurable than ever, and she was lost.

CHAPTER TWENTY-ONE

After all Rafe's talk about taking her, she expected to find herself on her back and full of werewolf cock as soon as his lips touched hers. What she got instead was a show of incredible restraint: Rafe pulled her into his arms, cupped her breast tenderly in his hand, and explored her mouth with deliberate passion while she clutched at his T-shirt and fought not to pull him down on top of her. The kiss lasted only a few sweet moments before he released her and backed away.

He averted his gaze and licked his lips. "I like protecting you."

Katie touched her mouth with her fingers, already missing him. "That was really nice."

"It was difficult to stop." Apparently determined not to tempt fate, Rafe not only closed his eyes but turned away as well. "Very difficult."

"You didn't have to stop." She braced herself for the potential consequence of her words. She was desperate for Rafe, even knowing that any coupling they might engage in now would be influenced by the powerful sway of the full moon. She knew it could be rough. Maybe even a little violent. But if it felt half as good as their wake-up sex, she was ready. "Maybe you just need to give yourself permission to do what comes naturally. And trust that if I can't handle it, you'll know. You'll know and you'll respect that."

Rafe shuddered. "I think right now we'd better stick to kissing—at least until I get better control over what you do to me."

"Fair enough." She bit her lip, hesitant to say more. But like Rafe only minutes ago, she caved almost instantly. "You know, we'll have to figure out how to be intimate during the full moon if we're going to be together." She held up her hand to forestall Rafe's protest. "If we're going to be together."

"I know." Rafe cleared his throat. "That's why I kissed you. To try and figure it out."

"Good. Don't hesitate to try again if the mood strikes."

He chuckled and rubbed his hands on his knees. "I won't."

Katie leaned away from Rafe and snuck a glance toward the front door. The knowledge that Lisa and her pack mates had congregated outside like a bunch of college kids waiting for a concert to begin was unsettling, even if she was pretty sure that they wouldn't attempt to engage them until after the sun set. If the other pack had planned to disobey their alpha, they would have ambushed them from the start.

"I want you to carry the revolver with you today." He touched her knee, but quickly withdrew. "Take it everywhere you go."

"I will." She tucked her legs beneath her on the couch, getting comfortable. "So other than boarding up the windows, what do we have planned for the rest of the afternoon? Looks like more target practice is out." She gave Rafe a playful wink. "I'm assuming sex is as well."

Rafe clearly struggled not to rise to her baiting. He clenched his fists in his lap, nostrils flaring, and took deep breaths before answering. The agony on his face shamed her for toying with his self-control. Flirting even mildly with him was flat-out cruel—she could see it in his every movement. She had to stop doing it, if she cared for him at all.

Before she could apologize, Rafe gathered his composure and spoke gruffly. "We could talk about tonight some more."

"Is it okay if we talk about something else for a little while?" She worried he would chide her for being silly. Because what was more important than preparing to defend their lives, right?

But he simply nodded. "What do you want to talk about?"

She hadn't thought that far ahead. All she knew was that she didn't want to think about being brutalized for just a little while. As she studied the strong lines of Rafe's face, she realized that there was only one thing she wanted to know about. "You."

"Me?" She couldn't tell whether he was pleased or embarrassed by the suggested topic.

"Of course. I want to know everything about you." She considered where to start. The fact that his upbringing obviously didn't resemble hers in any way piqued her curiosity. "What were you like as a kid?"

Rafe's expression turned to stone. "Angry."

That surprised her. "Just angry? All the time?"

"Most of the time." He hesitated, choosing his words deliberately. "My mother died when I was three years old. At the time she and my father lived right outside of town. One full moon, a human shot and killed my mother. The man swore he thought she was a wolf attacking his sheep. The dead sheep bolstered his story. When the police started to investigate, my father felt that he had no choice but to take me and disappear. That's when we joined the pack. My dad blamed himself because he'd insisted on living among humans, because he loved human culture and technology. He didn't want to live in the woods like an animal just because he spent part of his life as one."

"I'm so sorry, Rafe." Her heart ached for the little boy Rafe had been, who'd been forced to grow up without his mother. She despaired that he couldn't currently tolerate physical contact, because she burned to hold him. "So that's why your father became a separatist?"

"Yeah." He stretched his legs out across the cushions.

She mirrored his action so that they rested side-by-side, their lower bodies touching from opposite ends of the sofa. Rafe tangled his fingers with hers, holding her hand loosely as he spoke. "He didn't hate humans, he just realized how dangerous they could be. I remember he always used to tell me that humans weren't bad, just different. And that they didn't understand us...and we didn't want them to."

"Was it a difficult transition for him to make, living out here?" She gestured around at the rustic cabin. "I mean, this is a pretty rough lifestyle for a guy used to living with the modern conveniences."

"Yeah, it was hard on him."

Deep pain lurked beneath his words, hinting at greater adversity than simply losing his mother. She sensed that whatever had caused it was also the source of his childhood anger. "Did something happen?"

If Rafe was surprised by the direct question, he didn't show it. "The pack was different back then. Our alpha was a guy named Cain. If you thought the Alpha you met last night was a hard-ass, then Cain would have scared the hell out of you. He was a huge guy, hairy, incredibly strong. He hated humans. He didn't go out and hunt them like Jack Devereaux's boys do, but he clearly felt that humans occupied a lower rung on the food chain. To him, separatism wasn't just a philosophy. It was an immutable law."

"So you're saying I should be glad I missed out on his reign."

"You would be dead if he was still our Alpha." Rafe spoke quietly, staring at her as though nothing else existed in the world except the two of them. "I would be too, for helping you."

The more she learned about Rafe and his culture, the better she appreciated what he'd risked when he'd decided to save her life. "That seems like a pretty extreme punishment for being humane."

"It was."

His word choice and somber tone didn't pass unnoticed. Nor did the slight flaring of his nostrils, or the tightening of his jaw. She knew without asking that they were touching on a painful memory. "We don't have to talk about it if you don't want to."

Rafe's mouth quirked into a rueful half-smile. "If you want to know about me, we probably should."

"Okay." She sat patiently and waited for him to reveal whatever it was that shaped him as a person. He clearly had some sympathy for human life and had exhibited a willingness to risk his own safety to protect it, despite being raised in an environment where such a thing would have been discouraged, even punished. Why?

"When I was seven years old, my father found a pair of hikers who'd gotten lost in the woods a few miles from here. They were college kids, unprepared for the elements, and they managed to get turned around and couldn't find their car for a week. By then they were out of food and struggling to find water. If Dad hadn't found them and brought them home, they would have died within the next couple of days." Rafe's gaze took on a faraway quality, the memory tugging at his lips. "I remember one of the hikers had this wristwatch. Star Wars...there was some kind of robot on the face. I thought it was cool so the kid gave it to me, to show my father his gratitude for saving their lives."

"Your father sounds like a good man."

"He was the most decent guy I've ever known." Rafe rubbed his thumb over her knuckles, once again in the present. "Anyway, Cain happened to stop by our place the morning after my father found those hikers. He came in and they were eating at our kitchen table and he just..." He shuddered. "He exploded. He killed one of the boys—the one who'd given me his watch—before I could even move. There was blood everywhere...all over me, all over breakfast."

Recalling Rafe's tender age, Katie sucked in a breath. "Oh, no."

"I froze in shock, but my father...well, I'd never seen him that upset. He dove in front of the other boy and shielded him with his body. He told Cain that he couldn't stand back and let him murder two innocent kids, and begged him to think about what he was doing." Rafe took a steadying breath. "So then Cain grabbed me."

Katie's stomach turned over. "Rafe..."

"He put his arm across my throat, cutting off my air. I thought he was going to kill me. So did my father. I could see it in his eyes." A raucous cheer arose from outside, setting Rafe on instant alert. He glanced warily over his shoulder at the front door. "Cain wasn't a killer because he got off on it, like them." He swallowed and refocused on her. "He told my father that by bringing those boys into our home, he'd put my life in danger. Dad insisted that they had no idea what we were and so there was no danger in saving their lives. He had planned to send them on their way that morning, none the wiser. But Cain wouldn't hear it. He said that any time we interacted with humans, we put ourselves at risk. And that he was trying to help my father understand how serious the pack was about our no-contact rule."

"You must have been terrified." Her heart broke for the little boy who'd been used as a pawn in such a deadly game. "What did your father do?"

"Cain told him he had a choice: kill the boy, or Cain would kill me. He wanted my father to truly accept that it was the human's life or mine, so that he would never be tempted to assist a human again." Rafe's emotion rose and tears actually welled in his eyes. "My father wasn't a killer. He didn't even like to hunt. If we hadn't needed to in order to eat, he wouldn't have. But when Cain gave him that ultimatum, I watched my father's face change. All of a sudden that boy didn't matter anymore. I did." He cleared his throat, straightening. "The boy saw it, too. The whole time he'd been sobbing and cowering behind my father, but as soon as Cain said that, he took off running for the door. My father tore his throat out before he'd made it five feet away."

Katie exhaled shakily. "That must have been difficult for him. Not making the decision, but living with having taken that boy's life."

"He didn't have to live with it very long."

Her free hand flew to her mouth. "No..."

Barely suppressed rage simmered beneath Rafe's almost deadly calm. "Cain tossed me aside and jumped onto my father. Beat him to death right in front of me with the same cast-iron skillet Dad had used to prepare breakfast that morning."

Katie literally felt like she would be sick. She put her hand on her stomach and exhaled uneasily. It took all her strength to open her mouth and speak. "I can't believe you had to see that. You were just a baby."

"Hey, I'm sorry. I didn't mean to upset you." Rafe scooted closer and curled his fingers around her ankle. "Take deep breaths."

When you hurt, I feel pain. She bowed her head and focused on not losing her breakfast. "This is from you?"

"Partially, at least." Rafe rubbed her calf, then gave her a tender squeeze. "This is a traumatic memory and I've never talked about it before. It's...intense. You're obviously picking up on my pain. That's how the bond works. For better or worse."

The urge to be sick receded, but a hollow ache remained. "It's not just our bond. That's an awful thing for anyone to have to witness. It's not hard to imagine why you were so angry."

"I stood there paralyzed the entire time Cain was killing my father. It was only after he was dead that I unfroze. I shifted—I was just a puppy then—and went after Cain like a full grown wolf. He had me pinned almost instantly. He just held me down until I was too tired to fight anymore. When I started to sob, he told me that as my alpha, it was his job to protect me. And that because my father had failed to do so, he'd had no choice but to put him down." Though this part of Rafe's story was no less tragic than the beginning, he kept his tone neutral and he seemed distant from the emotion he described—like he was protecting her from it. She covered his hand with hers, keeping them connected as he continued speaking. "He took me home with him. Told me he'd raise me as his own and teach me to be a 'real' wolf."

"Did he?"

"I lived with him for only a week. The entire time, he just kept telling me how weak my father had been. That he was a disgrace to the pack, that he'd failed me. When I cried that first night with him, he beat me until I literally couldn't cry any more. And then he beat me every night after that, until the day Cooper and our current Alpha—whose name is Derek—came to see him."

Katie desperately hoped this was the turning point in Rafe's story. She couldn't bear to think of the suffering his former alpha had caused. This was an authority figure, a man he was supposed to have been able to trust. No wonder Rafe had grown up so angry. "Did they know what Cain was doing to you?"

"They figured it out pretty quickly. They knew he'd killed my father." Rafe met her eyes. "Despite the brutality of the beatings I endured, my healing ability meant that there wasn't a scratch on me. It didn't matter, though. I think it was obvious that I was terrified of him."

"So what did they do?"

"Derek told Cain that he thought maybe I should stay with him or Cooper for a while. That after what had happened, I needed some time to grieve and recover. Cain told Derek that I was a weak little pussy because my father had raised me that way, and that it was up to him and him alone to straighten me out." His mouth twitched as he no doubt relived that day. "That's when Derek challenged him—his leadership. Apparently Cain's punishment for my father was extremely polarizing for a pack already beset by political unrest."

"So that's how Derek became your Alpha?"

Rafe nodded. "Cain had no choice but to fight him. They went outside in front of Cain's place, where most of the rest of the pack was waiting. The fight lasted for probably fifteen minutes, but it felt like forever. I was scared about what would happen if Cain won. The entire time I thought about shifting into a wolf and just running as fast and as far as my legs could take me. But I knew I'd never survive on my own. I wasn't exactly a city kid, but I wasn't a survivalist, either."

"And you were only seven."

"Yeah," Rafe murmured. "I was seven."

It was difficult to wrap her head around the idea that Rafe had witnessed at least three separate killings within a week, all at such a tender age. When she was seven, her biggest concern had been how to convince her parents to adopt a kitten. They had, of course, because they were amazing parents who'd given her the kind of childhood Rafe no doubt couldn't imagine. Eyes stinging, Katie came forward onto her knees and threw her arms around Rafe, gathering him in a tight embrace. He returned her hug, no doubt on instinct, but stiffened. Aware that she'd once again crossed the line and made him uncomfortable, she reluctantly pulled away. "Sorry."

"No need to apologize." He caressed her cheek, staring at her with an expression of pure wonder. "I'm okay, you know. It was a long time ago."

Katie sniffled, nodding rapidly. "I know. I just wish..." She hesitated. "I wish I'd known you then."

Rafe chuckled and dropped his hand to entwine their fingers. "You wouldn't have liked me much. I was a bad boy."

"I doubt that."

Scoffing, Rafe said, "Well, I wasn't a good boy."

"I imagine you were a troubled boy." Unable to stay away, Katie traced his jaw line with her thumb. "And who could blame you?"

"After Cain was killed, I got passed around to various

members of the pack. I'd stay a month here, three months there, but I never had a permanent home again." He gestured at their surroundings with unmistakable pride. "Not until I built this place when I was seventeen years old."

"Seventeen?" Katie was floored. "I wasn't even doing my own laundry at seventeen."

Rafe smiled. "I grew up fast. It wasn't what I would have chosen, but I had to. After my father died, my childhood ended. Don't get me wrong...my pack-mates were good to me. They kept me alive at a time when I had no survival skills and no kin, but after Dad died, I had to look out for myself. I was no one's first priority. And I didn't trust anyone, least of all those with authority."

"What about Susan? When did you meet her?" She tried to keep her tone light, hating the jealousy that swept through her at the thought of Rafe loving another woman. It was almost painful to think of him with someone else.

"I was sixteen. She was twenty-two." The warmth in his eyes hinted at the importance of Susan's place in his early life. It wasn't difficult to understand why. With no family, a lover must have quickly become the center of his world. "She just turned up one day—no family, no friends—looking for the security and protection of a pack. Alpha agreed to let her join. I was living with him at that time, and he put her in the bedroom next to mine for a few months. We hit it off almost immediately. She was my first everything."

Any jealousy she'd been harboring dissipated at the realization that Susan had been a friend for Rafe at a time when he'd clearly felt totally alone in the world. "I can't imagine how devastated you must have been when she disappeared."

"I was destroyed. I built this cabin for us. I thought we would grow old here together, maybe have some pups. But we only lived here for two months." He stopped talking suddenly, giving her a careful sidelong glance. "It was a very long time ago."

Knowing he was concerned about her reaction to the talk of his long lost love, Katie shook her head. She wasn't worried about competition. Rafe belonged to her, and she to him. The only thing she felt about Susan was sorrow that her disappearance had caused young Rafe yet another heartbreak. "Have you been alone since?"

"Yeah."

She recalled Rafe's confession the night before when she'd asked about condoms. He'd wanted babies with Susan, and now he wasn't sure that he could impregnate her. That kept spontaneous sex nice and simple, but it also meant they couldn't fulfill the dreams Rafe once had. Dreams that she had, as well. "Do you still want pups?"

He avoided her gaze. "I told you I don't think that's possible for us."

"But if it were?"

Rafe's jaw tightened. Before he could speak, a muffled thump drew their attention to the front door. A louder thud brought both Rafe and Shilah to their feet. Rafe held up his hand as he walked to the door. "Stay there."

Katie huddled on the couch, happy to obey. "Be careful."

Rafe walked to the door and looked out the peephole. Then he jerked back as another thump shattered the quiet. Glowering, Rafe stalked back and forth a few times before peeking out again. "They're throwing snowballs."

Her instinct was to giggle at the absurdity of their weapon of choice, but Rafe's obvious frustration took the humor out of the situation. "Ignore them."

Rafe let out a truly inhuman growl and pounded his fist against the door. "Fuck them."

Fury poured off him in palpable waves. Without thinking, Katie got off the couch and walked to stand behind him. Her only desire was to soothe Rafe's temper, to somehow draw him back inside their own private bubble. With so little time before he transformed, she didn't want to spend even a moment wallowing in anger and frustration about the situation

151

outside. She touched his shoulder. "Come sit with me."

He shrugged away from her. "I need to go outside to get some supplies so I can secure the windows. Do you have the gun?"

"It's on the coffee table." Katie didn't like the idea of Rafe coming face-to-face with Lisa and her thugs while he was so upset. "Rafe, the windows can wait. Let's finish our conversation."

Rafe whirled around and stared her down. "Like hell it can wait. And I told you to keep that gun on you. At all times."

She didn't know what else to do but answer his anger with tenderness. Moving slowly, Katie looped her arms around Rafe's neck and rested her head against his chest. His heart hammered beneath her ear as his entire body vibrated with fiery rage. Afraid that he would fly apart at the seams, Katie squeezed him as tightly as she dared. Eyes closed, she put every ounce of her concentration into passing calm, soothing energy from her chest into Rafe's. She had no idea what she was doing, but there was no denying that Rafe been able to create a palpable effect on her mood by doing something similar. Even if she wasn't supernatural, maybe it went both ways.

She felt the change immediately. His shoulders loosened and his breathing evened out. His hands came up and splayed across her back, possessive and reverent at the same time. He spun them in place so her back was against the door, then leaned against her with a shudder. She buried her face in his neck, stroking her hands over his shoulders. Another snowball hit the door, but she didn't react—nor did Rafe. He just leaned into her harder, breathing deeply as his heart rate eased.

Relieved that she'd somehow defused the situation, Katie reached up to play with the fine hairs on the back of his neck. "I'm enjoying getting to know you better. Let's keep doing that for just a while longer." She kissed the side of his throat. "Please."

He bumped his hips into hers and rumbled deep in his chest. Still rock hard, for once he didn't pull back when his cock pressed into her belly. A moan slipped out from between her lips unbidden, a trill of pleasure skittering up her spine. Her arousal triggered an instant change in their embrace. Rafe slid his hands around her waist to her lower back, then moved down to squeeze her ass. His fingers sought out the cleft of her buttocks, exploring her through her pants. Breathing that had slowed turned ragged as Rafe's touch grew more demanding.

She couldn't allow things to get out of control. Not unless she was prepared to risk another round of Rafe's self-flagellation. Summoning her will, Katie put her hand on Rafe's chest and gently pushed him away. At first she thought he wouldn't go, but after a moment of resistance, he retreated. Nostrils flaring, he stared at her with hungry, entreating eyes.

Once green eyes that now glowed unearthly amber.

CHAPTER TWENTY-TWO

Katie's startled gasp sent Rafe stumbling away from her. His wild, luminous eyes instantly lost their amber sheen, reverting to pretty green and transforming him back into the man she'd already come to love. He turned and hid his face, cursing audibly under his breath. With that, the peace she'd created for them vanished. Awkward silence lingered in its place.

She wanted to tell him that everything was okay—that she was okay—but her throat wouldn't work. While she'd understood that touching him carried the possibility of unchecked passion, she hadn't expected that at all.

Rafe curled his hands into fists, knuckles going white. "I'm going outside."

She stepped out of the way without protest. "Rafe, I'm sorry. I was startled. That's all."

He brushed past her, then hesitated with his hand on the doorknob. "Get the gun. Whatever happens, do not come after me."

"All right." Hating that her reaction to his appearance must have seemed like disgust, Katie reached for him but stopped short of making contact. "Please be careful. I want to finish our conversation."

He grunted, then opened the door and stepped outside to a round of jeers and catcalls. He slammed the door in her face before she could make out what was being said, but she didn't need to hear specifics to know that it was going to take all of Rafe's considerable resolve not to rise to their baiting. Between his pent-up sexual energy and his simmering rage over their threats to her life, Rafe had to be on the verge of explosion. She just wished that he would let her do something to help. Even with his eyes gone wild and a sky-high libido, he still hadn't attacked her. The opposite, in fact—he'd allowed her to push him away.

Rafe wouldn't hurt her. She knew it in her bones—all she had to do was figure out some way to make him see that, too.

Sighing, Katie jogged to the coffee table and snatched up the revolver. She didn't trust Lisa and her friends not to instigate trouble. More directly, she didn't trust Rafe to keep his cool in his current state of mind. There was too much bottled up inside him, and it made him vulnerable to the threats and taunts she knew were being hurtled at him outside. Aware that Rafe wouldn't approve, she took a chance that everyone was too distracted with antagonizing each other to notice as she cracked open the front door an inch.

The first thing she heard was a crude remark from Lisa. "Driving you crazy, isn't it? I could smell her cunt from here. It's only a matter of time before you tear that bitch to shreds."

"Back off." Though Katie couldn't see anything through the narrow opening she'd created, Rafe sounded like he was standing close to Lisa. Too close. "Let me pass."

"Or what?" Lisa snorted. "You ready to go against your Alpha and attack me? I'm not ready to cross mine."

"Then get the fuck out of my way!"

Rafe's booming voice echoed off the bare trees and set Katie's heart racing. She tightened her grip on the gun, ready to use it. If he started a fight, she wouldn't be able to stand by and not try to help. *Even if that's exactly what he's asking me to do tonight.* She closed her eyes and waited, hoping that nothing would happen that forced her to disobey Rafe. She wanted to do as he said and stay put, but not at the cost of letting this situation escalate out of control. If they injured or killed Rafe now, her life was forfeit. Even if she did manage to somehow hold them all off for the night, there would be no happy ending.

Rather than react to Rafe's outburst with violence, Lisa laughed derisively. "Shit. You are frustrated, aren't you?" He didn't answer. She increased her volume, as though he was walking away from her. "I know you've fucked her at least once. You reek of it. What's wrong? Are you afraid of frightening her? Breaking her?"

Rafe's heavy, deliberate footsteps ascended the porch steps and came closer. Katie pulled the door closed, muffling the sound of Lisa's taunting words. Breathless, she stepped to the side and waited for Rafe to return to safety. Instead, she heard him turn and clomp back down the porch stairs for another trip to the shed. Concerned that Lisa would really amp up her venom now, Katie immediately eased open the door again. After a brief hesitation, she summoned her courage and widened the opening so she could glimpse the confrontation.

She could only see Lisa's shoulder and half her face because a wooden support blocked the rest of her view. It was more than enough to witness the viciousness in her every movement. Lisa stepped in front of Rafe as he tried to pass. "Was it worth it? Killing my mate for a human you can't even touch? One too fragile to satisfy a wolf's needs?"

"Katie is worth a hundred of your mate." Rafe shouldered his way past her, striding past a dark-colored wolf who sat erect and watched the proceedings with unwavering attention. "More, even."

"I don't know about that, but she sure does taste good," shouted a familiar male voice. The biter.

"Is that right?" Lisa waited until Rafe approached her with an armful of wooden boards, then lunged at him to knock a few off the top into the snow. "Does Katie taste good?"

An unfamiliar male voice called out, "If the rest of these

fools leave her alive until tomorrow morning, I plan on taking my time and finding out just how sweet she is. There's nothing quite like human pussy. Am I right?"

Rafe bent, disappearing from view, then straightened with the boards once again stacked in his arms. "Anyone who touches Katie is going to suffer a particularly painful death. That's a promise."

The naked brunette who'd gotten fucked on the ground sidled up to Rafe and reached between his legs. "As painful as that massive hard-on you're wielding?"

White-hot anger surged through Katie as the stranger fondled her bond-mate. Rather than pull away, Rafe stood his ground and stared down both women blocking his path. "Remove your hand or lose it."

"You can't tell me this doesn't feel good." The brunette leered, moving her arm in a slow rhythm that suggested just how intimate she was getting with Rafe. "That human of yours obviously can't take care of you the way you require. But I can. Seems like the least I could do before we kill you tonight."

Rafe lunged forward, shoving past the women with an aggressive growl. "No, thanks."

Lisa grabbed a hammer from atop Rafe's stack of supplies as he walked past, then drew back to swing at his head. Katie burst out of the cabin without thinking of the consequences. She raised the revolver, took quick aim, and pulled the trigger. Sparks flew as the bullet struck metal and the hammer flew from Lisa's hand. Ten heads swiveled to stare at her in shock. Katie's hand shook as she realized what she'd just done, and how easily she could have missed her target. Even though she hadn't hit Lisa or the other woman, her impulsivity might have just started a war.

Rafe pointed at the door. "Go inside. Now."

Katie turned and fled without looking back.

CHAPTER TWENTY-THREE

Rafe stormed into the cabin moments later. He dumped a load of wooden boards and tools just inside the door, then stepped outside for another armload of stuff. Katie stood by silently, afraid of the rebuke she knew was coming. He closed and secured the door, then walked to where she leaned against the kitchen table. Folding his arms over his chest, he raised an eyebrow as though waiting for her to speak.

She wasn't exactly sorry about what she'd done. Perhaps Rafe would have anticipated the attack if she hadn't intervened, or perhaps he would be lying in the snow with a crushed skull. "She was going to hit you."

"I know." Rafe handed over the hammer. There was a shallow dent roughly halfway between the claw and the head, an inch above the handle. "That was an amazing shot."

Surprised by the lack of censure in his voice, Katie met his gaze. "Thank you."

"I'm not going to scold you. You acted to protect me and, as a bonus, you just showed those idiots that you aren't some silly, defenseless human. I know they're reconsidering their chances now." He gave her a tight smile. "At least a little."

"I got lucky," she admitted in a whisper. Turning the hammer over, she marveled at the placement of her bullet. She'd been confident in her aim, but not that confident. She wasn't a bad shot, but luck no doubt also played a role. "I could have killed her. Or you."

Rafe shook his head. "Nah. You have a prodigious talent and you made exactly the shot that you intended. I'm willing to bet you could do it again right now."

She wished she could be so certain. "No, thanks."

"Yeah, that's probably best." He ducked his head and smiled crookedly. "You scared the hell out of her, you know."

"Good." Relaxing now that the threat of a lecture seemed to have passed, Katie straightened. "I didn't like that other one touching you."

"I know. I could feel it from thirty feet away." Rafe dropped a quick kiss on her forehead, then took back the hammer and walked to the pile of wooden boards in the foyer. "I didn't like it, either. Believe me."

Katie followed him to the curtained window next to the kitchen table. He secured the first board across the center of the frame, driving the nail into the wood with one aggressive motion. Riveted by the flexing of his muscular arm, she debated whether to ask what she knew was an extremely loaded question. She didn't want to start a fight, but Lisa's mocking tone kept ringing in her ears.

"What is it?" Rafe barely looked at her as he pounded another nail into a second board, slowly blocking off the light from outside. He no longer seemed angry, but instead crackled with a new kind of energy. A decidedly sexual energy.

She took a deep breath, then asked what she burned to know. "Do you think they're right?"

He positioned another board. "About?"

"That I can't satisfy you the way you need."

Rafe stopped mid-swing. Lip twitching, he gave her a sidelong glance. "Last night was the single best sexual experience of my life." He scanned her up and down, then turned back to the window and began to hammer with renewed vigor. "You satisfy me, Katie. Believe that."

"So then why have you been suffering with this all day?" She waited until he drove the final nail into the board, then stepped behind him and slid her hand around the front of his linen pants. He was hot and thick and throbbing, hips jerking

160

involuntarily into her caress. "Let me take care of you. You'll function better with a clear head."

He pushed her hand away and reached for another board. "For fuck's sake, I can go a few hours without—"

"During the full moon?" Katie challenged. "Really? Can you?"

"I'll take care of it myself." Rafe positioned the piece of wood over the last open space. "After I finish this." He stepped to the side, putting distance between them, and swung the hammer with a frustrated snarl. His emotion got the best of him and his aim was off. Yelping, he grabbed his thumb in his fist and squeezed hard enough to turn his knuckles white. "Fuck."

"No, I think we need to take care of this now." She hooked her finger in Rafe's belt loop, pulling him closer. Adrenaline continued to surge through her veins after her showing outside, and she needed an outlet. So did Rafe. Now was the time to prove that she could keep him under control. Pushing lightly against his shoulder, she placed him on the wall next to the partially-boarded window. "How's your hand?"

"Healing." He wiggled his fingers, looking none the worse for his crushing injury. "Listen, maybe you're right. Maybe I should take a few minutes to clear my head. You and Shilah can wait for me in the guest room. It won't take long."

Katie shook her head. "No. Here."

Rafe gaped at her as though she'd just suggested they go outside and roast marshmallows with their new friends. "With you?"

"With me." She'd misstepped by allowing Rafe to see how badly his glowing, wolf-like eyes had startled her. Now more than ever, she needed to demonstrate acceptance and trust—and by doing so, earn his trust in return. "I won't touch you unless you ask me to. I'll just watch."

He tilted his head back with a resigned sigh. "What if I lose control and do something you don't want?"

"I'll tell you to stop." She drew her fingernail in a line down the center of his chest. "And you will."

Doubt shone in his kind eyes. "You have no idea what you're playing with, Katie."

"Then show me." She nodded at his tented pants. "Take out your cock."

Shuddering, Rafe exuded a curious mixture of embarrassment, fear, and unchecked need. "Katie..."

"Be a good boy and obey your bond-mate," Katie murmured. "Please."

His nostrils flared as he tugged down his pants. "Even if my bond-mate is being a very bad girl?"

A little shiver of excitement curled in her belly as he revealed his swollen cock. She'd never seen a man so aroused before. It looked almost painful. Licking her lips, she forced her attention back to his face. She had to control this situation. He would never trust her otherwise. "Especially because I'm being a bad girl."

Rafe wrapped his hand around his length and exhaled shakily. "I can smell how wet your pussy is. It's driving me fucking crazy."

"Sorry." She batted her eyelashes and shot him her most playful smile. "You're not the only one who's feeling the full moon."

He chuckled and stroked himself with purpose. His gaze dropped to her chest. "Take off your shirt. Let me see your breasts."

She didn't plan to let him actually fuck her—only because she intended to prove a point—but she was happy to provide him inspiration for release. Reaching for the hem of her shirt, she put on a little show that led to a clumsy approximation of a striptease. It wasn't a move from her usual bedroom repertoire and she doubted she pulled it off the way she'd envisioned it in her head, but Rafe was clearly riveted. Enjoying the rush of power she got from his obvious hunger, she unhooked her bra while Rafe pumped himself into his fist. She tossed it onto the floor without looking away from his face, not wanting to take her focus from Rafe's body language for even a second. An explosion was coming. The air around them hummed in anticipation of it. And she had to be ready.

His willpower dissolved within the span of a few fevered strokes. He lunged and caught her around the waist, pulling her to him roughly. Then he grabbed two handfuls of her ass and rubbed his cock against her through her pants. A throaty groan died in his throat when Katie planted her hand against his chest and pushed him away. He stared at her with unblinking eyes that were once again a glowing, unearthly amber, then reached for her a second time.

Speaking in the calmest voice she could manage, Katie said, "No." Chest heaving, Rafe appeared to struggle to obey her command. Determined not to allow him the opportunity to ignore her, she pushed against his shoulder until his back hit the wall. "Stay right there. You don't get to touch me right now."

Rafe whined, a sad, wholly wolf-like sound from the back of his throat. Then he closed his eyes and took three deep, measured breaths. When he looked at her again, it was with very human guilt. "I'm sorry."

"Don't be." She dropped her gaze to his still-throbbing erection and nodded. "Keep going."

He didn't argue with her, which told her that he was very horny indeed. "It's just...not easy." His breathing grew labored as the speed of his hand increased. "Seeing you, like this. And not touching."

Taking pity on him, Katie decided that a little physical contact would be acceptable. After all, they would need to negotiate sex during the full moon at some point. For her sake, if not for his. "How about I touch you?"

Rafe's throat bobbed. "Yes."

Clearly he was no longer concerned with protecting her virtue. Relieved that she was so far in control of their encounter, she stepped closer and put her hand on his cock and her mouth next to his ear. "Remember, keep your hands to yourself."

He pushed away from the wall and tucked his hands behind his back. "I will."

"I know you will." Katie kissed his stubbled cheek, then drew away so she could watch his face as she slid her hand to the base of his cock. His jaw tightened and he hissed as she cupped his heavy balls. Pleased by his responsiveness, she ran her fingers along his length to caress the tip. "Or else I'll stop."

Rafe shivered and bucked his hips, encouraging her to grasp him and give him a few slow strokes. "You usually this bossy?"

"Only when the situation calls for it."

His eyes grew heavy-lidded and a grin played on his lips. "You really are an amazing woman."

"You're just saying that because I've got your cock in my hand."

He barked out a strained laugh. "That's only a small part of it."

Humming, she stepped directly in front of Rafe and worked his cock with both hands. "There's nothing small about you."

Rafe leaned forward and pressed his forehead against hers. He inhaled, shivered, then murmured, "I wish I was inside you."

"Close your eyes," Katie whispered. When he obeyed, she tightened her grip on his now-slick erection and massaged him firmly. "That's my pussy wrapped around you. Do you feel it?"

Rafe's breathing hitched and he rumbled out a groan. "Yeah."

"You're filling me up, Rafe, and it feels so good." Sensing his impending climax, she quickened her movement. He'd enjoyed talking last night, so she planned to finish him off with her words. "I'm so tight and you're so fucking big. Don't stop.

Don't stop fucking me. Make me come all over your big, hard cock."

Another growl spilled from Rafe's throat as he reached for her again. His fingers found purchase on her hips, digging in as his entire body stiffened. Vibrating with animalistic energy, he managed not to take control and instead kept perfectly still.

"Good boy," she said, then stroked him to shuddering, grunting climax. His body quaked for what felt like forever, before all the tension seemed to drain away, leaving him limp against the wall. She drew away, unsurprised to find amber eyes staring back at her. Without allowing herself to hesitate, she pressed her lips to his in a passionate kiss.

He kissed her back, breaking away only when the hand he used to caress her face began to tremble. His eyes had returned to normal and he was as relaxed as she'd seen him all day. "Thank you," he mumbled, tangling his fingers in her hair. "You're right, that really helped."

"Told you so."

He snorted. "I love you, Katie. I really do."

That made her grin like an idiot, no matter how crazy she found the idea of being in love after only a day. Because she loved him, too.

CHAPTER TWENTY-FOUR

Satisfied that she'd managed to defuse Rafe's sexually-fueled hair trigger, Katie picked up the hammer and hefted it with purpose. "Let's finish the windows now."

He took the hammer from her grasp and returned it to the table, then hastily tucked himself back into his pants. "What about you?"

What about her? She ached. But no matter how badly she wanted him, she couldn't let Rafe reciprocate. It was too risky. After the victory they'd just had, she feared pushing him too far for the sake of her own libido. Calling up her most breezy air, she said, "I'm fine."

"Bullshit."

"I'm not the one dealing with the moon." She patted his chest and stepped past him to reach for the hammer again. "And I think we should stop while we're ahead."

"Tell me the truth. Do you want me to touch you?"

How could she deny that when he could literally smell her? "Of course. But it's not necessary and we have a lot to do before tonight."

Rafe raked his gaze over her bare chest, a growl rumbling from deep in his throat. "I bet I can make you come in ten seconds flat. Just give me that—ten seconds."

Ten seconds. Maybe he could keep the wolf under control for that long. Of course, that assumed he could make good on his bold claim. The possibility that he might did nothing to quell her fierce arousal. She could feel her resolve draining away. "I don't know. It usually takes me longer than that."

"Ten seconds. All I'll do is put my hand inside your panties. Don't let me do any more than that. You don't even need to get undressed."

She doubted that her blue jeans were enough to protect her from his animalistic urges, but the more he spoke, the less she cared. The fact that he seemed confident in his ability to pleasure her quickly without succumbing to his baser urges made it impossible to say no. She wanted it so badly that she couldn't summon the will to refuse.

"Ten seconds?" Katie unbuttoned her blue jeans but made no move to pull them down. "Show me."

Rafe hooked an arm around her waist and pulled her close. His free hand slipped between their stomachs, surprisingly gentle fingers tickling her bare belly. She squirmed within his embrace, her laughter turning into a moan when he moved down and eased his fingertips beneath the elastic waistband of her panties. He played with the material for a brief, teasing moment, then slipped inside and sought out her wet heat with his whole hand. He parted her with deft fingertips, coming to rest over her slippery, engorged clit. Katie held her breath—his touch was somehow already so familiar and it felt so good.

"Eight seconds left," Rafe whispered, then closed his eyes in apparent concentration.

The orgasm exploded deep within her belly, taking her legs out from beneath her. Rafe tightened his grip and kept her on her feet, his chest heaving against hers. It was as though he was sending energy directly into her clit through touch alone, triggering wave after wave of delicious pleasure that only seemed to intensify the longer it went on. Katie cried out in shock at the strength of her full-throttle climax, and at the way it rendered her unable to do anything except clutch at Rafe's biceps, boneless within his powerful embrace.

She didn't know how long it lasted. More than ten

seconds. Far more. She never wanted to come down, but eventually her frail human body couldn't take anymore. Weakly, she pushed at Rafe's shoulders and shook her head, overcome. "Please stop."

He pulled his hand from her panties and the pleasure ceased, leaving blissful contractions and aftershocks in its wake. Katie didn't release Rafe—she held on tighter, stunned by what had just happened.

"Was that okay?"

The uncertainty in his voice snapped her out of her stupor and forced an incredulous laugh from her too-dry throat. "Uh, yes." She loosened her death grip on his arms, shifting, whimpering as another aftershock rippled through her. "Rafe, what did you do to me?"

"I thought that was obvious." Confidence crept into his voice. His eyes sparkled.

"I mean, was that some sort of werewolf trick?" Katie looped her arms around his neck, sighing as his chest hair brushed against her erect nipples. "Did you know that would happen?"

Rafe shook his head. "I'd heard stories about bonded sex." He pulled her closer, both hands on her bottom—safely on the outside of her blue jeans. "I was hoping that would feel good for you. Honestly, I pretty much winged it."

"It was incredible. And it didn't even take you ten seconds."

He growled and nipped at her throat, hands tightening on her ass. "Fuck, I want you."

"Me too," Katie said, but pushed him away and stepped out of his embrace. Her legs trembled as she forced herself to put distance between them. "But we've got a lot to do and I'm saying no."

Rafe inhaled deeply, hands curling into fists, eyes igniting with fiery need. A low rumble from deep in his chest made him sound more like a wolf than a man. Katie shivered, caught between desire and the mild, instinctive fear the now-familiar sound provoked. Rafe leaned back against the wall and closed his eyes. "I understand."

Longing rang clear in his chastened voice. It took everything she had not to go to him and fall into his arms. The only thing that stopped her was her fear of what she might initiate. And how Rafe would feel if he lost control. "The full moon sucks."

He surprised her with silent laughter that made his shoulders shake and put a genuine smile on his face. "Yeah, it kind of does."

"Tomorrow, when this is all over..."

Rafe nodded and pushed off the wall, exhaling. He got the hammer off the table and went to nail another board in place. "We'll celebrate."

෴

It took them an hour to finish boarding up the windows. Katie followed Rafe around the cabin, offering help where and when she could. Mostly she tried to stay out of his way, aware that he was having an increasingly difficult time keeping his composure. Only two o'clock in the afternoon and already she could see the growing influence of the moon. Rafe's movements and vocalizations grew more primal by the minute, and Katie could feel his pent-up aggression stirring and roiling within. Though she had a bad feeling that boarding the windows was a silly, futile gesture, the task gave Rafe an outlet for his aggression and that was exactly what he needed.

When he nailed the last board in place, Katie looked around, wishing for another. They had another six hours to kill before he would need to go outside and face their enemies. She questioned Rafe's current capacity for small talk and doubted that he had a closet full of board games somewhere. How they would pass the time when all either of them really wanted to do was fuck, was beyond her. She almost suggested they brave the inevitable taunts and jeers and go for another round of target practice, but she knew that Rafe's struggle to hang on to his humanity was no doubt shared by the other werewolves outside, and for them there was no fighting against their beastly natures. Stepping outside now would be like tossing gasoline onto a fire.

She'd rather brave the heat inside the cabin.

Rafe placed the hammer on a shelf near the hallway that led to the bedrooms when he was finished. "Remember this is here, if you need it."

She sincerely hoped that she wasn't going to be engaging in the kind of close combat where a hammer would come in handy, but she nodded. "Thanks."

Sweat soaked through Rafe's thin T-shirt, evidence of his exertion since their brief sexual encounter. The release she'd given him seemed to have improved his aim, but each swing had been harder than the last, until she'd grown concerned he was going to put the hammer through the thick log wall. She'd said nothing, content to let him release his primal urges in a relatively innocuous fashion. Yet after all that, he looked only mildly satiated, staring at her with palpable heat as he stripped the damp shirt over his head.

"I'm going to shower."

Katie nodded absently and tried not to stare. Rafe's lean, muscular torso dripped with perspiration. His musky, pleasant scent hung heavily in the air between them, literally making her mouth water. She'd never enjoyed sweaty hugs from ex-boyfriends, so she was mystified by her reaction to Rafe's natural aroma. It was probably pheromones. Or something. Forcing her gaze from Rafe's chest to his eyes, Katie nodded again. "Okay."

"Will you wait for me in my bedroom?" He jerked his head toward the front door. "I don't feel comfortable leaving you alone out here. Even with Shilah."

The brown mutt lifted his head from his place on the floor, next to the kitchen table. His ears were alert, but his face remained open and friendly. Katie regarded him fondly. "Yeah, Shilah doesn't seem like much of a threat."

"Oh, he'll protect you as best he can. I have no doubt about that." Rafe crouched down, calling the dog to him. Shilah dashed to his side, happily accepting the affectionate strokes that Rafe bestowed upon him. "Unfortunately, he's a mere Canis lupus familiaris. So he's at a bit of a disadvantage with my kind. Especially outnumbered."

Shilah leaned against Rafe's legs and panted with a doggy grin on his face. "He loves you."

"I love him." Rafe scratched behind Shilah's ears, and Shilah closed his eyes in clear pleasure. "He's my brother."

The sight of Rafe—shirtless, beautiful, strong Rafe—lavishing his dog with affection stole Katie's breath and filled her chest with a powerful feeling of deep, limitless love. This was her family now. These two recluses, a werewolf and a mixed-breed dog. She never would have believed it possible to feel about anyone the way she felt about them.

Rafe raised his gaze to meet hers. "Us, too."

Katie blinked back tears. She didn't have to say a word for Rafe to know exactly how she felt. It was the same for her. Both Rafe and Shilah wore their love and loyalty plainly. "I know."

Arms flexing, Rafe stood and gestured toward the hallway. "Will you stay in my room? It really will make me feel better."

"Of course." Pleased that Rafe was actually conversing with her again, Katie followed him willingly. "Maybe after you shower you can tell me more about being a werewolf. I'm sure there are things I should know."

His hand found the small of her back and he guided her to his bedroom door. "I'd rather talk about you." He urged her into his room, stepping away after a brief caress on her hip. "You can tell me what it was like growing up human."

That sounded like a safe way to spend the countdown to the full moon. "Deal."

Rafe left her with a tender smile that was in stark contradiction to the heated lust in his eyes. He closed the door behind him, but not before checking, "You've got the gun?"

She held up the revolver, which had been tucked into the back of her blue jeans. "Got it." As soon as he left the room, she placed the gun on the nightstand and flopped onto his bed, anxious and exhausted and thrumming with unspent sexual energy—despite the strength of the orgasm Rafe had given her only an hour ago. Who said she wasn't dealing with the full moon, too? This was torture.

To distract herself, she lifted the leg of her jeans and inspected the wound on her calf. Once again, she'd nearly forgotten it was there. Whatever Rafe had done to her had not only taken away her pain, but it appeared that her torn flesh was already healing itself. Not at the rate that Rafe could manage, no doubt, but much more quickly than she'd ever seen her own body accomplish. The bite looked days old, maybe even a week—certainly not like it had happened less than twenty-four hours ago. Shivering, Katie lowered her pants leg and lay back. She stared at the ceiling while she tried not to dwell on memories of her attack, but rather thoughts of her rescuer.

The shower came on in the bathroom and she shivered, all too aware that Rafe was naked on the other side of the wall. Naked and...wet. And no doubt rock hard. Katie exhaled and rolled onto her side, bringing her knees to her chest in an effort to distract herself from the stunning arousal she felt lying in Rafe's bed, surrounded by his scent, listening to him soap his naked body. She tried to think of other things—the pile of work that was no doubt waiting for her back at home, the murderous thugs lurking around outside at that very moment—but her mind kept going back to Rafe. The way he'd slipped his hand into her panties. How he'd felt inside her last night and this morning.

"This is crazy," Katie murmured to herself. No sooner had

the words left her mouth than a delicious wave of ecstasy rolled through her belly and settled squarely between her legs. She moaned in surprise and squeezed her thighs tightly together. "Shit." Another wave of pleasure, this one nearly kicking off a bona fide orgasm. Katie closed her eyes and took calm, measured breaths.

This was really crazy.

A low, muffled groan from the bathroom confirmed the source of her surreal ecstasy. With her eyes shut, she was able to focus on the sound of Rafe—and more importantly, the feel of him. Even without seeing him, she knew he was jerking off. Of course he was. It was the smart thing to do, during this rare moment apart. And it was probably necessary for his continued sanity as dusk approached. Except—

Katie moaned quietly as breathtaking pressure built in her womb. Unable to keep still, she rolled onto her back and stared at the pattern of the wood grain on the ceiling, biting her lip as the shared sensation with Rafe grew more intense. She was certain he was going to make her climax without even touching her, which was absolutely amazing—and exciting. Yet she wanted to rub her clit so badly she ached.

She succumbed to the urge almost immediately. Unbuttoning her jeans with shaking hands, she plunged the right one into her panties as soon as she had access. Pure relief spread throughout her body, but her muscles remained tense and her breathing only grew more labored. She glided her fingertips through her slick arousal, shuddering at the overwhelming sense of satisfaction that the caress brought. A quiet moan escaped her lips, and Rafe answered it through the wall.

Could he feel her pleasure, like she felt his? She hoped so. Eager to enhance his masturbation session—and hers— she moved her fingers down to tease at her opening. The contact felt so good that her hips lifted on instinct to allow her fingertips to slide inside. She groaned quietly, then grinned at a grunt from the next room. That was a good sign. Pressing in deeper, she lay the palm of her hand over her sex and rubbed herself sensuously.

"Fuck." Rafe gave a muffled shout. Then he let loose a snarl that raised the hair on the back of her neck and caused her pussy to contract, hard, sending her over the edge once again.

Unable to cope with any more stimulation, Katie pulled her hand from her panties and rolled onto her side. She curled into the fetal position and closed her eyes, riding out her climax in desperate silence. One moan at the wrong second and Rafe could be here and inside of her before she could summon the strength to say no.

Finally the pleasure ebbed and she could breathe again. The water turned off in the bathroom, signaling that Rafe was also finished. She didn't know how long it might take him to get dressed, but she was certain that she didn't want to be in this state when he returned to the bedroom. She sat up with effort, wiping her hand on her panties—like that would disguise her scent—then fumbling to fasten her jeans. She spent the next two minutes schooling her breathing and trying to think about happy memories of home. About anything but Rafe.

He returned to the bedroom wearing no shirt and a clean pair of sweatpants. Clearly embarrassed about his state of undress, he barely met her eyes and rumbled, "Closer we get to dark, less I can stand wearing them."

"Them?"

"Clothes." He gestured down at the pants, which failed to hide his unflagging hard-on. "I'll keep these on. I just can't tolerate the shirt anymore."

"That's fine. I'll control myself." Katie admired his broad chest, trying not to react to the sight of so much skin. She remained sitting on his bed, not trusting her legs to support her.

Rafe's nostrils flared and he visibly fought not to come any closer. She knew without him saying that he was aware of exactly what had happened in his bed. "Why don't you wash up and then we can talk?" His gaze moved over her body, then the mattress. "In the den."

CHAPTER TWENTY-FIVE

He was waiting for her on the couch when she returned to the den, two glasses of water and two sandwiches on the coffee table in front of him. He didn't look up at her as she entered the room, too busy staring at his sandwich like he wanted to devour it in one bite. Surprised that he'd bothered to wait for her, she said, "Go ahead and eat."

Rafe startled, acknowledged her with a brief nod, then picked up the thick sandwich laden with nothing but meat and took a ravenous bite. His eyes glowed briefly amber at the first taste, and Katie nearly hesitated before sitting down beside him. That he seemed more interested in lunch than her reassured her that he hadn't noticed her slight lapse. She still believed to the bottom of her soul that he would never hurt her, but those eyes were difficult to get used to.

"I didn't think you would want quite as much meat as me," Rafe mumbled between bites. "But there's plenty in the kitchen, so help yourself."

She eyed the generous mound of thinly sliced meat and vegetables he'd prepared for her, amused at his concern. "This is more than enough."

He grinned. "We've been working up an appetite today. Figured we could use the energy for tonight." He took another giant bite, rumbling in satisfaction. "I know I'm starving."

Katie nibbled at her sandwich as she studied him as

subtly as possible. His muscles were bunched and tense, his entire body wound tight. "This must be exhausting for you. Having your body hijacked, spending the entire day in overdrive."

Rafe shrugged. "I'm used to it by now. It's not usually this bad." He glanced at her, then away.

She picked up on the subtext. "I'm sorry I'm making things difficult." Reflecting upon that statement for a moment, Katie sighed. "Really, I've made your entire life difficult. No matter how tonight ends, I can't imagine that you'll be able to simply fall back into your old routine. You'll have blood on your hands and a human girlfriend that your friends despise."

He polished off his sandwich, brushed his hands on his pants, and turned to touch her knee. Comforted by the heavy weight of his hand, she managed another bite. She wasn't hungry, but Rafe was right—she needed the energy.

"I don't want to fall back into my old routine." Rafe sounded so sincere that Katie didn't doubt him for an instant. "You weren't a part of that routine and that means it's not worth missing for even a second. Understand?"

She nodded, throat stinging. "Okay."

Rafe squeezed her knee. "Now tell me about being a kid. I'll bet you were a spirited little thing."

The affection in his voice made her feel cherished in a way she'd never come close to experiencing. With all of the sexual intensity between them, moments of quiet warmth had been difficult to find today. But here Rafe was, closer to sunset than ever, and he'd just made her feel as adored as she ever had. "I was precocious. A know-it-all. I watch home movies and cringe."

"I like a woman with confidence." Rafe sat back and put some distance between them.

"My older sister Erin is the same way. We used to butt heads a lot. She's even more stubborn than I am. We would fight like crazy—drive mom and dad nuts—but we were always best friends." Katie smiled as she thought about Erin, then ducked her head when tears threatened to spill over. "I really hope I get to see her again."

Rafe took her hand, stroking his fingers over her wrist. "You will." He lifted her face with his other hand. "What about your parents? Do you still have them?"

"Yes, and they're still married. They live down near San Jose. Erin lives in San Francisco, with me." She paused, then said, "Not with me. Close to me."

"I'm sure they're worried about you." Regret colored his tone. "I'm sorry I wasn't able to let you contact them."

"Soon enough," Katie said in as light a voice as she could manage. "Maybe tomorrow the roads will clear and we can drive to town."

He swallowed. "Yes, hopefully. The good news is that it's stopped snowing, and the sun was shining when I went outside earlier. I won't be surprised if some of the snow melts off today."

"That is good news." Aware that they needed to pass the time with innocuous conversation, Katie returned to answering Rafe's question. "I was always interested in art. I started drawing with crayons and colored pencils when I was three or four years old—not your typical pre-school drawings, I guess. I started to focus on graphic design in college, but as a teenager I did mostly charcoals and pencil drawings. I still do, for fun."

"I'd love to see your work."

"I'd like that." Warmed by the genuine interest Rafe exuded, Katie said, "My parents were afraid that I would graduate from college and become a starving artist, but I was always too practical for that. That's where computers came in. Luckily, that allowed me to develop a reasonably lucrative career that's still related to my passion."

"I've always been into photography, myself," Rafe murmured.

She thought back to the pictures that lined the walls of the guest room. They were beautiful—she'd even thought so when she'd been convinced that Rafe was a serial rapist and/or murderer. "You took the pictures on the walls?"

Sheepish, he tipped his head. "I'm not artistic like you are, but I enjoy taking pictures."

"You're very artistic. There were some gorgeous shots." Katie made a mental note to examine his work again. That he had creative tendencies reassured her that perhaps they were well-suited for one another in more ways than just having a supernatural connection. "My sister is a general surgeon. That's one area where we couldn't have been more different. She was the practical one, I was more of a dreamer."

"I hid the photography from my pack mates for a long time. I knew I'd be ridiculed for having such a 'soft' interest."

"As far as I'm concerned, your social circle would benefit from a little more softness." She touched Rafe's foot, hoping to lighten the mood, but he recoiled as though burned. He shot her an apologetic look and she reassured him with a tentative smile. "You're a good man. A good wolf."

Rafe didn't look convinced. "I wonder how your family would feel about me."

"If they knew everything or if they got a censored version of your biographical information?"

Rafe's chuckle was tinged with sadness. "The censored version would probably be safest."

"Then they'll love you." She poked him with her toe, just enough to get his attention. "What's not to love?"

She hated the brief flash of self-loathing that passed over his face. "You obviously don't belong in my world, but I worry that I would be just as out-of-place in yours."

"Unless you go wolf right in front of my family, trust me, you'll compare favorably to my ex-boyfriends. You're the kindest, most considerate, well-mannered man I've ever dated." She paused, embarrassed to realize that she was admitting a shitty taste in men. "I've never had a guy make me feel as genuinely loved as you do."

"I can't say I'm sorry that I get to be that guy," Rafe murmured, "but I do regret that no one has ever given you a better twenty-four hours than we've just spent. Or made you feel more loved." Familiar guilt tightened his features. "You deserve better."

Katie shook her head. "I'm happy with what I've got." Crazily, it was true. Despite the fear she'd felt since meeting him, despite the danger, she considered herself lucky. To be alive, and to have found this surreal connection with another living creature. Even if he wasn't the same species as her. She giggled quietly—could her ever-pragmatic sister even believe the truth about her new boyfriend? "Erin will be happy I've found someone who treats me well. The guy I was with before my most recent ex wasn't very nice. To say that Erin was upset when she found out is an understatement."

Rafe went very still, eyes glowing dangerously. "Not nice how?" His words came out as a fierce snarl. Just like that, he looked ready to kill a man he'd never met. For her.

Alarmed by the intensity of his reaction, Katie waved off his concern. "He was a jerk, that's all. Mostly during arguments. Called me names, got slightly physical once or twice." She'd left him the day he'd smacked her across the face during a screaming match over the fact that she'd been asked to work late. Prior to that night, the worst David had done was grab her arm and squeeze. A blow to the face had been the last straw. The rising fury in Rafe's expression made her wish she hadn't brought up the subject. "I left him before it got too bad, Rafe. I swear."

His anger swiftly turned to sorrow. "And now you're with me."

She didn't know if it was their encounter that morning or his potential for unconscious violence during the full moon that brought such remorse to his tone. Either way, she still had faith that he would only ever protect her. "You've never hurt me," Katie said quietly. She touched his leg, aware that it would incite fierce desire, but held him back with a sober look.

"You won't."

He stared at her until his eyes threatened to spill over. "I honestly couldn't live with myself if I did."

"I know." She brought her hand to his face, unable to stop herself though she knew her touch would be torture. He surprised her by placing his hand over hers, then he turned and kissed her palm. Katie exhaled. "We'll figure this out, Rafe. I swear."

Nodding, he cleared his throat and looked away. "Have you ever been in love before?"

"I thought so, once. In college." Her second boyfriend had been a sweet enough guy—except for his fear of monogamy. Unfortunately, she'd only discovered that flaw after two years and no-doubt countless affairs. "At the time I felt strongly about him. Way more strongly than he felt about me, as it turned out. It seems a little silly now, looking back." She paused. "It doesn't compare to the feelings I have for you."

"Of course not." Rafe managed a self-deprecating smile that didn't reach his eyes. "He didn't have the ability to join your soul to his while you were unconscious. So I had an unfair advantage."

"I'm not convinced I wouldn't have fallen in love with you even if that hadn't happened."

A wistful shrug. "Guess we'll never know."

"If we were meant to be bonded, I'm pretty sure it would have happened whether I was conscious or not. Besides, I don't really care how we got here." She scooted slightly closer, and he finally allowed her to make eye contact. "The important part is that I do love you—and I trust you with my life."

"Good thing." He tried to force humor into his voice, but couldn't produce convincing levity. "Because I don't think you have much choice."

Katie glanced at the front door, then the boarded windows that blocked the outdoors from view. What was the other pack doing? Was Lisa plotting a particularly twisted revenge or simply stewing in her hatred? She mentally reviewed the group outside and shuddered. "The one who bit me is out there."

"I know." Rafe bared his teeth. "Can't wait to bite him."

Gross, but she appreciated his desire for vengeance. Clearly the moon was bringing out Rafe's primal side in a big way.

Despite his bravado, it was hard not to worry about how he would manage to not only subdue the monster who'd so easily taken her down with one bite, but also nine of his meanest friends. This morning she'd allowed Rafe to convince her that he had the situation under control, but this close to sundown, it seemed like he was facing an impossible task—one suited to an action movie where happy endings happened only because of audience demand and not reality. Fear of losing him clutched at her insides, and she struggled valiantly not to throw herself into his arms and refuse to let go.

"What's wrong?"

She shivered at the quiet concern in his suddenly gentle voice. "I'm scared."

"Katie—"

"I know you're strong, Rafe, but so are they. And there are so many of them."

He put his hand under her chin and turned her away from the front door, forcing her to look at him. "I'm the good guy. I'll be fine."

How she wished it were that simple. "But—"

Rafe stopped her mouth with his. She grabbed his biceps on instinct, at first pulling him close, then, remembering his fragile state, she hastily pushed him away. Or at least she tried. He tightened his grip on her arms, not allowing her to retreat. Despite his persistence, the kiss itself was almost undemanding—not at all like their frenzied coupling that morning. It filled her with the most amazing sense of peace and reassurance, like everything would be okay as long as they were together. She relaxed and kissed him back, allowing their intimacy to chase away her fears. By the time they broke apart minutes later, foreheads pressed together, Katie's panic had receded to a manageable level. Though she would never totally shake her fear of losing him, somehow he'd passed her his confidence and faith that they would be all right through the joining of their lips.

Incredible.

"No more worrying about me," Rafe rumbled. He eased back and reclined against the other end of the couch, chest rising and falling rapidly. "You should go nap. I doubt we managed more than four or five hours of sleep last night, and you'll need all the energy you can get."

She hated the thought of being away from him for even a second. "Will you nap with me?"

"Can't." His hand dropped between his legs and he adjusted his visible arousal with a subtle wince. "No way I can sleep this close to sun down."

Then she wouldn't either. "I'm not tired."

"Katie, you're going to need the rest. Trust me. Falling asleep is not an option once I transform. You're going to have to be on guard all night long and that won't be easy if you're exhausted." He nudged her with his bare foot, the simple contact sending a shiver down her spine. "How about if I stay with you while you sleep?"

Knowing he was right, she gave in with a reluctant nod. "I just hate to waste our last few hours together."

"It's not a waste." Rafe stood and offered her his hand, then pulled her to her feet and into his arms. She snuggled into him happily, all too aware of his erection pressed against her stomach. "Consider this nap an investment in our future. The more well-rested you are, the better chance we both have of making it through tonight. Okay?"

She stepped back and took his hand, leading him to the bedroom behind her. "Okay." He stopped when they reached the doorway. Katie took another couple steps, then turned to face him. "Will you lie down with me?"

She expected an argument, so was shocked when he simply nodded and approached the bed. "Give me the gun. I'll keep watch."

His compliance inspired her own. Katie handed over the gun and automatically began to unbutton her jeans. Remembering herself, she looked up at Rafe and tilted her head. "Do you mind?"

He stood at the foot of the bed, staring. Swallowing, he rasped, "No, get comfortable."

Not interested in drawing out the situation, Katie quickly shed her pants and crawled beneath the comforter. Exhaling, she burrowed into the surprisingly cozy bed and rolled onto her side. She closed her eyes and waited, hopeful that Rafe would join her. After a few tension-filled moments, he did. He lay on top of the comforter, on his back, and when she opened her eyes to check how he was handling being so close to her, she found him staring straight ahead at the door.

"Thank you for staying," she murmured, and closed her eyes again. Looking at him made it more difficult not to use him as a pillow. She yearned for his touch and his scent surrounding her so much it hurt.

A strong arm slipped beneath her shoulders and pulled her closer. "Come here."

She went willingly. Resting her head on his firm shoulder, she relished the heat of Rafe's bare skin against her cheek. And quickly—more quickly than she ever would have imagined—the steady thrum of his heartbeat lulled her into peaceful slumber.

CHAPTER TWENTY-SIX

She woke up to Rafe squeezing her tightly, mild panic in his voice. "Katie, wake up."

Her heart rate accelerated as she struggled into consciousness. What time was it? Was Rafe ready to transform? Was the battle about to begin? Panicked, Katie shot into a sitting position and braced herself for the worst. Had the other pack decided to ambush them? "What? What's happening?"

Rafe put his hand on her back and she instantly relaxed. Everything was still okay. At least for the moment.

"I need to go outside soon. I figured you would want a little time awake before that happens."

"Of course." Katie dropped her head into her hands and exhaled, shaken by how unprepared she'd felt when she'd thought the moment had arrived. "Thank you."

"Also, I'm finding it incredibly painful not to mate with you." He winced slightly, then amended, "Make love with you."

"No, I understand." She scooted away from him, then fished over the side of the bed for her jeans. "Sorry."

Rafe caught her wrist in his large hand. He stroked his thumb over the inside, as though checking her pulse. "Don't be. It was wonderful to hold you like that. You're so beautiful...so soft."

His grip tightened slightly. Katie pulled away and stood,

certain that if she didn't, Rafe would succumb to his urges and leap on top of her. With her back to him, she fumbled on the ground for her jeans. She could feel his eyes on her ass as she zipped up. After taking a moment to collect herself, she turned back to Rafe with a smile. "It felt good to be held."

This time she wasn't even surprised to find his eyes glowing. An hour before transformation—she was probably lucky that he'd had the willpower he clearly did. Even now she could see his determination dissolving a little as he stared at her.

He rubbed his hands on his thighs, struggling outwardly to control his actions. She could feel him thinking of breaking down and indulging his instincts. He would ask for her consent—she was sure of that—but she had no idea whether either of them would be able to control what happened after she gave it. Though she believed in her heart that Rafe would never ham her on purpose, she knew he would never forgive himself if he got too rough or injured her right before the big battle.

Being the responsible one sucked. "No," Katie said with less conviction than she'd hoped to convey. "Tomorrow—not now. It's too late."

Anguish washed over Rafe's handsome face. "I know."

"Use that desire as motivation." The advice was as much for her as it was for him. "To make it through tonight."

"Protecting you is my motivation. I don't need anything else."

Emotion threatened to overwhelm her. Soon, she was going to have to send her bond-mate outside to face a gang of murderous werewolves alone. Because of her. Because he'd saved her life and she'd rewarded him by running off and finding the worst kind of trouble.

Rafe shook his head. "This wasn't your fault."

"If I hadn't run away—"

"It would still be the full moon tonight. We would still be alone in the woods with wolves on the prowl." Despite his coherent speech and the rather salient point he was making, Rafe appeared more untamed than she'd ever seen him. His eyes still hadn't reverted back to human form, and she wasn't sure they would before morning. "You would still be a fresh piece of meat for those animals to devour."

Katie flinched at his blunt words. "Right."

"And I would still be ready to die to protect you," he said, voice softening.

"I know." Unsure how to respond to his heartfelt words without initiating physical contact, Katie gestured at the door. "We should probably go out there. Get ready."

"Probably." Rafe sighed and walked stiffly to the door. Shilah jumped up from his place on the floor when Rafe stepped into the hallway. "Give me a five minute head start, will you?"

"Of course." She knew exactly how he planned to spend their time apart. She was already throbbing in sympathy. "I'll wait here."

Rafe managed an embarrassed smile. "You'll know when I'm ready."

"You're right." Katie chuckled, blushing along with him. "I will." She spoke up before he could walk away. "Think of me?"

He snorted. "Like I can think of anything else."

 catso

He was done in just over four minutes. Katie lie panting on the bed for another minute after that, overcome by the psychic vibrations of Rafe's pleasure. This time she hadn't touched herself at all, but this orgasm had been no less intense than the last. In fact, she wasn't sure if her legs still worked. She allowed herself to bask in the afterglow for a brief, glorious spell, then forced her body into motion. After a trip to the bathroom for a hasty clean-up, she walked to the den to find Rafe pacing in front of the couch.

Naked.

Stunned and turned on by the unexpected sight, Katie stopped and stared. His muscles flexed and jumped as he strode aimlessly back and forth, reminding her of a caged tiger. His nostrils flared in time with the rhythmic rise and fall of his broad chest. When he caught sight of her on his next turn, he barely slowed his pace and greeted her with a wordless grunt.

She stated the obvious. "You need to go outside soon."

"I can make it another forty-five minutes or so." His hand drifted between his legs and he stroked himself as he eyed her breasts. She was almost relieved when he swiveled on his heel to walk the other way. "Maybe less."

"I don't want to send you out to them before it's absolutely necessary." Katie folded her arms over her chest to shield herself from Rafe's penetrating, unearthly stare. "I want to be together, every second we have."

Facing her once more, Rafe came to an abrupt stop and jerked himself off roughly. "I'm sorry, this is incredibly inappropriate—"

"Don't be silly." Quite frankly, she was impressed that he could still manage multi-syllabic words. "Do what you need to do."

Rather than take her invitation, Rafe growled and released his cock. Then he gestured with his head. "Actually, there's something I need to show you. Consider it a last resort."

She followed his gaze to the far corner of the room, on the ceiling—to what looked like an attic hatch door. Stunned that she hadn't noticed it before, Katie said, "What's up there?"

Rafe stalked across the room and grabbed a ladder from behind the couch, then climbed on top and pushed the hatch up and off the opening. He leapt into the attic with startling ease before poking his head back into the den to beckon her forward. "Come on. Quickly."

Ignoring her twinge of anxiety, she rushed to scale the ladder and grasp Rafe's offered hands. He pulled her into the attic as though she weighed nothing at all. After steadying her by the shoulders, he handed her a flashlight that she hadn't even seen him find. "Be careful to only walk on the joists."

She turned on the flashlight and illuminated their spare surroundings. The attic was larger than she'd expected, and so cold she could see her breath in the air. There was a small window at either end, enticing her with the soft light that filtered in from outside. Now that she was trapped indoors, she'd never craved the outside world so keenly. Katie took a ginger step toward the closest window, but Rafe put his hand on her shoulder.

"Don't let them see you."

"Why not? They know I'm in here." She shrugged away from him and cautiously made her way to the window.

"I don't want them to get them any more worked up than they already are."

Staying well away from the opening, Katie stepped to the side and angled her head to peek outside. Immediately she saw two naked men locked in a heated struggle. One drew back his fist and punched the other in the face. He returned the blow without flinching. Katie winced when the first man delivered another brutal hit to his pack-mate's temple. "I'm pretty sure they're too busy to notice me."

She startled when Rafe stepped behind her. He gazed over her shoulder at the fight, the heat of his body scorching hers. "Fighting and fucking. And they think humans are less evolved."

Katie tried to ignore his masculine scent at her back. Instead she focused on the view the window afforded. "Why didn't you mention the attic when we had time to work out a plan? If I brought the gun up here during the fighting—"

"Absolutely not."

She turned, surprised by just how close Rafe was standing. His erection bumped against her hip and he groaned, nearly tumbling off the joist he was balanced upon. Ignoring what had just happened, Katie said, "Why? If I could take out even a couple of them when the fighting starts, that's fewer for you to face alone."

"You don't even have a rifle."

"I don't need a rifle." Katie threw back her shoulders and challenged him to say otherwise. "You know I don't."

"It doesn't matter. I don't want you drawing attention to yourself during the fighting. I want them focused on me. Only me."

"But I can actually help—"

"No." Rafe leaned closer, invading her space. "Walking around up here is tricky, especially at night. If something happens to your flashlight, it'll be dark. Too dark to defend yourself. You could get cornered. Believe me, they'll find a way to get up here if that's what they have to do to get to you. Or you could take one wrong step and come through the ceiling on top of them."

"I could get cornered downstairs just as quickly. Maybe even quicker. Let's face it—if they get into the cabin, I'm in trouble. I'll have nowhere to go."

He pointed at the window behind her. "No, listen, the window opens. You can climb out onto the roof. Look to the left and you'll see what I mean. But I don't want you to even consider doing that unless you're trapped and you have no other choice. The roof will be slippery, and there's a big risk of falling and breaking your leg or worse. Not to mention, the second you open that window, they'll smell you. They'll know exactly where you are."

A sickening wave of vertigo swept over her at the thought of actually choosing to escape out a second-story window with more wolves no doubt waiting below. "Trust me, that's definitely my last resort."

"You're afraid of heights," Rafe murmured, as though committing an important fact to memory. He reached out like he wanted to touch her, but held back, grimacing. "I'll do everything I can to make sure you don't run out of options. Honestly, I don't want you up here tonight unless you're actively running from them. I only showed you this as a worst-case scenario—that's it. I don't want them to see you in the window. I don't want your scent on the wind because you're leaning outside, even from up here. Inside, they won't be able to smell you. So I want you to stay inside, with Shilah, and hunker down and hide. If any wolves get in here, shoot to kill." He paused. "Remember, any wolves."

Stark frustration threatened to shatter her composure. She knew Rafe was only trying to protect her, but he obviously didn't understand that she had the same desire to defend what was hers. "Why won't you let me help? I'm a good shot, Rafe, and you know that. I can make your job easier—I could help protect you." She searched his face, frustrated by the lack of discernible human emotion she found there. He stared through her, his entire body coiled like a snake about to strike. "I don't want to see you get hurt, either."

"We're not talking about this." As if in pain, Rafe curled his arm around his stomach and walked stiffly to the open hatch. "I said no."

"I don't remember agreeing to let you call all the shots," Katie sniped at his naked back. She couldn't help it—nothing elicited her temper like having a man boss her around. "It'll be so chaotic down there once the transformation happens that I doubt they'll realize where a few stray shots came from. And that would be two or three fewer of them to gang up on you."

"Enough." Whirling around, Rafe stared at her with eyes that glowed menacingly. "Now get downstairs."

She dug in her heels instead. "We're bonded, Rafe. Our lives are interconnected. So why don't I get to help protect you? Is it because I'm a woman? If that's what you—"

"Because you're human," Rafe roared. "Goddamn it, Katie. Do you understand that they're out there salivating over what they want to do to you? I can barely control myself with you smelling like that. How do you think they'll react if you open the window? It'll drive all of us crazy. And you're so goddamn fragile. You can't even heal yourself if you get injured! So don't be stupid about this, or I swear—"

In his pre-transformation state, her bond-mate cut an imposing figure. His deep voice shook the walls, impassioned and containing barely suppressed rage. Rather than shrink away, Katie stood her ground. "Or what?" She let the challenge hang in the air.

He deflated. "I'm not going to able to do this unless I know you're going to stay safe. So please, Katie." Gentling his tone, he said, "Please."

It was clear from his bearing that he was in no condition to argue. Taking pity on him, she decided to let the matter drop. There was no point in upsetting him in the last few minutes they had together. "All right. No shooting." Unless it's necessary.

She kept that caveat to herself.

He held out his hand. "I appreciate that you want to protect me. I do."

She made her way back across the joists, then laced their fingers and squeezed lightly. "And I appreciate that you're afraid for me."

Rafe said nothing as he helped her down through the hatch and into the den. He left the hatch open and the ladder poised beneath. "Just in case," he said, then walked back to the couch and sat heavily. He bowed his head and scrubbed at his face with his hands. "Soon now."

Katie sat beside him. "Does it hurt?"

"What?"

"Transforming." She ran her gaze along his lean, muscled body, trying not to linger in any one place too long. Besides his still-glowing eyes, he looked entirely human. Deliciously human. The thought that his body would soon undergo a forced metamorphosis—one that would strip away his human conscience—was unnerving. He exuded an animalistic energy that both frightened and excited her. "Does it hurt to transform?"

"Only for a minute." He lifted his face. "Then there's nothing."

"Is it scary?"

Rafe allowed a brief smile. "A little. But I'm used to it." He hesitated, then said, "I remember the first time. I was six years old and scared to death. My father took me into the woods and held my hand until it started. In the morning I woke up right next to him. I'm pretty sure we stayed together the whole night."

"That's sweet." She tried to imagine Rafe as a pup and couldn't hold back a fond giggle. "I bet you were adorable."

He grunted.

Very aware that their time together was ticking away, Katie wished that he was capable of a proper goodbye. Not goodbye, she amended silently. Until tomorrow. She wanted to kiss him so badly it hurt. Holding back was torture.

"I'm not telling you goodbye," Rafe muttered. "This isn't goodbye."

"I know." Katie closed her eyes and concentrated on her breathing. The knowledge that Rafe would soon leave her to spend a terrifying night alone made her stomach rumble in anticipation. Nausea overwhelmed her.

Clearing his throat, Rafe husked, "But just so that nothing is left unsaid, know that I'm glad I found you the other night. I'm glad I brought you home with me." His large hand landed on her knee. "The only thing I regret is not protecting you better."

She shook her head. "You protected me just fine. I'm the one who ran out into the night without a plan." Her mind wandered to the small crowd gathered outside, all of them determined to avenge their pack-mate. "If it weren't for me—"

"Zeke deserved to die. You think you're the first woman he's hunted down?"

Katie shivered. She knew she wasn't. "But his son..."

"That's on Zeke. And me. Not you." Shuddering, Rafe leapt up from the couch and jogged to the front door. He eased it open a few inches, peeked outside, then shut it quickly. A ripple of fear unsettled the air around them—Katie didn't know whether it originated from her or Rafe. "Katie, I think it's time."

No. It was too soon. Far too soon. Panic overwhelmed her need for caution and she ran across the room to grab Rafe's arm. "Please…"

He stared down at her with cold amber eyes. "You know I can't stay. Another five minutes and I won't be safe for you."

A quiet sob burst from her throat as she threw her arms around Rafe's solid torso. "I love you. Survive, do you understand? Whatever you have to do, just survive."

Rafe palmed her ass, squeezing and releasing her buttocks in a slow, rhythmic caress. "You, too. Remember what I said…the attic is a last resort. Not a plan."

Katie chose her response carefully, wanting to leave her options open. "I remember."

He moved his hand between her legs and rubbed her sensuously through her pants. "If they get inside, aim for their heads. Don't hesitate. If it's a wolf and it's coming after you, kill it. Period."

His bold touches were distracting, but she managed to focus on their meager plan. There was no way she would be able to shoot Rafe even if he did come inside, but she didn't plan to tell him that. There was no time for another argument. "Got it."

"Start with the shotgun and move on to the revolver only when your shells run out. Don't let yourself get spotted through any windows—if we're lucky, they'll be so busy with me that they'll forget about the hot piece of human ass I've got hidden away." Rafe paused but never stopped fondling her. She knew he regretted his word choice, but his self-control was clearly slipping. "Sorry."

"No, I'm glad you think my ass is hot," Katie said. It was

196

the truth. Crude as they were, his blunt words really did flatter her in some strange way. And his candor was just plain amusing.

"No matter what happens, don't come outside before the sun is up tomorrow morning. Bring a weapon when you do. I'll try to be back inside as soon as I can, but if you haven't heard from me before noon, I want you to take my truck and drive into town. Don't stop for any reason." He moved his hands to her back and simply held her against his chest. "The keys are next to the icebox. Take the road to the highway and go right. I love you."

He tried to release her but she clung to him tighter. Things were moving too fast. She wasn't ready to say good-bye. "I don't want you to go." The thought of sending him outside to face those animals made her stomach churn. "Please don't go."

Rafe buried his nose in her hair and inhaled. "I need you to be brave, darling. For me."

She would feel braver if she were able to do something other than hide away from the fighting. Rafe's plan left her helpless, which made it difficult to gather her courage. But his body seemed to vibrate against her, and his chest heaved, and she knew in her gut that he needed to leave the cabin—now. "I promise." She stood on her tiptoes and kissed his surprisingly soft lips. "Kill them all."

He bared his teeth in a malevolent grin. "I will." Nipping at her throat with sharp teeth, he exuded danger. "I'll see you tomorrow."

She released him only because she knew his time was up. As he turned and stalked to the front door, she murmured, "Be careful."

Rafe threw open the door without looking back. A raucous cheer arose from outside, and Katie glimpsed the crowd that awaited him. It had grown. Naked men and women—all of them with glowing eyes—froze in place and turned to face them. Lisa cackled cruel laughter, then the rest of her friends joined in. There were more than ten of them now. Katie counted at least fifteen. Maybe more.

"Ready to die?" Lisa snarled.

"No." Rafe stepped onto the porch and shut the door behind him. Stumbling forward, Katie pressed her ear to the wood just in time to hear his next words. "But I hope you are."

Katie closed her eyes and locked the door behind Rafe. The longest night of her life had just begun.

CHAPTER TWENTY-SEVEN

As soon as Rafe was out of her sight, panic set in. The noise level outside exploded as shouts, snarling, and cruel taunts filled the air and set Katie's heart racing. Shilah trotted to her side, a line of fur raised down the center of his back. Whining in the back of his throat, he leaned against her thigh in a protective stance. Katie patted his head, then rushed to the kitchen window, cursing the boards that blocked her view of the scene outside. She didn't know how to cope with not knowing what was happening. Being trapped inside—blind—while the man she loved faced impossible odds was torture in the purest sense of the word. In a way, she almost resented Rafe for expecting her to do it.

Almost, but for the simple fact that she understood the need to keep one's bond-mate safe. She felt that same desire deep in her soul—so deep that she wasn't sure she could obey Rafe's command to hunker down and hope for the best. Nothing he'd told her was incorrect. He did have physical advantages over her in this fight. He also had a psychological advantage. He could defend himself using pure animal instinct. She was stuck with her very human fear and anxiety, and she wasn't sure how she would react if she truly did bring even more trouble down on herself. If she ended up getting herself killed, it would almost be like she was killing Rafe, too. So he was absolutely right. It was probably dangerous for her to do anything except hole up with a weapon and wait for morning.

But how could she do nothing? He was even more outnumbered than they'd realized. How could she not help him when she knew she was capable of at least evening the odds a little? If she hid in his bedroom with a shotgun, Rafe could be torn apart outside within minutes. Then what? Even if she managed to fend off every werewolf in the forest, she would greet the morning as a widow. And she would never forgive herself for not following her heart.

Shilah growled at her feet as though he was privy to her thoughts and did not approve. "Quiet," she scolded him, then pressed her ear to the window and strained for some clue about what was happening.

A male shout. "Did you save any for us, traitor? I can smell her all over you."

Then a woman. "Took her for a ride after all, didn't you?"

A familiar growl from just on the other side of the window, probably near the porch steps. "Let's take this into the woods. This isn't about her."

"Like hell it isn't." Lisa. "That bitch is the reason my Zeke is dead. Tearing your bond-mate apart will be the highlight of my fucking night."

"Shutting you up will be mine." Rafe sounded like he was moving away from the cabin—toward the wolves that hungered for his blood. "I can promise an excruciating death to anyone who even comes close to touching her. But only if she doesn't blow your fucking head off with her shotgun first."

From somewhere in the distance, a tormented scream cut through the din of the crowd. Then another. Nearby, Rafe wailed and a wave of intense discomfort washed over Katie. Like she was about to burst out of her own skin.

Lisa's voice, sharp with excitement: "Getting close. You ready?"

A fresh jolt of pain had Katie bent at the waist, trying desperately not to pass out. She stumbled away from the window and knelt next to the kitchen table, sucking in deep breaths while she fought to push through the agony that poured from Rafe's soul into hers. She could feel his suffering in her bones, could taste it as a metallic tang in the back of her throat. Shilah woofed quietly and nudged her with his nose, as though encouraging her to stand. Balling her hands into fists, she rested her head atop them on the floor and listened to the godawful racket outside. The inhuman din sent a chill up Katie's spine. She knew what it meant. They were transforming.

The worst of the discomfort subsided within a minute—though it felt like she'd been trapped in Rafe's psychic pain for hours. As soon as she was able to catch her breath, she waged a silent, internal battle about what to do next. She'd promised Rafe no shooting. She'd assured him that she remembered the attic was her last resort. And yet all she could think about was fleeing upstairs so she could assess the situation from above. Nobody would know. She didn't even have to open the window. Well, unless an incredible opportunity presented itself. Otherwise, she could just watch.

Surely Rafe didn't expect her not to watch.

Katie rose to her feet. The ladder in the den, perched below the attic hatch like an invitation, proved too tempting to ignore. Before she could second-guess the decision, she tucked the revolver into her jeans and grabbed the shotgun from the kitchen table. Sprinting toward the ladder, she reasoned that the attic might actually be the safest place in the cabin. Even if it was dark and the footing treacherous, at least there was only one way in or out. If any wolves got into the house, she could simply sit across from the hatch and shoot whatever made it upstairs.

She scaled the rungs in three desperate steps, pushing the shotgun up ahead of her. Shilah ran circles around the bottom of the ladder, barking and growling and contributing to the growing chaos in the air. "Quiet, Shilah!" she shouted. "Go lie down."

Shilah jumped up and placed his front paws on the middle rungs. He gave a muffled bark, then another, almost as though he was scolding her disobedience in Rafe's absence.

Katie waved him away. "I need to protect your daddy. You want to protect me, you stand guard down here. Let me know if anyone gets inside."

Shilah whined, but didn't move from his spot on the ladder. She climbed the rest of the way into the attic, ignoring the sounds of canine protest below. Once upstairs, she moved across the floor slowly, careful not to slip off the joists and prove Rafe right about the danger of walking around. The space was already noticeably darker than it had been only fifteen minutes ago. Moonlight illuminated each end of the large room, but left a patch of inky blackness in the middle. Once again, Katie chose the path of least resistance and made her way to the same window where she'd seen the two men sparring earlier. Confident that the moon's glow adequately lit her path, she turned off the flashlight, not wanting anyone to see her from the ground.

Aggressive noises filtered in from outside, though it sounded like the heat of the battle was located on the other side of the cabin. Not dissuaded from her initial course of action, Katie balanced on the joists and crouched beside the window so she could peek outside. A dark shape streaked out from the edge of the trees and quickly ran beyond her line of sight. She cursed under her breath, then pulled the revolver from her jeans and flipped the safety off. Aiming ineffectually through the glass, she waited for more movement.

Just as she was ready to give up and make the long walk to the other side of the cabin, where she could hear snarls interspersed with the occasional yelp, two wolves raced into view, then turned to follow the first wolf she'd seen. She didn't think about consequences or even give herself time to consider the wisdom of taking a shot. Instinct took over. She lowered the revolver and yanked the window open in a mad rush. If she could take out an isolated wolf or two away from the main action, perhaps she could remain out of sight, on the periphery. If she were lucky, no one would catch her scent clear on the other side of the cabin. She would make sure that any wolves unfortunate enough to enter her sights wouldn't have the chance to alert the rest of the pack.

Almost as soon as she opened the window, both wolves skidded to a stop. They each began to turn in circles, noses in the air. Alarmed by how right Rafe had been about how powerfully their senses were attuned to the smell of human, Katie scrabbled with the revolver for a frantic moment before aiming at the wolf on the left, which was buff-colored and larger than its grey-and-white companion. As the beast swiveled to face her, raising its head to stare directly into her eyes, Katie exhaled and pulled the trigger.

The wolf fell and hit the ground as a nude, motionless man. His companion snarled and leapt toward the cabin. Seconds away from losing her line of sight on the smaller wolf, Katie aimed and took another shot. Then another. The small wolf's head snapped back and a visible spray of dark blood stained the snow below. She caught a glimpse of a naked female corpse—perhaps the brunette who'd put on that sordid sex show earlier—before she eased away from the window and into the shadows, paranoid about the deafening crack of her gunfire. Her chest rose and fell as she fought to catch her breath, overwhelmed by the reality of what she'd just done. She had just ended two lives.

Two human lives, for all intents and purposes.

Because they weren't just wolves, were they? Just like Rafe wasn't just a wolf. They had folks who loved them. Mates. Children. A pack. They had probably even been capable of love and kindness, in their own way.

Katie forced those thoughts from her head. Those 'people' she'd just shot looked at her and saw a meal to be consumed or a body to be violated for their sick pleasure. Their pack-mates were attacking Rafe right now. They would have killed her or Rafe in a second, given the opportunity.

She might be the only one saddled with the burden of a moral code tonight, but she wasn't going to let it prevent her from doing whatever it took to survive. Or to protect what was hers.

Full of renewed determination, Katie took a deep breath and moved to the open window again. She raised her gun to aim, then froze, horrified by the sight that greeted her below. Four wolves stood over the bodies of their companions, each of them staring up at her with glowing eyes. Startled into action, Katie fired a wild shot that went far left of her intended target. Each wolf took off in a different direction, all of them advancing on the cabin. For seconds that felt like hours, Katie sat paralyzed, listening. Downstairs, Shilah barked madly as the sound of shattering glass filled the air.

The windows.

Aware that Rafe had probably only bought her a few minutes with his quick boarding job, Katie struggled to her feet and hopped from one joist to the next until she reached the open hatch. She slid the cover into place to seal the attic off, then rushed to the opposite window, determined to take another peek outside before she had to turn her focus toward defending herself. If she had any chance of helping Rafe in whatever battle he was fighting, she had to take it. Now that she'd taken that first shot, there was no point in stopping now.

The barking downstairs hit a frenzied pitch as Katie reached her destination. The sound of Shilah in full protective mode sent guilt crashing over her. She'd left Rafe's dog—his brother, for God's sake—downstairs by himself, unprotected and hopelessly outmatched in any kind of fight with a supernatural canid. Her conscience tugged at her to go get the shotgun and protect Shilah, but her legs stopped working at her first sight of Rafe locked in epic battle.

His dark form was unmistakable in the moonlight, a lone figure encircled by five wolves. Surrounded by his enemies, he betrayed no fear or hesitation. Every time a wolf launched itself at him, he engaged it with fierce, murderous intent that left her shaking. He was so very powerful, but at the same time, he had never seemed more vulnerable. Though he was clearly capable of self-defense, the night was young and there were at least four other werewolves who could potentially lose interest in breaking into the cabin and seek out Rafe instead. And who knew how many more lurked out of her line of sight? No one—not even a bad-ass werewolf—could withstand an hours-long onslaught, hopelessly outnumbered, without sustaining serious injury. Or worse.

Ten yards away from where Rafe faced off against his attackers, four more wolves were tussling with a fifth. Katie wasn't sure what to make of that battle. So far it seemed as though the other pack ran together. It was possible that one of Rafe's own pack-mates had come to his aid and engaged them in a fight.

She hoped so. They needed all the help they could get.

Just as she had that thought, a loud crack sounded from below and Shilah snarled with a ferocity she'd never heard before. Another snarl filled the air, deeper and more menacing, before the worst dog fight she'd ever heard in her life broke out downstairs.

Shilah was in trouble.

CHAPTER TWENTY-EIGHT

Katie got up and promptly slipped off the joist she'd been balanced on, putting her foot through the ceiling of what she suspected might be the guest room. "Shit," she muttered under her breath. She was going to hear about that one later. At least she hoped she would.

Wrenching her foot from the hole she'd made, she rushed to the hatch as quickly as she could manage in the dark. The horrific sound of Shilah in full-out combat with a giant wolf scared her more than almost anything else that had happened so far. She was suddenly, keenly aware of just how badly she'd failed Rafe's dog. If she'd stayed downstairs, she could have blasted the intruder with her shotgun and saved him from the injuries she was certain he was sustaining. And if she'd listened to Rafe, the wolf might not have broken in at all.

Katie made sure the safety was engaged on the revolver and tucked it into the back of her jeans, then grabbed up the shotgun with one hand while she wrenched open the attic hatch with the other. It sounded like Shilah and the wolf were fighting near the kitchen, so she figured she'd peek her head down and try to attract the wolf's attention. Hopefully he would disengage with Shilah and come for her, and she could put a bullet in his head without putting Shilah in the line of fire.

She was comfortable with that plan until the moment she lowered her head through the opening and came eye-to-eye with a second werewolf who stood with its paws braced high up on the ladder. The wolf was so tall that its hot, sour breath washed over her face and triggered bile to rise in her throat. Jerking backward, Katie brought up the shotgun and clumsily aimed it down the hatch, but the wolf caught the barrel in its powerful jaw and tugged it from her hands with a single violent yank. Her best weapon clattered to the floor below, useless. Somewhere in the house, Shilah yelped and the dog fight fell silent.

Heart rending even as it exploded in terror, Katie grabbed the panel and tried to shove it back over the door. The wolf managed to shoot up the ladder, crashing into the barrier and breaking it into pieces. Adrenaline rushed through her body and took over her reactions. She couldn't die. If she died after defying Rafe, she would have ruined his life for no reason other than her own stubborn stupidity. Determined not to let both of them down, she grabbed the revolver from her pants and scrabbled backwards a few feet, aiming at the illuminated square in the middle of the dark attic. She had to take them out as they came up to her. There was no other choice.

A flash of memory washed over her. Rafe standing beside her on the porch. Target practice. The safety.

She remembered to flick it off at the same instant that the wolf finally powered its way up the ladder and into the attic. Trusting her instincts, she aimed and fired at the dim shape that advanced upon her. The first shot was a hit, judging from the high-pitched yelp that coincided with the ear-shattering crack of the revolver discharging in such an enclosed space. Yet it barely slowed the wolf down. The beast slammed into her, all muscle and teeth and claws, knocking her backward so that she landed awkwardly with a joist digging into her spine. Pain radiated up her arms, but she forced herself to raise the revolver anyway and deliver a second shot directly between the malevolent eyes that stared down upon her.

She knew it was a kill shot because the wolf transformed into a man right on top of her. He was heavy and naked, and being trapped beneath his bulk atop an uncomfortable, narrow piece of wood threatened to send her into total panic. It was only the knowledge that there was at least one more wolf downstairs, possibly more, that allowed her the presence of mind to crawl out from beneath the dead werewolf. Turning where she sat, she aimed at the hatch and waited for more.

No one came.

She could hear something pacing in the room below, its breath coming in hot, heavy snorts, but for whatever reason, it didn't seem able to pursue her as the other wolf had. Or maybe that's just what it wanted her to think. Without taking her eyes away from the hatch opening, Katie planted her free hand behind her and tested her ability to stand. Her legs were shaking so badly she didn't trust them to carry her. Lowering herself to the ground once again, Katie exhaled slowly and battled the tears that threatened to fall.

Shilah wasn't barking anymore. He wasn't even whining. He's probably dead. Katie choked back a sob at the stark thought. And if he is, it's my fault.

But there was a chance he was still alive, right? Until she saw his body with her own eyes, she had to believe he was alive. And until she knew otherwise, she had to do everything she could to help him. She may have failed him once tonight, but she wouldn't do it again.

Steeling her nerve, Katie took a deep breath and got to her feet. She kept her gun trained on the hatch opening, ready to pull the trigger at the first sign of movement. Though she could still hear the battle raging outside, her focus narrowed to nothing but getting to Shilah. She had to trust that Rafe could hold his own—at least until she dealt with the trouble that she had caused.

She approached the hatch with an overabundance of caution, creeping centimeter by centimeter through the dark. When she finally got close enough to the opening to peek downstairs, she found the ladder lying on its side and a frustrated-looking wolf staring up at her. She noted the blood on the wolf's fur as she put a bullet into its skull. It crumpled to the ground, a limp, dead man that she didn't recognize. All too aware that her gunshots had to be catching the attention of every wolf within a half mile radius, she waited silently for another one to appear. But nothing stirred downstairs.

Not until she heard a pitiful cry. Shilah. Alive.

જ્ર૦

All thoughts of caution flew out the window. She lowered herself to the attic floor and stuck her head through the hatch opening, scanning the den for any sign of intruders. The room was trashed—couch cushions torn open, the coffee table overturned—but everything was eerily still. Another weak cry pulled her attention toward the kitchen, where she thought she caught the barest hint of movement out of the corner of her eye.

She looked down at the floor of the den, a good eight feet below where she crouched. If she hung on to the edge of the hatch and dropped straight down, she would only fall a few feet but would almost certainly land on either the leg of the fallen ladder, her shotgun, or the body of the dead wolf. She could easily twist her ankle with this maneuver, and that was assuming she wasn't going to be ambushed by a hidden enemy while she hung there unarmed.

The memory of Shilah's cries spurred her on. She fumbled in her pocket for ammo and reloaded the revolver, happy to buy herself a moment of mental preparation for what she was about to do. Tucking the gun into her jeans yet again, Katie wiped her palms on her shirt and carefully stuck her feet through the opening in the ceiling. She waited to see if anything reacted to her movement, then—when all remained quiet—she turned and got on her knees so she could try and lower her body through the hatch without releasing her iron grip on the edge. It wasn't as easy as she'd hoped. She was halfway down, stomach pressed tightly against the edge of the opening, when a rustling sound, then a low growl, set her adrenaline racing.

Afraid to take any more time—and aware that the only way she could easily go was down—she slipped off the edge and swung wildly for a moment before letting go. As predicted, she landed awkwardly, one foot on the dead man's thigh and the other on the barrel of the shotgun. Her ankle rolled and she fell hard on her ass just as a dark shape sailed over her head. Without conscious thought, she grabbed the shotgun, swiveled it around, and blasted the scrappy wolf who had already turned to charge her again. The impact threw him backwards against the wall, and he slumped over, suddenly a very dead man.

Katie stood up, wincing at the sharp pain that shot through her ankle. She'd sprained it in the very least, which was scary as hell. She still had hours left to go. From here on out, she had to try and avoid further injury. That meant not taking unnecessary risks. Chastising herself for her carelessness, she limped to the kitchen with the shotgun held out in front of her chest.

Shilah lie motionless under the kitchen table. A streak of red across the wooden floor made it clear that he'd crawled there after the fight ended, either to seek safety or die alone. He wasn't dead, but his wounds seemed serious. Far more serious than she felt capable of treating.

"No," Katie whispered. She sank her fingers into a clean patch of fur on Shilah's neck, eyes glued to the blood that oozed from several deep lacerations on his chest, sides, and face. His back leg was mangled and hung limply from his body in a way that chilled her to the bone. Despite his battered state, his eyes were open and alert, and he gazed at her with so much loyalty and trust that Katie's composure shattered and she burst into tears. "Shilah, you're okay. You've got to be okay."

His tail thumped weakly against the floor, reassuring her

that even if he was down, he wasn't ready to give up. She wasn't, either.

Drawing a breath, Katie got to her feet and took stock of the situation. Cold air filtered in from a window at the far side of the den, where the boards Rafe had nailed down had been smashed to pieces. She decided her first priority had to be blocking off the opening. She couldn't concentrate on caring for Shilah until the cabin was secure. With that in mind, she limped to the large oak bookcase that sat against the wall next to the window, propped the shotgun on the floor at her side, then used both hands to sweep books off the shelves and onto the floor.

Afraid that she was making too much noise but unsure what else to do, Katie kept one eye on the window as she emptied the bookcase. She fully expected another group of wolves to burst through at any second, but although she could clearly hear the fighting continue to rage out front, there was no sign of movement in the jagged slice of outdoors she could see through the hole the intruders had left. Once the bookcase was clear, Katie planted her hands on the side and shoved with all her might.

She managed to move the heavy piece of furniture a couple of inches before she had to rest. The scuffle in the attic and her fall from the hatch had definitely taken a toll. Her ankle throbbed and it was difficult to catch her breath—from exertion or panic, she wasn't sure. All she knew was that she would give anything for Rafe's strength right then. She closed her eyes briefly, reaching out with her mind to try and latch onto their connection. She was certain he was still alive, if only because she hadn't experienced the gut-wrenching pain she sensed would come with his death. His presence within her was still strong despite their separation—by distance and species—and his energy centered her and gave her renewed focus.

Opening her eyes, she gave the bookcase another shove. Three more inches. Then she pushed again, straining and struggling until she managed to move it directly in front of the broken window. Without allowing herself time to breathe, she hastily refilled the shelves to provide extra weight to the obstacle she'd created. She doubted it would keep out a determined wolf all night, but at least she would hear it coming.

Living room secured, Katie snatched up the shotgun and ran back to the kitchen. Her heart stuttered at the sight of Shilah lying with his eyes closed, but he opened them as soon as she knelt by his side. "I don't know what to do," she whispered to him. His tail wagged weakly at the sound of her voice. His obvious happiness at her mere presence tugged at her guilty conscience. "I'm so sorry, boy. So sorry."

Shilah nuzzled her hand with his nose, snapping her back into focus. She knew what to do. She had to clean his wounds, just as Rafe had cleaned hers the night before. As long as she did everything that Rafe had done—short of healing Shilah with her hands, of course—there was a chance that he would survive. She just needed to keep Shilah alive until Rafe returned in the morning. Then Rafe could fix him.

That's what she had to tell herself. Rafe could fix him.

The first thing she had to do was move Shilah to the bathroom. Not only would it be difficult to bring first-aid supplies to him, but they were too exposed in the kitchen. Here they could be rushed from all sides. The bathroom was a somewhat fortified position. At the very least, she could shut the door and hopefully have time to pick up her weapon before anyone broke through.

Unfortunately, moving Shilah to the bathroom required picking him up. There was no way to do so without hurting him, she knew, but her bigger concern was the possibility that she could make things worse. Some of the lacerations on his body were deep. She was scared to death that she would lift Shilah up and find herself fighting to keep his vital organs inside his body. But what other choice did she have?

"No choice," Katie murmured. She also had no other

213

option but to leave the shotgun behind as she carried Shilah to the bathroom. Using both hands, she very carefully eased her hands beneath him and attempted to lift his limp body to her chest. He was a big dog—sixty-five pounds at least—so she only managed to raise him a few inches off the floor. He left behind a small pool of blood, but mercifully, his only reaction to being moved was to whimper in the back of his throat. "Sorry, boy." She glanced around, looking for options, then set him on the runner below the sink. It would be far easier to drag him than carry him.

She moved him to the bathroom as quickly as she dared, afraid to waste any more time before addressing his wounds. She had no idea how much blood a dog his size could lose before needing more, but she wagered he was already pushing the limit. She was pretty certain that blood loss and the potential for internal injuries were her biggest concerns. There wasn't a lot she could do to address internal injuries, but she could sure as hell stop his bleeding.

Luckily, she'd left the bathroom door open earlier and was able to drag him right in. His front paws twitched after she stepped away, as though he wanted to jump up and follow her. She held out her hand to stop him. "Stay."

He lay his head on the floor and stared at her with plaintive eyes. Heart breaking, Katie backed out of the bathroom and ran down the hallway toward the kitchen. Her singular focus was on getting the shotgun so she could examine Shilah more fully. So far she hadn't observed any obviously fatal wounds. It was almost unbelievable that Shilah was alive at all, and that he'd been able to hold his own against a larger and more powerful opponent. What a tough dog.

As she approached the kitchen table, the hair-raising sensation of being watched swept over her. She slowed her pace and looked around, unsettled by the feeling that she wasn't alone. After moving around unhindered since killing that last wolf in the living room, she'd simply assumed that she'd taken care of all the intruders. Now she wasn't so sure. Perhaps she wasn't giving these wolves enough credit. One of them could be biding its time, stalking her and waiting for the perfect moment to pounce.

No sooner had she thought it then something heavy slammed into her from behind. Already reaching for the shotgun, the barrel slipped out of her grasp as she fell to the kitchen floor. Determined not to get pinned on her stomach, she rolled onto her back and saw two things simultaneously: the yellow eyes of the wolf that had bitten her twenty-four hours ago, and the tantalizing shape of the stock of the shotgun hanging over the edge of the dining room table.

The biter held her down with his front paws, lips drawn back in a feral grin. Saliva dripped from his wicked jaw onto her face, turning her stomach. Before he could sink his teeth into her for a second time, Katie did the only thing she could think to do. She drove her fist into the center of his throat. The wolf let out a satisfying yelp, so she punched him again. He swiveled his head and caught her wrist with his teeth as she drew back her fist for another go, tearing her skin as she snatched her hand out of his jaw. Visceral emotion surged through her—anger at this wolf and his buddy for creating this whole mess, fear that Shilah was bleeding out at that very moment—and she jammed her thumb into one of the wolf's yellow eyes with a ferocity that shocked even her.

The wolf roared in pain and turned his head to the side, trying to get away. Unconvinced that she could reach the shotgun from her position beneath him—not without getting chomped in the process—Katie pulled her thumb from his eye socket and scrabbled to reach the revolver that dug into the small of her back. Wrenching it out from beneath her with a cry of relief, she disengaged the safety and pointed the muzzle directly at the wolf's head. Then she pulled the trigger, sobbing as the wolf's remaining eye went blank and he transformed into the man who had traumatized her so badly the night before.

215

Having his naked, dead weight on top of her was almost too horrific to bear. She pushed at his shoulders frantically, rolling out from beneath him with a tremulous whimper. Uneasily aware that she was on the verge of a genuine emotional meltdown, she set the revolver on the floor beside her. Then she grabbed the shotgun from the table and cradled it to her chest as she tried not to lose her composure.

Four wolves had descended upon the cabin after finding the two bodies she'd left outside, and now four corpses littered the floors of Rafe's home. There was a good chance that she'd just killed the last of the intruders, but she wouldn't put money on it. The biter had lain in wait for a good ten minutes while she barricaded the window and carried Shilah to the bathroom, biding his time even when she'd been vulnerable to attack, so it stood to reason that yet another wolf could be doing the same thing now. Maybe they enjoyed toying with humans just as much in wolf form as they did when they were human. In any event, she had to search the cabin before she could focus on Shilah. She needed to be certain they wouldn't be ambushed again.

She struggled to her feet only because she knew Shilah's life depended on her not shutting down completely. It took every bit of her courage to walk into the den, shotgun at the ready, and check the closets. She was nervous about finding another wolf lying in wait. Frankly, she couldn't believe she was still alive. She'd killed six werewolves tonight. Six. Even if she'd made a mistake in leaving Shilah to fend for himself, those were six wolves who wouldn't join in an attack on Rafe. That had to give him a better chance of survival. Maybe something good would come out of her stubborn impulsivity, after all.

She conducted a cautious search of every room before concluding, gratefully, that she had managed to kill every werewolf that had broken into the cabin. Trudging her way back to the bathroom, she tried to guess just how much time had passed since she'd left Shilah. It felt like hours. Perhaps it was only ten minutes. It was impossible to tell—time had lost all meaning. Wolves continued to fight outside, but for now, no one else seemed interested in breaking in. Hopeful that she would finally have time to work, Katie went to her patient, nervous about what she would find.

Shilah's ears perked as she entered the room, but he betrayed no other sign of movement. Closing and locking the door behind her, Katie leaned the shotgun against the sink and sank to her knees for her first good look at Shilah's wounds.

He was a mess. There was no other way to describe it. His coarse brown fur was matted with tacky blood, pink tissue peeked out from deep slices on his chest, and the corner of one ear had been torn clean off. She blinked back tears as she searched through the medicine cabinet for supplies. "We're going to fix you up, boy. Then when your daddy gets home, he'll really fix you. I know he will."

The quiet thump of Shilah's tail against the floor encouraged her that she wasn't just being overly optimistic. Shilah was a strong dog, clearly, and if he'd held on this long, surely he could make it until morning. Pleased when she found a first aid kit that included needles and suture thread, she only hoped she could successfully close the wounds that required stitches. Of course, before she could do that, she would have to wash and disinfect them. She grabbed the antibiotic ointment, disheartened to find half the tube gone. She hated to use all the medical supplies on Shilah when she was worried that Rafe would need them tomorrow morning, but she couldn't not treat Shilah's wounds.

She would just use the ointment sparingly—and hope that Rafe's ability to heal himself would come into play when this long, hellish night was over. Because she needed him back with her.

Now.

CHAPTER TWENTY-NINE

Somehow, she was able to clean and stitch Shilah's wounds in relative peace. She could hear the occasional muffled snarl or howl from outside, but there were no obvious attempts to break in to the cabin, and nobody tried to breach the closed bathroom door. Time faded away as she meticulously washed each gash on Shilah's body, her entire world narrowing to the injured dog in front of her. Certain that Rafe wouldn't mind, she borrowed his razor and shaved the fur away from the lacerations she felt were deep enough to require stitches. Then she went to work creating the sloppiest sutures she'd ever seen.

Shilah lay perfectly still for nearly all of her tending, only twitching and pulling away during her first couple of tries with the needle and thread. Soon she fell into a comfortable rhythm with her needle work and Shilah relaxed, watching her with alert brown eyes. She was relieved to discover that none of his injuries seemed particularly life-threatening, save for one deep cut on his side. Katie wasn't certain whether it was deep enough that she needed to worry about internal bleeding, but that wound made her nervous. So did his leg, which was twisted and nearly severed at the knee.

"I'd give anything for an emergency vet right now," Katie murmured to him. Considering her options briefly, she pulled off her shirt and wrapped it tightly around Shilah's leg, creating a tourniquet. This was one injury she simply didn't know how to treat. She suspected he would need a cast—or God forbid, an amputation—and she was in the position to provide neither. All she could do now was keep him comfortable and get them through the rest of this hellish night.

Exhaling shakily, Katie stroked Shilah's head and tried to decide what to do next. She could either defend this position or else move Shilah to Rafe's bedroom and defend that one. Though she hated the idea of moving Shilah again, the small, confined space they were in made her nervous. If a wolf did break into the bathroom, there would be very little room to maneuver. Shilah could easily get caught up in a fight that his body was in no condition to survive.

That settled it. She had to move Shilah somewhere safe.

Not about to make the same mistake as last time, she took the shotgun and walked through the cabin on another security sweep. She visited every room and opened every closet door, unwilling to get surprised again. Satisfied that they were still alone, she tucked the revolver into her jeans and left the shotgun on Rafe's bed. Spotting Shilah's dog pillow in the corner of the room, she carried it to the closet, opening the door and arranging it safely inside. She could hide Shilah in there for the night. That way, even if wolves broke in, he would be safe from harm.

Satisfied with her plan, she made the short trip to the bathroom next door and dragged the rug Shilah still lie on down the hall and into Rafe's bedroom. He seemed to snuggle into her body as she picked him up and carried him the short distance to the closet, and she pressed a kiss to his uninjured ear and whispered, "You're a good boy. Thank you for trying to protect me."

He turned his head and licked her face. Placing him on his bed with a tired groan, she closed the door nearly all the way, but left just enough room that she could see him and he could see her. Then she pushed Rafe's dresser in front of the closed bedroom door, blocking the only way in and out of the room. Shilah whined as she went to sit on the bed, but quieted when she held up her hand and gave him a firm look.

"Now it's my turn to protect you," she told him. "No arguments." Scooting backwards so she could rest against the headboard, she held the shotgun on her lap, pointed at the door, and waited. And she tried not to think about whether Rafe was still holding his own. If she felt their connection get severed while she was sitting inside—safe—on his bed, she wasn't sure she would ever forgive herself. Of course, if she left Shilah and he died, she'd never forgive herself for that either. Frustrated by her dilemma, wishing for sunrise, Katie gave Shilah a smile she didn't feel. "Don't worry, boy, it'll be over soon."

She wished she believed that.

〇〇〇

Katie couldn't remember having spent a longer night in her life. Not when she'd been trapped in her snow-covered car alone, waiting for rescue. Not that evening in college when her mother called to tell her that her father was in emergency surgery after suffering a heart attack. The only memory that even came close was the time she was six years old and convinced herself that there was a monster in her closet when her mother left the door ajar after her bedtime story. She'd been too frightened to get out of bed, or call out for her parents, or sleep. So she'd lain there for hours, staring into the inky depths of the closet and praying that the boogeyman wouldn't come for her.

Waiting for morning to come—and Rafe's torment to end—was infinitely worse than all of those tense nights combined. Once Shilah was settled and she had nothing to do but watch the door, she began to notice that some of the pain that radiated through her body didn't seem to be the result of her own injuries. It was Rafe, who had to be exhausted and hurting. He'd been fighting for hours at that point with hours left to go, and it was obviously taking its toll.

All night she strained to hear the sound of fighting, uneasily aware that it was her best indication that Rafe was still standing. The only other noise in the room was Shilah's labored breathing and the riot of anxious thoughts in her head.

She hoped Rafe would return to her as soon as the sun came up. That he would be in one piece. That Shilah would be all right, and that Rafe would forgive her for allowing his dog to get into a fight unaided by her marksmanship. His potential anger with her for going against his wishes was the least of her worries. What would happen if he didn't come back? What if she couldn't even find him tomorrow morning? Or she did find him, but with injuries too severe for her to treat? She didn't know what she would do if he was killed. Take his truck and Shilah and simply leave? And what then?

Katie jolted awake at the realization that she'd dozed off. With no windows in the room and no alarm clock on the nightstand—proof of the polar opposite lifestyles she and Rafe led—she had no way of knowing how long she'd slept. The first thing she did was roll out of bed and go to the closet to check on Shilah, whose rhythmic breathing had slowed but not stopped. His eyes were closed and his paws and nose twitched in fitful sleep. Relieved, she stood and stretched, determined not to join him in slumber again.

That's when she noticed that something was different. The air was too still. Too quiet. Walking to the barricaded door, Katie tilted her head and listened.

She couldn't hear the sound of fighting anymore.

Which could mean anything. Heart pounding, Katie braced herself against the dresser with both hands. She put her head down and closed her eyes, trying to reach out with her mind and body to feel Rafe. Before she'd never had to put any effort into their supernatural communication. It had just happened. Rafe had just been there. Now there was…nothing.

That didn't mean Rafe was dead. Did it? Her knees

wobbled and threatened to give out, but then she sensed...not nothing. The sensation was weak, thready, barely there—but it was something.

Shoving the dresser away from the door, she had a fleeting worry that morning hadn't yet arrived. She'd promised Rafe that she wouldn't go outside until the sun was up, but she would be damned if she was going to wait in his bedroom any longer. Not when his presence within her was as weak as it had ever been. Shilah whimpered from the closet as she snatched up the revolver, then the shotgun, but she silenced him with a single look. "I'll be right back. You stay. And be quiet."

She turned right after she left the bedroom and conducted a stealthy search of the guest room before venturing down the hall. She wasn't going to make the same mistakes as she had last night. Even if the eerie silence suggested that the threat was over, complacency could get her killed. She checked every room in the house except the attic, trying not to let her gaze linger on the corpses she'd created only hours earlier. Once she was satisfied that she was still alone, she went to the kitchen window and pressed her eye against a narrow gap in the boards. Daylight greeted her.

Relieved, Katie walked to the front door and moved to unlock it. Then she hesitated. Daylight didn't mean she was safe. No matter what their alpha had decreed, the other pack had suffered heavy losses throughout the night, six by her own hand. And she was still standing. Whatever peace treaty the two alpha wolves had forged to avoid a pack war was very likely null and void after the carnage she and Rafe had inflicted. Who was to say that Jack Devereaux wasn't standing on the other side of the door, waiting to tear her apart the moment she walked out?

She dropped her hand and took a step back. The smart thing would be to go up to the attic and look out the windows before she ventured outside. At least that way she could survey the landscape and check that nothing but Rafe was still moving. If he was still moving.

"Stop it." The sound of her own voice was shockingly loud, yanking her back from the edge of the abyss that beckoned when she thought of losing Rafe. She couldn't succumb to the aching loss that threatened to consume her. He wasn't dead. She'd felt something. She had.

Knowing it was the right plan made it no easier to return to the den and set the ladder back under the still-open hatch. It was hard enough to be around the bodies of the wolves she'd shot downstairs. The thought of having to see the one who'd come at her in the dark attic scared the hell out of her. Just thinking about the way he'd leapt upon her made her stomach clench. But there was no choice—not if she wanted to help Rafe.

Katie put down the shotgun and climbed the ladder slowly, feeling each and every hit she'd taken over the past thirty-six hours. Her muscles quivered from a mixture of fear and exhaustion, and despite her trepidation, when she got to the top she hauled herself into the attic and collapsed with a grateful sigh. All she wanted to do this morning was curl up in bed with Rafe and allow her body to heal, but instead she was lying face-to-face with the corpse of the man who'd fucked his female friend on Rafe's lawn the day before. Blood pooled around his head and his chest, where her blindly fired bullets had left neat holes. His lips were still drawn back in a terrible, ghastly snarl.

Shivering, Katie got to her feet and pointed the revolver at the body as she cautiously stepped around it and made her way to the window that overlooked the front of the cabin, from which she'd last seen Rafe. She paused before she looked outside, afraid that she would need a moment to prepare for the sight that might greet her. She had no idea what to expect. What kind of trouble they might still be in.

The thought that Rafe might still be in danger propelled Katie forward. She pressed her hands against the chilly glass pane, going boneless when the clearing came into view. The snow-covered ground was littered with blood and torn-off limbs and crumpled human forms, not one of them showing any sign of life. Nothing stirred. Her gaze skittered from one body to the next, searching for the familiar form of her lover among the victims of his wrath.

She recognized Rafe the instant she saw him. He was sprawled on his back in the center of the carnage, and mercifully, he was in one piece. Or at least he appeared to be. He was clearly unconscious, covered in blood, and frighteningly still. She scanned the surrounding area for another second or two, then hurried to the other side of the attic as quickly as she could. She spared only a passing glance out the back window, unsurprised to see the carcasses of the two wolves she'd shot and nothing else.

That was good enough for her. The dust had settled, the casualties were high, and Rafe could be bleeding to death even now. She had to go outside and get him.

She made it downstairs and to the front door without questioning her decision even once. Rafe had spent an entire night protecting her. Now it was her turn. Katie disengaged the lock and cracked open the door, peeking outside before taking a cautious step onto the porch. The chilly morning air stung her nostrils and brought tears to her eyes, which she wiped away in a hurry. She'd left the shotgun behind, aware that she couldn't exactly carry it and Rafe—something she was increasingly worried she would need to do. The revolver was her only line of defense. As she stepped off the porch and into snow that wasn't as deep as it had been the day before, the handgun hardly felt like protection at all.

She'd never seen so much blood and gore. Some of the dead werewolves had literally been torn apart, others eviscerated. As she made her way through a small group of bodies, she saw something that turned her stomach. Rafe's pack-mate Cooper lay on the frozen ground with his throat torn out and both legs bent at odd angles. His sightless eyes stared at the startlingly blue sky above.

Katie said a silent thank you to his friend for the help, then stepped over a severed hand to get closer to where Rafe had fallen. That's when she heard a soft crunching sound from her left, in a stand of trees. She turned and raised the revolver on instinct. Almost like she knew what the hell she was doing.

Lisa stared back at her, closer to Rafe than she was. Her slim, nude form was also smeared with blood, and though her gait indicated pain and exhaustion, her malevolent eyes were wild. She carried a large rock that Katie worried was intended for Rafe's skull. Lisa bared her teeth in a ferocious snarl as she openly appraised Katie from head to toe. "He's dead, bitch."

She flicked her gaze to Rafe for only an instant before returning her attention to Lisa. "No, he isn't."

Lisa took another step closer to Rafe. "Well, he will be in a minute."

Lowering the gun, Katie fired a shot that landed mere inches from Lisa's bare foot. The bullet threw up a spray of snow and stopped the other woman mid-step. "Stay the fuck away from him," Katie said, and took her own step forward.

"And if I don't?" Lisa scanned her body with a look of disdain. "You don't scare me, you human piece of trash. I can tear you apart right now. Make you beg for mercy...wish you'd never been born." She grinned, then licked her lips. "Pity Rafe won't be awake to watch, though."

Katie aimed at the center of Lisa's forehead. "Last I heard, your alpha said no picking fights."

"That was before you two wiped out a third of our pack. I'm guessing he might feel differently now."

Katie held her finger on the trigger, ready to apply pressure at the slightest advance from the other woman. "I promise you, if you do anything except turn around and go home, I'm going to put a bullet in your head. I will make your little boy an orphan. I don't want to, but I will."

Her words seemed to strike a chord. Lisa's shoulders dropped and she stared at Katie with an expression of pure hatred. "You don't actually think this is over, do you?"

Gazing around at the bodies surrounding them, Katie said, "Haven't enough lives been lost?"

"Not the right ones." Lisa's fury was palpable and frightening. Eyes glowing, she seemed to struggle not to leap forward and attack.

Katie tightened her hand on the gun, wholly prepared to pull the trigger. She wouldn't hesitate to do it, no matter how much she despised the thought of killing an innocent child's only living parent. She and Rafe hadn't survived this long only to be separated now. "Don't make me do this to Ben. Please don't. Just leave. Go home to him."

"Only because I want to be there when he wakes up." Lisa tossed the rock in her hand in Rafe's direction. Katie's heart stuttered until it landed feet from his head, sparing him further injury. Then anger surged through her and she moved forward, but Lisa stopped her with a mocking smile. "I'll see you next month, Katie. And the month after that. Until one of us is dead." She turned her head and spat onto the ground, aiming at Rafe but falling short. "If Rafe's Alpha lets you live, that is." She walked backward, retreating without taking her eyes off Katie. "Looks to me like you just created one hell of a mess, human. Good luck convincing his pack that keeping you around is worth a war."

Katie shivered, and it had little to do with the frigid air. She knew Lisa was trying to threaten and upset her, but there was truth in her words. How would Rafe's pack react to what had happened? They weren't exactly sympathetic toward her to begin with, and that was before she'd murdered rival pack members in cold blood. Aware that words couldn't begin to fix anything, but compelled to say something anyway, Katie said, "I'm sorry about your mate. It's not your son's fault that his daddy attacked me. It's not your fault, either." She watched Lisa's face, curious how she felt about her mate's activities. If he hadn't come after Katie, he would still be alive. "He should have been home with you."

"He loved to go hunting. And I loved for him to do it. Nothing got him worked up like playing with a human woman before he came home to me." Lisa lingered by the edge of the trees with a sneer on her face. "Zeke was a predator. You're prey. He attacked you because that's how nature works. But you know how nature doesn't work?" She gestured at Rafe, then at her. "You two are an abomination. You're disgusting. And I promise you I won't stop hunting you until you're screaming for mercy with my teeth in your throat."

Katie had to forcibly stop herself from physically recoiling. She readjusted her aim, somehow holding her arm steady. "Get the fuck out of here."

Lisa growled, then shifted into wolf form. She hobbled away slowly, clearly more affected by the nightlong battle than she'd let on. Katie trained her gun on Lisa's back and watched her slow retreat, not lowering the weapon until she was long out of sight. Afraid to drop her guard but all too aware that Rafe's time could be running out, she waited for a minute or so after losing sight of Lisa, then reluctantly pocketed the revolver and ran to Rafe's fallen body.

His skin was frighteningly cold—far colder than she'd ever felt him. His blue-tinged lips brought her heart into her throat, but it was the red blood streaked across his chest, thighs, and face that really worried her. She ran her hands up the chilled, tacky plane of his chest, then pressed her fingers to his neck to search for a pulse. He was alive, but in rough shape. Though she saw no wounds that appeared to be fatal, the fact that he hadn't yet regained consciousness concerned her deeply. That Lisa was awake told Katie that it was past time for Rafe to rouse from his moon-induced sleep, but he didn't stir even when she bent and pressed her lips to his in a quick, desperate kiss.

"Please, Rafe." Katie laced her fingers with his and squeezed, waiting for some sign that he could hear her. "Wake up, baby. I really need you to wake up."

He didn't move. Katie raised her head and scanned the

tree line, then the unmoving bodies around them. They were incredibly vulnerable out in the open like this. For all she knew, Lisa wasn't the only rival pack member who'd survived the night. She needed to get him into the cabin as quickly as she could. As long as they stayed outside, they weren't safe. But she had no idea how to move an unconscious man of Rafe's size the thirty yards to the cabin, then up the porch steps and inside. If he wouldn't wake up, she was in for a long, difficult task that would leave her completely exposed and helpless if Lisa or her friends decided to return.

Panic surged through Katie and she put her hands on his shoulders, shaking him hard. "Rafe!" She waited for his eyelashes to flutter, for a groan—some sign of life. But there was nothing.

A crushing wave of despair threatened to derail her. Rafe was alive, yes, but something was very wrong.

Katie stood up and, after a final glance around, slipped the revolver into the back of her jeans. Then she bent and grabbed Rafe beneath the arms. Summoning all the strength she had remaining, she grunted and dragged him a couple of inches across the slick snow. She had to stop and rest almost immediately. His limp body was impossibly heavy, and her ankle and hand throbbed from the events of the night before.

"Shit." Tears slipped out of her eyes and froze on her cheeks, drawing her attention to just how frigid the morning air was. Nervous about letting her emotions get the better of her, she searched the trees once more, ready to draw the gun and defend Rafe to the death. Still quiet. Giving his arms another tug, Katie managed to move him a few inches closer to the porch before his foot got caught on the leg of the dead body lying beside him. No matter how hard she tugged, the corpse held him stubbornly in place. Exhausted, she let go of Rafe's arms and fell backwards into the snow with a frustrated cry. "Fuck."

"You look like you could use some help."

Startled by the quiet female voice at her back, Katie leapt

to her feet and whirled around as she withdrew the revolver from her jeans. An attractive brunette woman stood beside Rafe's porch, not ten feet away, completely nude and wearing an expression of genuine concern. She narrowed her eyes when Katie pointed the gun at her head, but didn't move.

"Don't come any closer," Katie warned in a tremulous voice. She swiped away her tears quickly, determined not to show any weakness. They might be the predators and she the prey, but she was damn sure going to do everything she could to defend Rafe. "Stay back."

The woman ignored her and took a step forward. "Is he alive?"

She aimed at the woman's forehead. "Stop or I'll shoot you. I swear I will."

The woman stopped. Then she sighed. "I came to help Rafe. Want to put down your gun and let me?"

CHAPTER THIRTY

Katie lowered the gun slightly, but didn't relax. "Who are you?"

"My name is Susan." She looked past Katie and frowned. "Why is he unconscious? Is he badly injured?"

Susan. The name tickled at her memory before she recalled why it sounded so familiar. "Rafe's Susan?"

A smile played at the corners of the other woman's mouth. "I haven't been Rafe's for a long time." She moved forward, hand up to forestall Katie's protest. "It's not safe for either of you out here. We can talk while we carry him to the truck."

"The truck? No, I need to get him inside so I can look at his injuries—"

"That's not a good idea." Susan lowered her hand. "As soon as the pack regroups and realizes the losses they've taken, they'll come for you. And it'll most likely be with Jack Devereaux's blessing—if not his help."

"We didn't choose this fight," Katie said. She kept the gun trained on Susan, afraid to trust her. "We were only defending ourselves."

"I know. But this," Susan gestured at the bodies lying around them, "is a pretty big fucking deal."

Katie wanted help so badly that she was tempted to simply pocket the revolver and hope for the best. She was almost certain she couldn't get Rafe into the truck alone. But the sudden reappearance of Susan after years missing seemed too coincidental to be true. Too easy. She didn't trust the situation any more than the woman who claimed to be Rafe's long, lost love. "Why are you here? What do you want?"

"I want Rafe to live. Now please." Ignoring the gun pointed at her, Susan closed the distance between them and knelt at Rafe's side. She reached to touch his throat, but Katie knocked her hand away with her foot. Susan narrowed her eyes, then snatched the revolver out of Katie's hand before she could react. "You're starting to test my patience," Susan said as she rose to her feet. For a breathless moment, she pointed the gun at Katie's head and stared hard into her eyes. Then she turned the revolver around and offered Katie the handle. "I could have killed you just now, if I'd wanted to." Katie took the weapon with a shaking hand and Susan knelt back beside Rafe. "I hope you'll take that as a sign of good faith that I don't particularly want to."

It was agony to decide whether to accept help from a strange werewolf after everything that had happened. This woman could be anyone. It was possible that Rafe's enemies knew about his history with Susan—especially if they were the ones responsible for her disappearance. This could be an elaborate plan to get her to drop her guard. But what other choice did she have? Unless she was willing to kill Susan right now, the only thing left to do was accept her help and pray that her trust wasn't misplaced. The fact that she desperately needed the help made the decision feel like it was hardly one at all. "Fine. Help me carry him."

Susan was far stronger than she looked. She grabbed Rafe by the arms and hefted him into the air, leaving Katie to pick up his feet and follow her as she carried him to the old Chevy pickup truck parked out front. Both the driver's side and passenger windows were smashed in. Yet another way the rival pack had entertained themselves during the run-up to the main event, she supposed. Nervous that they'd caused more serious damage, she checked the tires. Snow was still piled around them, but hadn't drifted high enough to block access to the passenger door. The good news was that the snow had probably protected the tires from vandalism. The bad news was that they wouldn't be able to go anywhere until they cleared it away.

As though reading her mind, Susan said, "Let's get him in the passenger seat and then I'll help you dig out the truck."

Nodding, Katie allowed Susan to support more of Rafe's weight while she tugged on the passenger side door handle. It was locked. "Shit."

"Where are the keys?"

Katie turned and looked at the cabin, then Susan. "Next to the icebox."

"I'll get them." Susan jerked her head at a patch of fresh snow beside them. "Let's just set him down. You can wait here and guard him."

Glad that Susan wasn't expecting her to leave Rafe, Katie nodded. "All right." Once they lowered him onto the snow, however, her paranoia kicked in. Did she trust Susan in the cabin alone? Shilah was in there. With the truck's windows broken, she didn't technically need the keys to get the door unlocked. But she would need them to leave—and that wasn't all she would need. Deciding to test Susan's willingness to bring her the keys before she mentioned Shilah or her purse, Katie said, "The kitchen is just through the front door. Icebox is on the left."

Susan gave her a smile tinged with sadness. "I remember."

Katie tried not to feel a twinge of jealousy as she watched Susan jog toward Rafe's cabin—nude, supple, and so very graceful on her feet. After only a couple of days with Rafe, she was starting to get used to seeing strangers naked. Yet seeing his ex-girlfriend that way was a unique experience. Though she didn't doubt the strength of her bond with Rafe for a second, it was still strange to witness the sudden reemergence of his first love. She was beautiful. Trying to sort through her mixed emotions about Susan not only made her head hurt, but also distracted her from protecting Rafe. Determined not to let her guard down, Katie pulled out the revolver, did a quick visual scan of the trees, then knelt at his side.

"Please, baby." She caressed his cool cheek, rough with stubble. "Please, please wake up."

The sound of a door closing jerked her attention back to the cabin. She stood up quickly, only barely resisting the urge to point the gun at Susan again. Nervous and on edge, she wasn't ready to trust anyone around the man she loved while he was totally helpless. Susan gave her a cautious look as she approached, shotgun cradled in her arms, and unlocked the door with a key fob. "Lot of bodies in there."

"I didn't invite them inside," Katie said pointedly.

Susan held up the shotgun and the rest of the shells. "You don't want to forget this." She walked to the truck and yanked open the passenger door, tucking the weapon between the seats. After sweeping her arm across the seat to clear the broken glass, she turned to Katie. "Any luck waking him up?"

Katie slipped the revolver into her pants, then grabbed Rafe's legs as Susan hoisted him by the armpits. "No. I don't know what's wrong."

They didn't speak as they wrestled his heavy weight into the seat. Susan leaned over his lap to buckle his seatbelt while Katie kept a watchful eye on the forest. It was almost eerily still. The sky was blue and clear, and sunlight shone down from above, illuminating the snow and making it seem to glow. If not for the fact that corpses littered the yard around them, it would be a beautiful day.

Susan shut the passenger door. "As soon as you have the chance, you need to hold him. Make sure your skin touches his. I don't know if it works the same with a human, but as his bond-mate, you should be able to send him healing energy. Just focus on your bond, on his heartbeat..." As though suddenly self-conscious about her nudity, she folded her arms over her chest. "It's hard to explain. Just want it, and trust your instincts."

Having been the recipient of Rafe's healing touch, Katie had an idea of what she needed to do. She just hoped she could muddle her way through the details. "I'll try. How long will it take him to wake up, if it works?"

"I'm not sure." Susan crouched and shoveled snow away from the tires with her bare hands. Her urgency quickened Katie's pulse and drew her attention to their surroundings once more. "Head south on the first road you come to. Then west when that road dead-ends. Turning east will take you right through their territory, and trust me, you don't want to go there."

Reluctant to put down her gun or use her bare hands to move snow out of the way, Katie kicked at the rear tire. Her head swam with questions, not least of which was how she would explain the unconscious, naked man who was covered in blood in her passenger seat if she did happen to make it to civilization. This was not a day she wanted to get pulled over. "Are the roads even safe to drive on?"

Susan gave her a meaningful look. "No less safe than staying here. You'll need to be extremely careful, obviously, but with the chains he has on the tires, you should be able to drive out as long as the weather holds."

Katie glanced into the truck at Rafe, who still hadn't moved a muscle. She wished desperately that he would show some sign of life. It was terrifying to see him so still and powerless. In fact, it was probably the scariest thing she'd seen so far. After only two days together, already she couldn't imagine her life without him. She looked back at Susan—the woman she suspected had chosen to leave him willingly. "So you never answered my question. Why are you here?"

"Because I care about Rafe. I want to see him survive this

mess."

"If you care about him so much, then where have you been?" Accusation sharpened Katie's tone and made her words come out harsher than she'd intended, but she didn't care. This woman's disappearance had caused Rafe immense worry and heartbreak, yet here she was—alive and well. "He thinks you're dead, you know. That the others murdered you."

"And as far as I'm concerned, it would be better for everyone if he kept thinking that."

Even if she'd wanted to keep a secret of this magnitude, Katie suspected their bond wouldn't allow it. "I can't keep this from him. I won't."

"I know." Susan sighed, then gazed through the passenger window at Rafe's prone form. "You two don't deserve this. He killed Zeke to protect his bond-mate. I understand that, even if most of my pack doesn't."

Susan's casual confession as to her affiliations turned Katie's marrow to ice. "You left him to join the others?" Having interacted with a few members of the rival pack, Katie wasn't sure what to make of this woman. She seemed too kind to be one of those animals. And Rafe had once loved her, which had to mean that she was almost certainly a different type of wolf than the rest of them. So why had she abandoned Rafe to run with a bloodthirsty gang of thugs only months after moving in to the home he'd built for them? "I don't understand."

Susan shook her head, a faraway look in her eyes. "I loved Rafe. Heart and soul, I loved that boy more than I had ever loved anything in my entire life." She kept scooping snow out of the way as melancholy crept into her voice. "Then one day I went out running not far from here and met Ian. At first I was actually a little scared of him. He was rough around the edges, with this nasty scar across half his face from one of the many occasions his father nearly beat him to death. He came on so strong it frightened me. Flirting, challenging me, following me when I turned around to go home. I could tell from the tone of his voice that he didn't want to hurt me, exactly, but he also didn't want to let me go."

"So you were kidnapped?"

"No." Susan met Katie's eyes. "I shifted into a wolf and ran from him. He followed. Ian is fast, incredibly fast." She smiled, and Katie realized that her voice was full of love for this other man. "He caught up to me. Tackled me. And as soon as his body touched mine, it happened." Susan sobered. "We bonded. Just like that. We both shifted back into human form, lying naked and tangled together on the forest floor. And suddenly that frightening, scarred man was my bond-mate. He was my destiny. So when he kissed me, I kissed him back."

Bonded. Katie understood the overwhelming power of that connection, knew how impossible it was to resist it. She was also completely aware of how amazing it felt to give in to the incredible intimacy of being connected to another person's soul. "You chose to leave Rafe, but only because it really wasn't a choice at all."

"Nobody knows why these things happen. But when they do, there's no fighting against it. I found my other half, and he wasn't Rafe."

Katie had a terrible thought. Had Susan's bond-mate been one of the horde they'd slaughtered? "Ian wasn't...he's not here, is he?" While she wouldn't have done anything differently—couldn't have done anything differently—she hated the thought that either she or Rafe had severed someone else's bond. Especially when that someone was Rafe's ex-girlfriend. "He wasn't killed last night, was he?"

"He's at home with our daughter." Passenger side tires clear, Susan moved to the other side of the truck and Katie followed. "When I left, I told Ian that I could never do anything to hurt Rafe, then or in the future. Ian is the only one in our pack who knows my full history, and he accepts that I will always hold a special place in my heart for my first love.

When Lisa asked him to join the pack here last night, Ian refused. We both stayed far away from that mess and I'm glad, because I'm not sure who I'd have fought for under the full moon."

That Susan still loved Rafe was clear. Yet she had caused him so much pain that it was hard to imagine how she could justify her lies. "Do you realize what it did to Rafe to think you'd been killed? He tried to get his Alpha to go to war with your new pack over your disappearance. When that didn't happen, he withdrew from everyone. He's lived all alone out here, missing his lover and resenting his pack for not believing him that something terrible happened to her."

"His Alpha knows what happened to me." At Katie's incredulous look, Susan nodded. "Ian and I went to see him shortly after that day in the woods. I felt I needed to tell him so that he didn't think about starting some kind of war. I begged him not to tell Rafe because I just couldn't..." She swallowed, staring at Rafe's naked, battered body. "I couldn't bear to hurt Rafe that way. I was young and selfish. It was easier for me if he mourned me instead of hated me."

"Do you really think he would have hated you? Surely he knew even then what it meant to bond. If you didn't mean for it to happen..."

"I don't know." Susan gazed at Rafe with unveiled tenderness, then crouched to clear away more snow. "He'll hate me now, that's for sure." Her eyes teared up, and she glanced at Katie self-consciously as she wiped her face with the back of her arm. "Tell him...tell him I'm sorry. I never wanted to hurt him. He was such a sweet boy, and I did love him. I really did."

"I'm sure he'll be glad to know that you're all right." Katie wasn't sure what else he might feel about this revelation—especially the fact that his own Alpha had hidden Susan's fate from him—but she hoped that his feelings for Susan were enough of a thing of the past that he wouldn't let it phase him too severely. "He loved you, too. Losing you hurt him badly."

She managed to hold her tongue a beat, then said, "I know it was easier for you that way, but it wasn't easier for him."

"I don't know about that." Susan's features softened. "Anyway, it all worked out for the best. If I hadn't met Ian that day, maybe Rafe and I would still be together. But I never loved him the way I love Ian, and Rafe never loved me the way he loves you. Believe me, I became an afterthought the instant you two bonded." Her voice caught, and she said, "Sometimes I wish I had bonded with Rafe, honestly. At the time I told myself he was a puppy dog and I needed a wolf, but after seeing how he's defended you..." She sniffed. "You're very lucky."

Katie couldn't disagree. "Things did turn out for the best. I'm just not sure that gets you off the hook for leaving the way you did."

"Maybe not. But hopefully he can at least appreciate that I came here to help you today." With that, Susan's manner became business-like. "Listen, you can't tell anyone I was here. That includes Rafe's Alpha. No one can know. I'm pretty sure the peace treaty between our packs won't survive what happened last night, and I don't want to be branded a traitor."

"I won't tell. I promise."

"And don't trust anyone. That also includes Rafe's Alpha. There's a chance he could choose to sacrifice the two of you if the alternative is a pack war."

Katie's head throbbed as the scope of Susan's warning became clear. Now they not only had to fear the rival pack, but Rafe's own friends. "Right. So don't stop for anyone, because they all want to kill us."

"Pretty much." Susan stood and surveyed the truck. "That will be good enough to get you moving." She gestured at the vehicle. "Which you should do. Now."

"Wait." Overwhelmed, Katie made a mental list of everything she needed that hadn't yet been packed. "I need something for him to wear once he wakes up. And we can't leave Shilah—"

"Shilah?"

Apparently the puppy had arrived after Susan left. "Rafe's dog. He was injured when wolves broke into the cabin last night. I tried to dress his wounds and stitch him up as best as I could, but I don't really know what I'm doing. I'm worried he won't make it."

"Where is he?"

"In Rafe's bedroom, in the closet. He's resting."

Susan glanced worriedly around. "Okay, let me go get him. I'll also grab a change of clothing for Rafe."

"And my purse, if you don't mind. From the guest room." Katie considered asking about her own clothes, but decided to just let it go. This gave her the perfect excuse to go shopping once she was back in San Francisco. "Thank you. I appreciate it."

"Just keep your eyes open while I'm gone." Susan ran back to the cabin, taking the porch steps two at a time.

Katie opened the driver's side door as soon as Susan went inside. She brushed the broken glass off her own seat, then opened the small door to the extended cab, relieved to find that the back bench was plenty big enough to accommodate Shilah. Aware that it would take Susan at least a couple minutes to gather everything, Katie shifted her focus to Rafe. Unhappy about the blood staining his skin, Katie knelt and gathered a handful of snow. She brought it to his chest and scrubbed over the tacky streaks of crimson, checking his reaction to the freezing wetness as she washed away blood and grime to reveal the smooth, tanned skin beneath. Hopeful that the shock of the cold snow against his bare skin would yank him out of his eerie sleep, her stomach turned over uneasily when it became clear that he wasn't feeling anything at all.

Desperate to wake him, Katie drew back and slapped him across the face. She winced at the impact, feeling the blow in her own gut, but when he didn't stir, she hit him again. "Wake up. Please." Still nothing. Recalling Susan's advice, she pressed her palm to his cheek and concentrated on willing Rafe's eyes to open. She imagined energy flowing from her hand into his body, healing him from the inside. After a few moments, the muscles around his beautiful mouth twitched.

The cabin door opened and closed again. Concentration broken, Katie pulled away from Rafe with a regretful sigh. Five more minutes and perhaps she could have woken him up. She glanced over her shoulder, at Susan approaching with Shilah cradled in her arms as though he weighed nothing at all. Perhaps it was best for Rafe to miss this part. Right now they needed to focus all their energy on escape, and nothing else. The truth about Susan's fate was sure to bring up complicated feelings that he didn't need to deal with while their lives were still in danger.

"It looks like you did a good job treating Shilah," Susan called out as she approached. "I also gave him a little TLC of my own. He'll be fine. You will need to take him to a vet for that leg, though. It may need to come off."

Katie's stomach turned over with guilt. Yet despite Susan's grim prediction, Shilah seemed perkier than he had since the fight. He wore a friendly doggy grin as Susan carried him to the backseat. Katie managed a genuine smile in return. "We'll take him. Thank you."

Susan settled Shilah on the bench seat, then backed away from the truck with a not-so-subtle glance at Rafe. She handed Katie the stack of Rafe's clothes that she'd somehow managed to carry with Shilah, along with her purse. "I don't recommend stopping before you hit the road west. I know you'll want to try and wake him up as soon as possible, but you've got to put as much distance between you and this place as you can. Understand?"

"Yeah, I get it." Katie closed the truck doors, then stood to face Susan. "Listen, thank you."

"Don't mention it." Susan quirked a frustratingly endearing smile as she handed over the keys. "Literally."

"I remember." Rocking back on her heels, Katie searched

for the appropriate parting words. The best she could come up with was, "Be careful."

"You, too." Susan snuck one last look at Rafe. "Take good care of him."

"You know I will."

Susan turned to leave, but before she took even a single step, she hesitated, then glanced back over her shoulder. "I don't know where you're going—and I don't want to know—but please remember that Rafe hasn't spent a lot of time around humans. It may take him a while to adjust." Worry clouded her pretty face. "Be patient with him, okay? Remember how out of place you feel here. He'll feel just as out of place in your world."

Katie wasn't sure that was exactly true. After all, Rafe wasn't likely to find hordes of people desperate to rape and kill him in San Francisco—or wherever they ended up. Still, she understood Susan's point. "I'll remember."

Susan tipped her head. "Take care of each other." She swiftly transformed into a wolf—a beautiful, buff-colored one that was far more graceful than intimidating—and took off running.

Katie didn't bother to watch her until she disappeared. As soon as Susan hit the tree line, Katie ran around to the driver's side of the truck and climbed inside. Fishing the key out of her pocket, she forced her numb fingers to fit it into the ignition. A whine from the backseat drew her attention to the rearview mirror, where Shilah stared back at her. She exhaled shakily. "I'm going to do my best to drive us out of here, boy." A sudden flash of memory sent a sick feeling to the pit of her stomach. Trying to keep her car on the slick road, only to end up stranded and alone. "Hopefully I won't lose control of the truck this time." Shilah sighed deeply, and Katie echoed the sound. "Don't worry, I'll stop to wake your daddy up as soon as I can. I don't want to drive in these conditions, either."

Unfortunately, Susan was right. She had no other choice.

CHAPTER THIRTY-ONE

The drive was a nightmare. Worse than a nightmare, actually, because the sickening slide of the tires around every curve made her feel out of control in a way that was all too real. The sensation took her back in time to only a week ago, when an ill-conceived trip into bad weather on treacherous roads had ended with her nearly freezing to death in a ditch. Driving with the frigid wind whipping against her face made her feel even more panicky. With no windows, they would have no protection from the elements if she wrecked this time.

She hoped that her decision to leave without waiting for the snow to melt wasn't the wrong one. If she had another accident, they would be sitting ducks for vengeance-seeking werewolves. Even if Rafe woke up, that would be an awful situation. If he didn't, she wasn't certain she could shoot their way out of it.

In the backseat, Shilah whimpered every time she hit a particularly rough section of road. More worrying was that Rafe made no sound at all. She strained to hear something— anything—over the crunch of the tires on the snow and the panicked rasp of her own breathing. But there was nothing. Rafe wasn't there.

Even though she still felt their connection enough to know that Rafe was still with her, the thought disturbed her immensely. How much longer until she felt nothing at all? Taking her attention off the road for only an instant, she scanned his slumbering form from head to toe. Was there some injury she couldn't see? He was littered with cuts and bruises, but nothing that explained his continued sleep. She yearned to pull over and try to wake him as Susan had suggested, but she intended to heed the warning to wait until they'd driven a few miles west. Just to be safe.

Safe. Katie tried to snicker, but couldn't seem to force her lips out of the tense line they'd formed. Right now she felt anything but safe. She hadn't felt safe since Rafe walked out the front door the night before.

When the road finally dead-ended, offering her a choice between east and west, Katie took the right-turn with a grateful sigh. Her relief immediately turned into horror when the truck's back-end fishtailed on the slippery surface, sending her careening toward the side of the road in what seemed like slow motion. She tightened her grip on the steering wheel, paralyzed for what felt like an eternity before instinct took over and she steered out of the deadly slide. From behind her came the sound of Shilah yawning loudly, clearly anxious, while Rafe uttered a moan that was so quiet, at first she wasn't sure that she'd really heard it.

"Rafe?" Katie pushed down on the brake, slowing to a tentative stop only yards away from the interchange. She touched his bare thigh, pleased to find his skin once again warm to the touch. "Sorry about that. If you want to take over behind the wheel, I'm all for it." When he didn't stir, she cradled his face in her hand. "I need you here with me, baby. Please come back to me."

He groaned, and her heart sang. Glancing around to make sure they were still alone, she pressed both palms flat against his chest, then bowed her head and focused all her longing for his company on their point of contact. All the love he inspired, her dreams of sharing a future with this man she just met, every intangible, illogical thing he made her feel—

244

she took all of those emotions, jumbled as they were, and channeled them into a yearning, all-consuming plea to the universe to release Rafe from whatever deep, dark place he'd fallen into.

"Wake up," Katie whispered, then sobbed quietly when Rafe's eyelashes fluttered. "Wake up, wake up."

The sound of a wolf howling in the distance shattered her concentration and raised the hairs on the back of her neck. Katie snatched her hands back and grasped the steering wheel, then let off the brake. They were obviously still in the middle of werewolf territory, which made stopping a very bad idea. As much as she wanted to revive Rafe, that couldn't distract her from the all-important business of securing their escape. She sensed that she would only need another minute or two to rouse him, but right now continuing their slow and steady pace toward civilization seemed like the wiser choice.

She didn't make it another mile before a second howl arose from behind them. Katie jolted at the mournful cry, then stiffened in dread as a reply came from somewhere north of their position, far closer than she liked. Already she was second-guessing her decision not to rouse Rafe. If they were going to be ambushed by wolves, she'd feel a hell of a lot better if Rafe were awake for the fight. Of course, her ultimate goal was to avoid a confrontation at all.

"Shit," she muttered. She tore her gaze away from the path ahead every few seconds, checking Rafe again and again. Each time her attention shifted to the passenger seat, she hoped to find green eyes staring back at her. Every time it didn't happen, her sense of desolation grew. "I don't know what to do." She spoke to Shilah as much as Rafe, not expecting an answer from either of them. She was on her own. This was her decision to make, and the consequences would be her responsibility to bear. "I want you awake. I know you want to be awake."

She tried to decide what Rafe would want her to do. She had no doubt that he wanted to protect her and would beat himself up over the knowledge that she'd had to fend for herself while he slept. But he would also want her to do whatever kept her safest. She just wished she knew what that was.

The back end of the truck slid this way and that as she rounded a bend in the road, sending her perilously close to the edge of the steep drop-off she'd been trying not to notice. She regained control within seconds, but the mishap left her sweating and trembling uncontrollably. One thing was certain—driving didn't make her feel safe. Neither did stopping. The reality was, there was no such thing as safe as long as they were trapped in the Sierra Nevada mountains. There were only different degrees of danger.

Katie felt like she was having an out of body experience as she slowly applied her foot to the brake and pulled to the side of the road. After only a moment of internal debate, she shifted into park. If she did this quickly, Rafe would be awake and he could help her make decisions. That was all she wanted right now. Someone to help her decide what to do next. Unbuckling her seatbelt, she climbed over the center console and straddled Rafe's hips as she took his face between her hands.

"Rafe, it's time to wake up now." She tried to sound calm, but her voice wavered and emotion came to the front. Her vision blurred and her eyes stung, but she blinked back the urge to burst into tears and forced steel into her voice. "Listen to me. I need you. I can't do this without you anymore."

He didn't respond. Sitting forward on his lap, Katie used her fingers to part his thick, dark hair and searched his scalp for signs of a head injury. If he'd suffered a hard enough blow to the skull, all the supernatural healing magic in the world wouldn't fix it. At least she didn't think it would. Yet Susan had seemed confident that she could help him. Recalling her advice to have skin-on-skin contact, Katie pulled her shirt and bra up in one motion, gathering them under her chin and pressing her bare chest against Rafe's. She rested her head on his shoulder, her cheek touching his, and whispered into his ear.

"I don't want to do this alone." Voice breaking, she clung to his naked body, comforted by the heat he exuded. She focused on how badly she wanted to be with Rafe, how empty she felt without him, and let the full scope of her love flow out of her and into him. He shifted ever-so-slightly beneath her, and Katie whispered, "Please don't make me do this alone. Help me."

Inspired by her favorite fairy tale as a child, she pressed her lips to his and gave him a chaste kiss. When that failed to rouse him, she increased the pressure of her mouth against his, then traced the tip of her tongue along his lower lip. He stirred beneath her, clearly aware and approving of her presence. Encouraged by the sudden, feather-light caress of his finger along the bare skin of her side, she squeezed him tight and wished with all her might that he would wake up and kiss her back.

And that's what he did.

One moment she was kissing an unconscious man, and the next, his tongue teased hers while one hand tangled in her hair and the other slid down to caress her ass. Breaking their kiss with a gasp, Katie sat back on his lap and sobbed in relief at the sight of his dazed, happy smile.

"That was a really nice way to wake up." Rafe released her hair and traced her mouth with his thumb. "Special occasion?"

She brayed loud laughter before dissolving into silent, quaking sobs. Exhausted from the effort of waking him, she collapsed onto his chest, grateful for the steady thump of his heartbeat against her breast. Not ready to move, she forced herself not to focus on the urgency of the situation so that she could enjoy the way his hands explored her body for another minute more. "Not really," she choked out.

Rafe moved the hand that had been stroking her ass to the middle of her back and held her close. "Shh, don't cry.

You're alive. I assume, despite how my head feels, that I'm alive..." He gave her a gentle squeeze and rubbed her lower back. "Everything turned out okay."

Katie shook her head. That wasn't true—not yet. The thought yanked her back to reality. As good as it felt to be held, this was no time for cuddling. She had to drive them out of there. She tried to climb off Rafe's lap, but he held her in place. Painfully aware that he didn't yet understand the full scope of what had happened while he was unconscious, Katie debated what to tell him now and what to leave for later. The most important thing was to express the urgency of their need for escape. The details—including Susan—could wait until they were safe. "We've got to keep moving. We're about five miles from the interchange, going west. The roads are awful, but we had to leave. I killed six of them and I didn't even stop to see how many you got. Lisa's still alive, though, and she's pissed, and I'm pretty sure we've got their whole pack after us now...maybe even your Alpha, too."

"Whoa." Rafe took her by the elbows and eased her back so he could look into her eyes. "You killed six of them?" Suddenly a bit frantic, he ran his hands over her body as though checking for invisible injuries. "Are you hurt?"

"A few cuts and bruises, but no big deal." She pulled her shirt and bra down and tried to climb over to the driver's seat again. "Let's talk while I drive—"

He put his hands on her thighs to keep her in place. "Wait. Did they hurt you?" He looked around the cab of the truck as though noticing where they were for the first time. "How did you get me into the truck? And where's—" He glanced into the backseat, reaching for his dog even as Shilah leaned forward to nuzzle into his touch. "What happened?"

The sound of another wolf howling pulled Rafe's attention out the driver's side window. Katie put her hand on his cheek and urged his face forward. She could feel his mind racing as he tried to catch up with the events of the past fourteen hours, then his body tensed when the danger of their present circumstances seemed to become clear to him. This time when she lifted off him, he let her go. She fastened her seatbelt and shifted the truck into drive, pulling back onto the road slowly.

"We had a long night." Katie cringed at the quaver in her voice. She was determined not to fall apart until they were safe in a hotel somewhere far away. Just thinking about being able to crawl into bed with Rafe—naked, warm, and secure—threatened to shatter her composure completely. "Shilah was injured when wolves broke into the cabin."

Rafe cursed under his breath. She tore her eyes away from the road ahead to give him a sidelong glance, and giggled in surprise to find him with both hands cupped over his crotch. "I want to hear all about it—seriously—but first please tell me you thought to grab some pants before we left?"

She jerked her head toward the backseat. "Next to Shilah."

He leaned over the center console and grabbed the extra set of clothes with a grateful grunt. "Good. If we're going into human territory, I want to be ready. I'll need to blend in."

Human territory. Katie recalled Susan's prediction about Rafe having a difficult time in San Francisco. She desperately hoped it wouldn't come true. It was clear that she wasn't safe in Rafe's world, which meant their best shot at a life together was in hers. Even if he experienced a bit of culture shock, surely he would adjust. At least he wouldn't have to fear for his safety—or hers. She was so lost in her thoughts that she nearly missed Rafe's strange silence after he tugged on his T-shirt. But an ominous quiet settled over them, making Katie's stomach churn and drawing her attention to the passenger seat.

"What's wrong?" Katie asked.

Rafe blinked and turned to her slowly. "Who helped you put me in the truck?"

She bit her lip, hesitant to go down this path while they were still fleeing for their lives. But she couldn't lie, and she could tell from the tone of his voice that he already knew the answer anyway. "It was Susan, honey. She showed up this morning when I went outside to find you."

He sat back in the seat, planting his hands on his knees and exhaling in a rush. After what felt like forever, during which time Katie didn't dare to take her eyes off the road, he pulled on his pants and socks. Once he was fully clothed, he said, "Do you want me to drive?"

Of all the follow-up questions he could have asked, that was the last one she'd expected. Katie shook her head. "Maybe in a little bit. First you should wake up—and we should talk."

"Apparently so," Rafe murmured. He rested his hand on her thigh, and the connection brought instant calm. "So let's talk. Tell me what happened...start from the beginning. After the transformation."

Surprised that he didn't want to hear about Susan first, Katie mentally reviewed the entire sordid tale. A fresh wave of guilt crept over her at the prospect of confessing how she'd barely even hesitated before ignoring his order to lay low and avoid confrontation. How could she justify disobeying him when the casualty of that rebellion was sprawled across the backseat for both of them to see? A lump rose in her throat, making it hard to swallow. "Rafe, I—"

His fingers tightened almost imperceptibly on her thigh. "Just tell me everything. Whatever it is, it's not nearly as bad as you think. The important thing is that we're both alive."

Katie exhaled. She knew better than to believe that Rafe could hate her for what she'd done. It simply wasn't possible. She was almost positive that there was nothing he could do to change how she felt about him, and trusted that that loyalty went both ways. Confident that their bond was strong enough to handle everything she was about to say, Katie did exactly as Rafe suggested and started at the beginning. "I went up to the attic after the fight began. I know you told me not to, but I couldn't stand not knowing what was happening. Not being able to see you when I could hear such awful noises—"

"I understand." Rafe gave her a gentle pat. "Honestly, I do. I'm not upset with you."

Unsure how he would feel once he knew the whole story, Katie decided to just get through it as quickly as possible. "When I got up there, I looked out the back window first. You were fighting in front with most of the wolves who were there, but I spotted two on the ground who were isolated from the others. I knew they were heading to help the rest attack you, and I honestly didn't even think—I just reacted. I figured if I could take out stragglers who were away from the main action, the other wolves would be too distracted with you to even notice. And that would mean fewer for you to fight alone." Aware that he hadn't liked that plan the first time she'd said it, she subtly checked Rafe's reaction to her confession. He was actually smiling. Confused, Katie said, "You really aren't angry?"

"I'm not angry. I'm not surprised, either." The fondness in Rafe's voice relaxed her instantly. "I was pretty sure you were going to do whatever you had to do to protect me. Obviously I didn't want you taking unnecessary risks, and I would have preferred that you just did as I asked and stayed hidden, but I can't exactly be upset with you for doing what I would have done, in your situation. You want to protect me just as much as I want to protect you. That's the nature of our bond. How could I ever hold that against you?"

Katie sagged in relief. "Thank you for understanding."

"That doesn't mean I'm thrilled, mind you." His obvious concern wrapped around her like a warm blanket, taking away the chill in the cab. When he stroked her thigh with so much adoration, it filled her with that feeling of safety and belonging she had been craving all morning. He chuckled. "I have a feeling the rest of this story will terrify me, but please keep going."

251

She knew that was true. The rest of the story terrified her, and she'd lived it. "It was just like you said. They smelled me as soon as I opened the window, but I managed to shoot them both. Then I ducked out of sight, honestly a little freaked out by the realization that I'd just taken two lives. Once I got my head back together, I looked out the window again and saw four more wolves standing over the bodies. They spotted me right away, so I took a shot at one of them, but I missed. Naturally, they all took off running. That's when I heard a window break downstairs." Katie tightened her hands on the wheel, tense and angry at herself in retrospect. That was the moment when she should have gone downstairs to protect Shilah.

"Then what?" Rafe asked in a gentle voice.

"I knew they would break in eventually, but I wanted to look out the other window before I had to deal with them. I wanted to see if I could help you. So I..." She swallowed past the lump in her throat. "I closed the hatch on my way past it. I went to the other window and saw you fighting. There were five of them surrounding you, and another group of wolves were fighting nearby." For the first time since he'd woken up, she remembered the somber news she had to deliver. "Rafe, Cooper is dead."

She felt the physical impact of the news as his body jolted beside her. "What?"

"I found his body this morning. That must have been him last night, fighting the smaller group of wolves beside you." Katie fell silent as the truck's tires struggled to maintain traction on the slick surface. Turning her focus toward driving while Rafe processed her words, she began to worry after he didn't speak for a long time. Guilt radiated from him, and stark torment. Without looking away from the road, she murmured, "It's not your fault, honey."

"I didn't honestly think anyone would come fight with me."

The agony he was clearly feeling made her insides ache. "He'd known you since you were a little boy. Even if you always felt like a lone wolf, he obviously cared about you."

"Obviously." From her peripheral vision, she saw him brusquely scrub the back of his hand over his eyes. "It doesn't feel right to just leave him. I know they're coming for us, but—"

"Cooper would want you to escape. Otherwise he died for no reason."

Rafe put his elbows on his knees and dropped his head into his hands. "I know. I just wish I could have at least told his mate. Taken his body to her..."

"I'm so sorry." Katie didn't think that leaving immediately had been the wrong choice, but she hated that Rafe hadn't had a chance for any type of closure before she took him away from his home—possibly forever. "You can call her from the city."

Sniffing, Rafe nodded and put his hand back on her thigh. "So you saw me fighting. What happened next?"

The knot in her stomach only got bigger. "Wolves broke in through one of the back windows. I heard..." She shuddered. "I heard Shilah fighting with one of them, and I panicked. I realized that I'd left him down there all alone..." A sob burst from her with unexpected force, all the emotion she'd suppressed for the past fourteen hours finally catching up with her. She stopped speaking, afraid that she wouldn't be able to continue driving if she attempted to tell the rest.

"Pull over." Rafe cradled her cheek in his hand, wiping away her tears with his thumb. "I can drive now."

She didn't argue. Even if he'd just woken up, she was exhausted and emotional and ready for a break. Steering the truck onto the side of the road, she shifted into park and unbuckled her seatbelt. Rafe put his hand on her back, coaxing her into another warm embrace. She held on tightly, greedy for the comfort. "When I went to help Shilah, there was a wolf on the ladder. He jumped up into the attic with me, and I shot him, but by that time the fight downstairs was over and Shilah was quiet. I had to deal with two more wolves before I found Shilah. He was in pretty rough shape. I spent the rest of the night cleaning his wounds and protecting him." She shivered, then burrowed deeper into Rafe's arms. "I'm so sorry. He needs to go to the vet. His leg is very badly injured."

Rafe hugged her tighter. "Katie, look at him. He's all right." He waited for her to glance into the backseat at Shilah, then caressed the small of her back. "You were trying to protect me. He was protecting you. Nobody had bad intentions, and everybody got through the night alive. Am I happy that you put yourself in danger? Not really. But we're all still in one piece, potentially because you did exactly what you did. I'd be a jerk to reprimand you now." He fell silent, and they breathed together for a few moments. Then Rafe murmured, "Especially when I wouldn't have listened to me, either. Not with my bond-mate in danger."

His empathy triggered a fresh flood of tears. That he understood why she'd done what she had meant everything. "I love you."

"I love you, too." Rafe released her with a final squeeze. "Now trade seats with me."

Katie climbed over him into the passenger seat, buckling the safety belt with shaky hands as he settled in behind the wheel. "Thanks for taking over. I'm so tired I'm ready to collapse."

"I'll bet." Rafe shifted the truck into drive and pulled back onto the road, resuming their torturously slow pace. "You said you killed six wolves, but you've only told me about five. Was the last one after you found Shilah?"

"Yes. He surprised me when I went back to the kitchen to get the shotgun after I moved Shilah to the bathroom." A chill shook her as she recalled their encounter. "It was the one who bit me. The one with Zeke. That was probably my closest call last night."

The blood drained from Rafe's face. "But you're all right?"

"I will be." Katie scooted over in her seat and rested her head against his shoulder. "How about you? How are you doing?"

"Happy to be alive." Rafe kissed the crown of her head. "Sad for Cooper. Confused."

She knew without asking. "About Susan."

"Yeah." He flexed his fingers on the steering wheel, jaw set in determination. "I'm ready to hear that part now."

Katie exhaled, not sure she was ready to tell it. But they had hours of driving ahead of them, Rafe needed to know what had become of his first love, and there was no point in putting it off the telling just because she was afraid of how he might react. She couldn't hide anything from him. She didn't even want to try.

So she started, once again, from the beginning.

CHAPTER THIRTY-TWO

Rafe listened quietly until she got to the part where she'd confronted Susan about her disappearance. Then he lost his cool. "So you're saying that she's been living with those psychopaths all this time?"

Katie winced at the anger in Rafe's voice, and at the sharp turn he took entirely too fast. She'd expected him to be upset, but now she seriously questioned the wisdom in timing the big reveal to coincide with their desperate escape down an icy mountain road. "She bonded with the guy. She didn't mean for it to happen. It just did."

The muscles in Rafe's jaw bunched. "How did it happen? Tell me what she said."

"She was out walking near your cabin and came across this man—"

"What's his name?" Rafe interrupted. When she hesitated to answer, he gave her an entreating look. "Please. I just want to know if I've met him before."

"Ian." Katie watched his face carefully. There was no spark of recognition in his eyes. "He didn't come to fight you last night." Dreading the impact of this next detail, she added, "He stayed home to be with their daughter. Susan stayed away, too. Said she wasn't sure whose side she would've been on if she'd joined the rest of her pack-mates."

The anger on Rafe's face vanished, replaced by a stony mask. "For years I imagined how they might have tortured her. How they'd made her suffer before they finally killed her. I've imagined her dying a hundred different ways, and she's been living only miles away with a bond-mate and a pup of her own?" His knuckles turned white as he gripped the steering wheel. "I don't understand why she would do that to me."

"She didn't want to hurt you." When he looked at her, incredulous, Katie shrugged. "I don't think she knew how to deal with breaking the heart of a boy she genuinely loved. She was young and selfish. It was easier for her if you mourned her, rather than hated her."

He cursed under his breath, turning hard eyes back to the road ahead. Then he exhaled and took his foot off the gas pedal, reducing their speed. "I'm sorry. I don't even know why I'm so upset. She bonded. And because she did, I had the chance to bond...with you." He gave her a look of apology. "If she hadn't left, I probably would never have found you that night. I might not have ever known what it's like to be connected to someone on this level. So in a way, I'm glad she did what she did. But it still pisses me off."

"Of course it does. She was your first love and she disappeared. You thought something terrible had happened to her, and you spent years trying to make the rest of your pack listen to your concerns. It's only natural to be angry when you find out it was all a lie. But she obviously loved you, and she does seem genuinely sorry about hurting you. I know she hopes that coming to my aid this morning has helped to right some of the wrongs she committed." Tightening her fingers on his thigh, she experimented with sending him calming thoughts. "As the woman who needed her help—desperately—I'm asking you to let her off the hook just a little bit. For me."

Rafe grumbled under his breath. "Aw, hell. I forgive her. Of course I do." He dropped a hand from the wheel to cover hers for just a moment. "At the end of the day, I'm thrilled that she didn't suffer some terrible death. And I'm happy that she's happy. I just wish she'd been straightforward with me. I would have been upset, sure, but..." He winced. "It would have been better than seeing her raped and murdered in my imagination night after night."

"Well, at least she's come clean now. She didn't have to help me get you into the truck, or give me her name. She risked the wrath of her own pack to come to our aid this morning. Even if the gesture is years too late, that has to count for something."

"It does." When the truck's tires spun suddenly on a patch of ice, Rafe eased off the accelerator even further. "But now I feel like an ass. I can't tell you how many times I butted heads with Alpha over Susan's disappearance. I called him a coward for not pursuing the truth about what happened to her. I was ready to start a goddamn war. I can't help feeling a little guilty about that, in retrospect, even if he couldn't have known that she was okay."

Katie bit her lip. This one was going to hurt. "Actually, he did."

Rafe went deadly still. "What?"

"Your Alpha knew. Susan went to him after her bonding. She didn't want him going after Ian's pack thinking that something had happened to her, but she asked him to keep it secret from you." Katie paused, afraid to say more. A fresh surge of rage rolled off Rafe and hit her in the gut. At the core of his intense emotion was the most profound sensation of betrayal she'd ever experienced. The potency of it took her breath away.

"I take back what I said about feeling guilty." His low voice sent a chill down Katie's spine. He slowed the truck even more, as though countering his blistering anger with an overabundance of caution. "And now I remember why it is that I don't need a goddamn pack."

Her heart hurt for him even as she found hope in the idea that he didn't need to be around other wolves to be happy. After the past forty-eight hours, she knew one thing for sure—

they were better off living as far away from his kind as possible. "I'm so sorry to be the one to tell you all this." She lifted her hand and, hoping he was receptive to affection, stroked the short hairs on the back of his neck. "But you deserve the truth—and I'm pretty sure I can't lie to you, anyway."

Rafe rested his head on the seat, tearing his eyes away from the road for a beat to search her face with an expression so open and sincere that Katie melted before he even spoke. "I wouldn't want it to come from anyone but you. Because I know you have my back, and you're literally the only living creature in the world—besides Shilah—that I can say that about. You've shown me that you'll be there even when things get rough. I want you with me when things get rough."

She leaned across the center console and kissed his stubbled cheek. "That's a promise."

He gave her a quick peck on the lips before she pulled back. "This Susan thing is a mind fuck, but I am okay. I swear. Or at least I will be." Exhaling, Rafe murmured, "Honestly, I have a feeling that all it will take is one night alone with you, safe from harm."

Despite her exhaustion, the thought of having Rafe back in bed—without anyone waiting outside to kill them—triggered powerful yearning. "Can you imagine? An entire night together without worrying about being murdered? Sounds like a dream."

Rafe's upper lip twitched in apparent amusement. "Doesn't it?"

Emboldened by the distance they'd put between themselves and the scene of last night's carnage, Katie slid her hand up the inside of Rafe's thigh. Running a fingernail over the length of his shaft, she murmured, "On that note, I'm looking forward to some very hot and explicitly consensual sex sometime in the near future."

For almost the first time since she'd met him, Rafe didn't tense up at the teasing contact. He didn't push her away.

Instead he hardened beneath her hand with a sensual groan. "That's a promise." Nostrils flaring, he sat in silence and thrust his hips into her touch, satisfaction ghosting over his face. His pleasure fed her own, and the fact that he finally seemed comfortable around her brought a profound sense of relief. Rafe shot her a sidelong grin, sharing in her happiness. "I will do everything in my power to ensure that the first two days of our relationship are the absolute worst we ever spend together. It's all uphill from here, sweetheart."

"I like the sound of that." Katie leaned back in her seat and exhaled deeply. Some of the tension in her muscles drained away, but she wasn't going to be able to truly relax until they were either at a hotel or her apartment in the city. Until then, anything could happen. A flat tire, a hidden patch of ice, a ferocious werewolf leaping onto the windshield.

Or a tall, well-built man waiting for them just around a curve in the road, rifle at the ready.

Rafe slammed on the brakes, sending the truck skidding across the snow and ice until it came to a shuddering halt only ten feet away from the man and the giant blue pick-up truck he'd parked across both lanes. Katie clutched at a leather strap that was attached to the ceiling of the truck and strained to see the face of the imposing figure who stared them down. She recognized him almost immediately, which wasn't surprising. She'd met him less than thirty-six hours earlier. It was Rafe's Alpha—and he scared her every bit as much now as he did then.

Maybe more.

"Fuck." Rafe checked the rearview mirror as though contemplating escape. The road was narrow and Katie was certain that he would never be able to turn the truck around before Alpha shot them both, if that was his plan. That he hadn't immediately raised his weapon and fired was encouraging, but the anger that burned in his eyes unfurled sick dread in her gut. Rafe took his hands off the steering wheel and leaned across the seat to block her body with his.

"Which gun do you want?"

She didn't register the question until he pressed the revolver into her palm. "This one," she confirmed, and held the weapon on her lap in sweaty hands. "What are you going to do?"

"Talk to him." Rafe glanced out the windshield, then unlocked the driver's side door. He spoke under his breath so Alpha couldn't overhear. "Or kill him, depending on how this goes down. I want you to stay in the truck with Shilah."

"Okay, but be careful." Katie blushed after the earnest admonition left her mouth. She knew by now that Rafe would do whatever it took to protect her. "Don't get killed."

Rafe reached into the backseat to retrieve the shotgun. He grabbed the door handle, but rather than open it, he gave her one last, loving smile. So much emotion passed between them that Katie had to grip the dashboard with her free hand to keep herself from flying into his arms. He murmured, "I love you, too," then climbed out of the truck, mouth set in a stern line.

Katie startled when he shut the door. Ramrod tense, she kept one hand on the revolver and used the other to clutch at the dash. She watched Alpha's face, hoping to discern his intentions, but he was impossible to read. Suddenly glad for the broken-out windows, Katie listened hard, prepared to jump to Rafe's aid at the first sign of trouble. After last night, she had no problem killing any werewolf who stood in the way of their freedom.

Rafe hoisted the shotgun and held it against his chest. "Alpha."

The powerful pack leader nodded in acknowledgment. "Figured you'd head this way."

"It seemed smarter than driving through their backyard." Rafe gestured at Alpha's weapon. "What's that for?"

Alpha grinned. "What's yours for?"

"Protection. In case you didn't hear, Katie and I have a few enemies." Rafe mirrored Alpha's casual air, doing an impressive job of looking completely unintimidated. "Fewer now than yesterday, though."

"That's what I hear." Alpha's attention shifted to the truck and he made eye contact with her through the windshield, then turned away dismissively. "I was told the human survived the night. Wasn't so sure you had, though."

"I'm fine," Rafe said. "Just eager to get Katie the hell away from here."

"Oh, is that what you're doing?" Alpha took a step forward, prompting Rafe to bring the shotgun down into firing position. Stopping short, Alpha clucked his tongue in admonishment. "You're going to kill me now?"

"Not unless you make me." Rafe hesitated, conflict playing out across his face. "Not if you let us go."

"So is this a one-way trip for you? Or are you still planning to drop her off at the nearest town and say goodbye forever?"

Rafe glanced into the truck, and Katie held her breath as she waited for his answer. There was no way she was letting him go. She refused. Rafe turned to Alpha. "I'm not coming back."

"You're willing to abandon your pack like that? For a human?" Alpha had the nerve to sound genuinely betrayed.

"It's not safe for us here—and not being together isn't an option. She's my bond-mate." Rafe hardened his expression, his own feelings of betrayal clearly coming to the surface. "You know all about how powerful a force a soul-bond is, don't you? So powerful that it compelled Susan to stage a disappearance and run away from me to join our enemies. So powerful that you chose to lie to me for years about the fact that you knew." Fire burned in his eyes. "You fucking knew."

If Alpha was surprised by Rafe's words, he hid it admirably. "You're right. A soul-bond between wolves is one of the most powerful forces in the universe. I saw that in my parents every day. Believe it or not, I also saw it in Susan and her mate the day they came to me. She was terrified for you to find out that she'd bonded with someone else. I agreed to keep her secret because I wanted to help protect that bond, and I honestly wasn't sure how you would react. I worried you would confront Ian and get yourself killed. Or kill him, and therefore Susan. You were still no more than a pup at that time, and I did what I thought was best. But I didn't enjoy deceiving you. Especially when you refused to stop inciting war with our neighbors over her imagined murder." He cocked his head as though something had just occurred to him. "Was Susan involved in last night's festivities?"

"It doesn't matter." Rafe lifted his chin. "Listen, Katie and I need to leave, now. You and I both know that it's only a matter of time before they come after us."

"Oh, I do know." Alpha snorted. "Jack Devereaux just called me with an ultimatum."

"Let me guess. You kill us to avoid retaliation on the pack, or you get ready for war."

"Give the wolf a bone." Alpha chuckled. Katie noticed that he still hadn't brought up his rifle to aim at Rafe or her, which was probably a good sign. At least she hoped it was. "Well, they don't want me to kill both of you. Just you, Rafe. Jack has requested that the human be turned over to their pack so they can have their fun with her before she dies."

Katie's stomach bottomed out. She tightened her grip on the gun, ready to defend herself in case Alpha followed through on his end of the bargain. She'd rather put a bullet through her own brain than be turned over to that group of savages. Movement from outside the car registered in her peripheral vision—Rafe, giving her a confident shake of his head. No. His silent promise not to let anyone violate her relaxed her only marginally. Terrified by where Alpha's threat took her imagination, she remained ready to start shooting at the slightest provocation.

Rafe turned back to Alpha and glowered. "That's not going to happen."

"It sounds rather distasteful to me, too. But it would certainly save your pack a lot of bloodshed." Alpha looked at

Katie again, then Rafe, as though trying to figure them out. "I'm guessing they took heavy losses last night, based on how pissed off Jack is, but I still don't relish the idea of a war with those sociopaths. There's a reason we've always done what we could to keep the peace with them. They aren't our enemies." His pointed gaze strayed to Katie.

Rafe bristled. "Katie isn't our enemy, either. And what's the point of a pack if not to stand up for their own?" His voice broke and he paused, clearly trying to reign in the resentment that Katie could feel simmering within him. "That said, I don't want a war, either. You and I both know that Katie will never be safe living out here, no matter who wins. She belongs with her own kind—and I belong with her."

"You would abandon your pack to fight the war you started so you can live among those who hate you?" Alpha cocked his head. "It's a whole different world out there. One that isn't friendly to wolves like us."

"We'll be fine." At Alpha's mocking snort, Rafe growled. "I will be fine. Just let us go. If we're not here, there's nothing to fight about. Just tell Jack you couldn't find me, that we escaped, and I promise to disappear forever. Tell Jack that if I ever come back, you'll kill me yourself." He gave Katie another sidelong glance, one that lingered. "Katie and I didn't choose this, but it's very real. She's done nothing wrong except be human in the midst of werewolves. And all I've done is protect my bond-mate. I know you don't want war, Alpha, but I'm pretty sure you do want to do the right thing." His jaw tensed. "Even if you haven't always."

Alpha seemed so unmoved by Rafe's words that Katie feared the scene was about to turn ugly. But rather than raise his weapon, he took a step forward. "I do want to do the right thing. And the right thing is to deliver the woman to Jack. One life to compensate for how many of his? And a human life, at that?" He offered Rafe a regretful shrug. "That is what's right. Whether you like it or not."

Rafe's expression turned to ice. "You can't take her life

without taking mine."

"What if I promised to let you leave?" Alpha took another step forward. "Jack wants you dead, so you can't stay. But if I give them the girl, they may forgive me for not being able to deliver your body."

"Let me go?" Rafe laughed. "If Katie dies, I'm as good as dead, anyway. We're bonded—I need her. More than that, I love her. You know goddamn well that I'm not taking that deal."

"Who's to say that your human-wolf bond even works the same as a real bond? It's possible that you could move on from this woman. Find another mate."

"There is no other mate for me." Rafe's confident proclamation sent a pleasant shiver up her spine. "And if you try to take her, I will protect her. Whatever I have to do."

"I don't want to kill you, boy." A note of subtle desperation crept into Alpha's gruff voice. "I swear I don't." The paternal affection in his words sounded genuine, reaching into her chest and gripping her heart in an iron vise. That was Rafe's emotion, no doubt, and it threatened to shatter her intense concentration on watching for Alpha's next move.

But she couldn't let her guard down. Not now. Not for even a second.

Twin howls echoed through the trees, so close to their position that she gasped in horror. She darted her gaze around reflexively, terrified that she would see approaching wolves, lamenting her distraction the entire time. From her left came an enraged growl, then the sound of bone slamming against bone. She looked back at the road just in time to see Alpha land hard on his back with Rafe on top of him. Alpha's head struck the ground with a sickening thud, but Rafe didn't back off. He held his arm across Alpha's throat, pinning him down.

"I don't want to kill you either, Alpha." Rafe spoke so quietly that Katie had to learn forward in her seat to hear. "But I will."

"Go, then," Alpha snarled. "And never come back."

Rafe hovered over Alpha's prone form, unmoving even as yet more howls filled the air. "I don't know how to trust you." His internal struggle over whether to kill the man who had helped raise him was plain to see, with or without their connection. She knew in her heart that he would prefer to avoid spilling more blood, but ultimately, he would do whatever was necessary to keep them both safe. "I want to believe that you'll let us go, but I'm not sure I can." Chest heaving, he seemed to press down harder on Alpha's throat. A fierce growl curled his lips. "Nobody hurts Katie. Not even you."

Unable to see Alpha's face, Katie held her breath as she waited for a reply. She half-expected Rafe to finish him off before he could manage one. But when Alpha spoke a moment later, he sounded surprisingly calm for a man on the brink of death. "Go on and get out of here, kid. Take your girl and disappear."

There was an interminable wait before Rafe answered. "And what will you tell Jack?"

"That I didn't make it in time to stop you."

Rafe bowed his head, obviously considering Alpha's offer. Body coiled tight with tension and rage, he looked wholly prepared to carry out a heartbreaking execution. So when he lifted his arm, easing off Alpha's airway, Katie went boneless with surprise—and, inexplicably, relief. Rafe grabbed Alpha's discarded rifle from the icy pavement beside his outstretched hand, then stood and backed away slowly. "You saved my life when I was a boy. Now we're even."

Alpha leapt to his feet so swiftly that Katie was certain Rafe had made a fatal mistake by showing him mercy. But rather than advance, he turned and walked to his truck in silence. Climbing into the driver's seat, he rolled down the window and pulled onto the shoulder of the road. Without meeting Rafe's eyes, he said, "Get the fuck out of here. You step foot in these woods again, you're both dead."

Rafe passed Alpha's rifle through the open window to Katie, then opened the door and got into the driver's seat without looking away from his former pack leader. "We're not coming back." Katie felt the finality of his declaration in the lump that rose in her throat. She put her hand on his knee, grateful to have him back beside her even as she mourned that being together came at the cost of the only life he'd ever known. Rafe shifted the truck into drive, then laced his fingers with hers. "Tell Natalia that I'm sorry about Cooper."

Alpha stared straight ahead, emotionless. "Right."

Rafe's hand tightened on hers. Under his breath, he whispered, "Keep hold of your gun until he's out of sight. Just in case."

"Okay." Katie adjusted her grip on the revolver as they drove slowly past Alpha's truck. He held the steering wheel in white-knuckled fists, his frustration palpable and downright unsettling. She kept her watchful gaze on his face until she couldn't see it anymore, and then she studied his tail lights in the rear view mirror, afraid that he would simply turn and follow them—perhaps even run them off the road. It was only after they'd driven a few miles without any sign of Alpha giving chase that she felt comfortable checking on Rafe.

His chest rose and fell rapidly. The energy that poured off him was so confused and chaotic that she struggled to comprehend how he felt about what had just happened. Betrayal, relief, sadness, anger, regret, worry, joy, uncertainty—the onslaught of emotion made her dizzy, almost sick to her stomach. Overwhelmed, she put her hand on Rafe's thigh to help steady them both. The instant she touched him, a profound sense of calm swept over her and chased away everything else, easing the tension in the car and making it easier to breathe.

Rafe exhaled slowly. "So that went well."

"It could have gone a lot worse." Startled to see the revolver still gripped tight in her hand, Katie set it in the center console. Then she balled her free hand into a fist, trying to stop its violent trembling. "Do you think he'll come after us?"

"Not if he wants to stay alive." As though sensing that his answer did nothing to allay her fears, Rafe gave her a tender smile. "No, I don't think he will. Even if he knew where we were going, he doesn't exactly venture into cities. None of my pack do. I doubt Jack's wolves will, either."

Katie nodded. She wanted to believe that. For the sake of her sanity, she had to believe that. "I can't believe he tried to get you to give me to them."

"He's an idiot," Rafe muttered darkly. "I would have killed him if he tried." His throat tensed, and Katie instinctively knew that he was imagining what would happen to her if she were given to Jack Devereaux and his pack as a plaything. Rafe's nostrils flared as he exhaled again. "I'll never let anyone hurt you, Katie. I promise you that."

She'd never believed in anything so strongly as she did that. For the first time in her life, she had a partner who would die to protect her. And she would do the same for him, without hesitation. "Me too," Katie said. Pleased when that earned her a genuine smile, she leaned across the console and kissed his cheek. "And I promise I'll do whatever I can to make living around us awful humans more bearable."

Rafe chuckled, then bared his teeth in a full-out grin. "I'm not worried."

Strangely, she wasn't either. She had no idea where they would go, what would come next, or how they would negotiate a relationship while coming from two such different worlds, but despite all that, she remained certain that as long as they were together, they would get their happy ending. And she couldn't wait.

CHAPTER THIRTY-THREE

Katie lie on her stomach across the surprisingly comfortable bed, cradling the hotel suite's phone to her ear. Freshly showered and wrapped in a fluffy towel stamped with the name of an expensive establishment she'd never splurged on before, she wanted nothing more than to curl up with Rafe once he finished his own shower. But first she needed to get through this one last phone call. Having already contacted her parents, the police, and a small list of clients to report that she was alive, all that was left to do was comfort her sister. Erin had burst into tears as soon as Katie said hello and was only marginally calmer after Katie explained that she'd been in an accident, had gotten rescued, then wound up stranded in the woods for a couple nights.

"Where are you now? Can I see you?" Erin sounded more like a little girl than Katie could ever remember hearing from her big, brave sister. "I was so worried, Katie. The police couldn't tell us anything except that search efforts wouldn't start until the weather cleared. We had your name and picture on the news, hoping someone could tell us something. We thought we'd lost you."

Katie's throat stung at the obvious anguish in Erin's voice. "I'm so sorry. I'm not even back in the city yet. This is literally the first chance I've had to use a phone since the accident. I was only able to drive out of the mountains this morning, and the roads were so bad that by the time I finally made it to

Sacramento, I decided that I needed a break." Not yet ready to get into all the details of the past week—including the fact that her new boyfriend had come along for the ride—she decided to play up her very real exhaustion to avoid a lengthy conversation. "I actually think I'll go to bed soon. I have a feeling it's going to take me a few days of rest to fully recover from the past week."

"How about I come up there and take care of you?" Clearly already making plans in her head, Erin said, "I can cancel my appointments for tomorrow, we'll go to breakfast at that little place in Old Town..."

Erin's hopeful lilt warmed her even as it made her cringe. She couldn't wait to see her sister again, but all she wanted to do right now was spend at least twenty-four uninterrupted hours with Rafe. As though answering her unspoken desire, Rafe opened the bathroom door and stepped out, still naked and damp from the shower. Making sure not to sound ungrateful, Katie demurred as gracefully as she could while admiring the most perfect male form she'd ever seen up close. "I appreciate that so much, Erin, but right now all I want to do is sleep for about twelve hours and then drive home. I promise to call you when I get there."

Erin couldn't hide her disappointment. "I understand, I just miss you. And I'm pretty sure that I won't be able to relax until I see for myself that you're all right."

Katie smiled at Rafe as he sat on the bed beside her. His hand immediately went for the bare skin of her calf, and stroked her gently. Basking in the closeness she felt simply being near him, she rolled onto her side and rested her head on his thigh. "Maybe we can meet for dinner tomorrow night? Somewhere in San Francisco, your choice."

"Are you kidding me? You're the one who nearly starved to death and got stranded in the middle of nowhere. Dinner is your choice."

Distracted by the teasing path Rafe forged up under the edge of her towel, Katie bit her lip and tried not to moan. The sensation of his fingers skirting up the back of her thigh to the curve of her ass rendered food the furthest thing from her mind. "I can't even think about eating right now. How about I call you tomorrow afternoon and we'll work out the details?"

"Sounds like a plan." Erin had gone teary again. "Were you hurt in the accident? Have you seen a doctor?"

The only one of them who had visited a doctor was Shilah. They'd found an emergency vet as soon as they made it to Sacramento, armed with the cover story that their dog had been attacked by some unidentified wild animal while they were camping in the mountains. The vet treated his wounds, prescribed antibiotics, and let them know how incredibly lucky they were that Shilah hadn't gone into shock from fear and blood loss. Despite Susan's prediction, the doctor was guardedly optimistic that his leg could be saved. Fitted with a bulky cast, he lie on the dog pillow the pet-friendly hotel had supplied, watching them with a shit-eating grin on his face. Really, what Shilah and Rafe had survived made her own bumps and scrapes seem trivial in comparison.

"I'm fine, Erin. I swear." She parted her legs slightly, allowing Rafe to slip his hand between her thighs. "I'm amazing, actually. I'll give you all the details once I get home." She wouldn't, of course, but not because she didn't want to. Terrifying as the entire experience had been, she was walking away from it with an amazing, gorgeous man who would fight and die for her. Katie wanted to trumpet that news far and wide—especially to her big sister.

Unfortunately, she didn't think Erin was ready to know exactly how special Rafe was. Intense supernatural bonds with werewolves weren't the kind of thing one casually announced to the world—or to one's family. Erin would never accept it. No man had ever been good enough for Katie, as far as Erin was concerned, and a lycanthrope was unlikely to change her opinion about Katie's taste in boyfriends.

"Okay," Erin said warily. "So you'll call me tomorrow?"

273

"Absolutely." Katie didn't have to force cheer into her voice with Rafe so close. He caressed her inner thigh softly, making no move to get any more intimate while she was on the phone. His solid presence at her side made her feel blessedly safe, pleasantly warm, and suddenly desperate to say goodbye to her sister. "I'm sorry again about everything. I hate that I made you worry about me all week."

"I'm sorry you had to go through that. Being trapped in your car…I can't even imagine how scary that was for you."

In retrospect, those five days alone had been one of the least traumatic parts of the entire week. Aware that there was no way to explain that, she sought to ease Erin's mind anyway. "It was awful, at times. But it wasn't all bad, I promise." She turned onto her back and smiled up at Rafe, who returned her smile while lightly grazing her crotch with his palm. "On that note, I love you, sis. I'll see you soon?"

"Count on it." Erin sniffled. "I love you, too."

"Bye." Katie put the phone back on the nightstand, then collapsed onto her back with a dramatic exhalation. "Well, that took it out of me."

Rafe loosened the towel from around her chest, allowing it to fall open and reveal her naked body. Despite the vaguely seductive gesture, he made no move to initiate lovemaking. Instead he rested his hand on her belly and searched her face. "Is everything all right?"

"Just reeling from the impact my disappearance had on everyone. My biggest client wanted to know if I was still going to meet my deadline next Wednesday—probably not, by the way." Work wasn't even on her radar yet. She couldn't think of anything that seemed more trivial than designing web graphics when her entire life had just changed in every possible way. "My parents…well, they were beside themselves. They've obviously been panicking all week. Erin, too. She was ready to drive up here tonight to make sure I was really okay."

"Did you want her to?"

Incredibly, Katie sensed that he would be cool with a surprise visit from her sister if that was what she wanted. But it really wasn't. Shaking her head, she murmured, "I want tonight to be about you and me and nobody else."

Rafe brushed his knuckles over her cheekbone. "I like the sound of that."

Not interested in being coy about her desires, Katie said, "I want to make love. With no fear, no protecting me from your lust, no reservations." She came up on her elbows and met him halfway in a deep, passionate kiss. When they broke apart, she whispered, "Just us, connecting. Enjoying this bond we share."

His fingers slid from her shoulder down over the side of her breast, eliciting a shiver that she felt to the tips of her toes. "I'd like that very much."

Certain that this was the perfect time to change the tone of their sexual relationship, Katie sat up and placed her hands on Rafe's chest, pressing him backwards onto the mattress. Clearly surprised by the dominant maneuver, Rafe stared up at her, smoky-gazed and compliant. "Taking charge?"

"As a matter of fact, yes." Kicking the towel she'd been wearing over the side of the bed, Katie straddled Rafe's hips and settled on top of him. He was already rock hard, his length nestled between her slick labia as though he was the missing piece of her puzzle. Groaning in satisfaction at even that slight bit of stimulation, Katie said, "Can you handle that?"

"I can definitely handle it." He moved his hands to caress her back, then dropped them to squeeze her ass and pull her wetness against his swollen cock. "Are you going to put me inside of you?"

Relishing the idea of being in control—and aware that Rafe was eager to prove that he wasn't always so insatiably dominant—Katie shook her head and gave him a playful smile. "Not yet. You have to earn it first."

Rafe raised an eyebrow. Any doubts she had about

whether he would enjoy her being on top vanished at the blatant arousal on his face. "How does one earn an invitation inside your beautiful body?"

She shot him a naughty grin as she climbed up his chest and planted a knee beside each of his broad shoulders. Threading her fingers in his dark hair, she held his head steady and lowered her wet folds onto his mouth. "You lick me until I tell you that I'm ready for more."

Never having taken on this role in the bedroom, Katie was surprised by how naturally it came to her—and by how much she genuinely enjoyed it. To her delight, Rafe's eyes sparkled as he stared up from between her legs. She moaned as he dragged his tongue through her wetness, teasing at her opening until she yanked on his hair and shifted her hips to guide his actions.

"That's right," she whimpered as he drew circles around her clit with the tip of his tongue. "That's so good, baby." She loosened her grip on his hair and stroked his head, pleased by how well he already seemed to know her body. Shocked by her own confidence when it came to finding satisfaction, she rocked her hips back and forth, using his whole face to stimulate her overheated flesh.

Rafe grabbed her ass, bringing her full weight down onto him with an appreciative groan. He was ravenous but respectful, gentle and loving and skillful in a way that curled her toes and made her forget all her lingering aches and pains. Lifting up slightly, she offered him a chance to breathe, then settled down once more with a contented sigh. He'd already pushed her so close to the edge and she had the fleeting thought that she should really stop this if she wanted them to come together, but she was physically incapable of moving away from the unselfish pleasure he provided. As though ensuring that she didn't go anywhere, Rafe tightened his grip on her ass, keeping her over his face.

Her orgasm hit her hard, causing her thighs to tremble and weaken and making her very glad that Rafe was holding her securely in place. Trusting him not to let her fall, she surrendered to the waves of ecstasy he created as he continued to lick and suck with passionate intensity. Finally she released his hair and planted both hands on the headboard, bracing herself as she lifted off his face and scooted backwards to sit on his chest.

Rafe took a grateful breath and grinned up at her. "That was the single most arousing thing I've ever experienced. Just so you know."

Crawling down his body, Katie stretched out on top of him, keenly aware of just how excited he was. His hard cock pressed into her belly and teased her with the promise of being filled, but he stayed perfectly still and didn't attempt to penetrate her. Tenderly, he put his hands on her shoulders and raised his head to give her a loving kiss. She smiled as she tasted herself on his lips, then ran her fingers gently through his hair. "Did I hurt you?"

He laughed. "Uh, no."

She grasped a lock of dark hair and tugged lightly. "Really?"

"If you did, it was a very good hurt." Rafe pushed her hair away from her forehead, gazing at her with unabashed adoration. "You're delicious. I could literally do that all night. The fact that you were forceful about it only made it hotter."

Katie parted her thighs just enough to allow his cock to slip between them, then undulated her hips, providing friction that brought immediate pleasure to Rafe's face. "All night sounds wonderful, but I think I'm ready for something else now."

Rafe ran his hands down her back. "Yes."

She giggled. "Yes, what?"

"Yes to whatever it is you're ready for."

Kissing the corner of his mouth, Katie murmured, "Are you always this agreeable?"

"I don't have anything not to be agreeable about right now." He tightened his arms around her in a careful bear hug.

"I've never been happier in my life."

"Me too." Katie spread her legs and planted her knees beside his hips. His stiff length pressed into her wetness, hot and throbbing and eager. He dropped his hands to his sides and balled them into fists. Enjoying the blatant desire on his face, she murmured, "Should I put you inside me now?"

Nostrils flaring, Rafe gritted his teeth as she reached between them to grasp his cock in a loose fist. She pumped him slowly, waiting for an answer. Finally he rumbled, "I want to feel you, sweetheart. Please." His throat convulsed, his jaw clenched. "Please let me in."

She bent to kiss one corner of his mouth, then the other, and guided the bulbous head to her opening. At first she rubbed him against herself experimentally, teasing them both with the barest hint of penetration, then she backed off and simply swirled the tip around her engorged clit, moaning loudly at how insanely good it felt. When Rafe closed his eyes, a tortured look on his face, Katie positioned him at her entrance again. "Am I being mean, tough guy? Teasing you like this?"

A low rumble of laughter bubbled up from deep in Rafe's chest. "It's okay. I like my women mean."

Katie chuckled. "I'll remember you said that." Taking mercy on Rafe, who steadfastly clung to his self-control, she sank onto him with a satisfied moan. "Oh, fuck that feels good."

He brought his hands up to caress her ass and nodded emphatically. "You feel perfect." He didn't attempt to guide her. He simply stroked her bare skin with tenderness that verged on reverence. "Thank you for this." He gave her a cautious squeeze, then tipped his head back and groaned as she lifted up then sank down again. "For that."

"You're very welcome." Reveling in the power trip he was encouraging, she leaned over so that her breasts brushed against his chest. Lips to his ear, she whispered, "Now I'm going to fuck myself with your cock until you come inside of me. Do you like that?"

Rafe inhaled swiftly. "I approve."

"Good." Katie kissed his ear lobe, then sat and planted her hands on his chest. She rolled her hips, pleased by his instantaneous reaction—a fluttering of his eyelashes, the tensing of his muscles beneath her hands. Taking her time, she settled into an easy rhythm of pulling herself off his cock until only the head remained inside, then sliding back down until she was fully impaled. Rafe's throat jumped as his attention dropped to her chest and the way her breasts bounced in time with her motion. Thrilled by his obvious inability to maintain eye contact, she lifted one hand from Rafe's chest and captured her erect nipple between her fingertips, pulling roughly. "You like these?"

Rafe nodded silently, seemingly at a loss for words. Locked onto the sight of her toying with her own breast, he seemed to forget that he was trying to hold back and met her next undulation with a powerful upward thrust. She cried out in surprise, then redoubled her own efforts as pleasure skittered up her spine and out through her limbs. He seemed to grow impossibly harder and thicker within her, stretching her so very close to her limit. Rather than be painful, the tight fit created the most exquisite sensation of physical intimacy she'd ever experienced. Katie placed both hands on Rafe's shoulders and dug in with her fingertips.

"Am I hurting you?" Rafe murmured. "Tell me if I am." He stilled his hips, but continued to encourage her to move atop him. "You're so tight."

It took all her concentration to vocalize a response. "No." She lifted up then sank down, again and again, chasing a climax that promised to shatter her completely. "Everything feels so good."

"Yes, it does." Rafe raised his hand and placed it on her cheek, love in his eyes. "You're beautiful, Katie. And I'm lucky." His nostrils flared as she tilted her hips to take him in as deeply as she could. "Stupidly lucky."

279

He'd just been forced to flee the home he'd built with his own hands—not to mention his pack—because she'd entered his life. His dog was practically crippled, also because of her. That he would still feel fortunate to have her was almost unbelievable—but then, she also felt lucky to have him. And that was despite the fact that their bonding meant that she'd become a target for psychotic werewolves. If that didn't prove that they were meant to be together, she didn't know what did.

Desperate to get closer, Katie lowered herself so they were chest-to-chest, adjusting her rhythm so she could continue to ride him while their bodies were flush. "Me too." As difficult as it was to choose her words with such incredible sensation building between her legs, she needed to tell Rafe something very important and didn't want to wait another moment. "I may not have had the opportunity to do so, but I would have chosen you. Even with all the problems that come from us being together—I'm glad you're mine."

He gave her a grin that lit her up from the inside. "I would choose you, too."

Unsure why they weren't kissing already, Katie licked at his lower lip teasingly. Rafe opened his mouth and accepted her inside with a contented groan. She quickened the pace of her hips, ready for them to come together. Matching her rising passion, Rafe tightened his arms around her and wrapped her in an embrace that made her feel as though nothing could hurt her. Even with her various bite wounds, strained muscles, and cuts and bruises, she felt no pain. There was no fear either, not even of the dark memory of fighting their way out of the wilderness. As long as she was with her mate, everything was okay. More than okay. Everything was incredible.

Nothing and no one had ever made her feel that way before. Breaking their kiss, Katie rested her forehead against Rafe's and whispered, "I'm going to come."

"Me too." Rafe moaned into her mouth. The raw noise

triggered her release, a powerful explosion that left her inner muscles clutching at his thick shaft, milking him of the semen he spilled within her. He dropped his hand to her ass and slipped his finger between her buttocks, sliding around in her wetness before moving to explore the tight ring of muscle that contracted slightly at his caress.

The unfamiliar touch intensified Katie's orgasm. She cried out and arched her back, begging for more. Rafe moved his finger back and forth over her anus, drawing out tiny noises of pleasure as Katie rode out her climax with total abandon. Just as her orgasm threatened to ebb, he pushed the very tip of his finger into her ass and set off a strong aftershock. Almost afraid to move for fear that any more stimulation would render her unconscious, Katie pushed her cheek against Rafe's and held on tight. Eventually the waves of pleasure receded until she could breathe again. Seemingly just as affected by his climax, Rafe's chest rose and fell in time with hers, his heartbeat pounding against her breasts.

When she could form a coherent thought, Katie said, "I really wish I wasn't too tired to do that again."

Rafe chuckled and kissed her hair. "Me too."

She lifted her head so she could stare down into his eyes. "We have really good sex."

"Amazing sex." He hugged her around the middle. "How are you doing?"

She knew he wasn't talking about their lovemaking anymore. She'd just endured a hellish week in which she'd almost died multiple times and had sustained multiple injuries that should really hurt more than they actually did. If not for the peace and safety he brought her, she would probably be inconsolable. "I'm good. More worried about you than anything."

"Me?" Rafe gave her an easy smile, and shook his head. "I've never been better."

"You've just left your home and your pack. You're about to live among humans for the first time in your life." Katie framed his face with her hands and kissed him again, lovingly. "Your entire world is turned upside down," she whispered. "Because of me."

"So is yours." He dropped his hands to cup her buttocks. "Being together won't be easy for either of us. That much is clear."

"I'll say. But I'm excited about it, just the same."

"Good. Me too." Rafe kissed her neck. "So am I meeting Erin tomorrow, or do you want to keep me secret for a while?"

She wouldn't be able to keep Rafe a secret for long. Not when she yearned to spend her every waking moment with him. "Tomorrow. She'll love you."

"I hope so." He kissed her throat again, tickling her with his stubble. "I'm pretty attached to her little sister."

Katie wiggled her hips. "Literally."

Rafe rewarded her with a light slap on her bottom. "Funny."

"I thought so." Sighing, Katie finally rolled off Rafe to lie at his side. She rested her head on his chest and curled her arm around his hard stomach, marveling at how well their bodies fit together. "If you don't mind, I'd like to go back to my apartment for a while. Feed my cat, get my life in order. Then we can talk about what happens next."

Rafe made a quiet noise of displeasure. "You have a cat?"

Katie picked up her head and fixed him with a sober look. "We have a cat."

"Wonderful." Quirking his lips, Rafe captured her mouth in another quick kiss. "We have a cat!"

Her giggle turned into a yawn. Now that she was safe, warm, and happy, her body was relaxing for the first time in days. To be able to curl up next to the man—or werewolf— she loved without fear of being murdered while they slept, well, it really didn't get any better than this. Katie closed her eyes, unable to resist the sweet lure of sleep. Before she let herself fall over the edge into unconsciousness, she murmured, "It'll all work out. You'll see."

Rafe tightened his embrace, radiating a joy she could feel. "I think it already has."

BIOGRAPHY

Meghan Malone grew up near Detroit, Michigan and now resides in beautiful Sonoma County, California. She lives with her partner Angie, their young son, and a genuine menagerie of pets. She makes her living doing web development, but dreams of the day when she'll be able to spend all her time writing down the stories that fill her head.